THE VILLAGE

Persephone Book N° 52
Published by Persephone Books Ltd 2004

Reprinted 2007

First published 1952 by The Cresset Press
© The Estate of Marghanita Laski
Afterword © Juliet Gardiner 2004

Endpapers taken from a printed cotton
designed by Margaret Simeon for John Lewis in 1946
© The Whitworth Art Gallery

Typeset in ITC Baskerville by Keystroke,
Jacaranda Lodge, Wolverhampton

Colour by Banbury Litho

Printed and bound by Biddles, King's Lynn

ISBN 978-1-903155-42-4

Persephone Books Ltd
59 Lamb's Conduit Street
London WC1N 3NB
020 7242 9292

www.persephonebooks.co.uk

THE VILLAGE

by

MARGHANITA LASKI

afterword by

JULIET GARDINER

PERSEPHONE BOOKS
LONDON

for
Rebecca Lydia Howard
and
her grandparents

Fictional villages are naturally supposed to be like real villages, and my Priory Dean is no exception. But since I have recently lived in two such villages, I should like to assure my friends in these, with all sincerity, that no one in Priory Dean is even imaginatively based on anyone I knew in either.

ML

THE PEOPLE

Major Gerald TREVOR, of Wood View, Priory Hill
Wendy TREVOR, his wife
Margaret TREVOR, his elder daughter
Sheila TREVOR, his younger daughter
Peterkins, the cat

Mr WILSON, Van Driver, of 15 Station Road
Edith WILSON, *née* HAYNES, his wife
Roy WILSON, Compositor, his son
Edie WILSON, House-Parlourmaid, his elder daughter
Maureen WILSON, Schoolgirl, his younger daughter
Gran, Mr WILSON's mother

Mr GRAHAM (deceased), of the Hall
Miss Evadne GRAHAM, his daughter
TALBOT, a maid

Dr GREGORY, of the Green
Mrs GREGORY, his wife
Dr Giles GREGORY, his elder son
Roger GREGORY, Medical Student, his younger son
Mrs SMITH, Housekeeper

Mr Ralph WETHERALL, Business Executive, of Green Lawns,
   Priory Hill
Martha WETHERALL, his wife
David WETHERALL, aged 5, his son
Caroline WETHERALL, aged 2, his daughter
Lt Toby WETHERALL, RN, his step-brother
Nanny

Mr George BRUCE, Junior Partner of Stalybridge, Son & Bruce, Solicitors, of Ridgeways, Priory Hill
Daisy BRUCE, his wife
Christopher BRUCE, aged 5, his son

Miss PORTEOUS, Retired Schoolmistress, of Kelmscott, Priory Hill
Miss Trixie BELTRAM, of the same address

The Rev Mr PAYNTER-SMITH, Retired, of Priory Hill
Mrs PAYNTER-SMITH, his wife

Mrs WINTERTON, Widow, of the Rowans, Priory Hill

Mr PENNYFEATHER, Retired Civil Servant, of the Thatched Cottage

The Rev Mr ROBINSON, of the Rectory
Mrs ROBINSON, his wife
Sally ROBINSON, his infant daughter

Mr JENKINS, Headmaster of the Priory Dean Elementary School
Mrs JENKINS, his wife
Jennifer Ann JENKINS, his infant daughter

Mr GREEN, the Ironmongery, of the Arcade
Mrs GREEN, his wife
Rosemary GREEN, his daughter

Mr Albert PICKERING, People's Warden, Chairman of the Parish Council, the Electrical Shop, of the Arcade
Edna PICKERING, his wife
Eileen PICKERING, Schoolmistress, his daughter
Ted PICKERING, leader of the Rhythm Ragamuffins, his son

Mr BROTHERTON, Stationer, of the Arcade
Mrs BROTHERTON, his wife

Miss MOODIE, Draper, of the Arcade
Paddy, her dog

Mr PARKER, Butcher, of the Arcade

Mr Jim WATERS, Licensee of the Master-At-Arms
Mrs WATERS, his wife

Mr TIMMS, Policeman
Mrs TIMMS, his wife

Mr PORTER, Taxi-owner

Mr ROWE, Farmer and Dairyman

Mr BIRCH, Gardener, of Station Road
Mrs BIRCH, his wife

Mr TAYLOR, Compositor (deceased), of Archery Lane
Mrs TAYLOR, his wife
Miss FAIRLIE, Infant Teacher, of the same address

Reg SUMMERS, of Station Road

Alice EVANS, Assistant at the Cake Shoppe

Jim –, employed at the Bentworth Paper Mills, Edie WILSON's
     fiancé

Bill COTTERELL, Gardener

Mr George WILKINS, Labourer, of Station Road
Mrs WILKINS, Charwoman, his wife
Louie, his daughter
Jenny, his grand-daughter

Mr CALDER, Scrap Merchant, of Station Road

Mr Alan THATCHER, Master Printer, of Bentworth Park
Sylvia THATCHER, his wife
Sandra THATCHER, his niece

Jill MORTON, of South Walbridge, friend of Margaret TREVOR

The TREMLETTS, of Fernlea, Priory Hill

Freddie –, Business Executive, friend of the WETHERALLS
Moira, his wife

Miss LATIMER, Headmistress of St Friedeswyth's School for
    Girls, Walbridge

Mr STALYBRIDGE, Senior Partner of Stalybridge, Son & Bruce,
    Solicitors

Miss CARTWRIGHT, Nursing-home Matron, of South Walbridge

Evelyn –, X-ray Dept, Walbridge General Hospital

Matthew –, Dentist, formerly of Walbridge

Sir Edward (deceased), of the Grange

The Rev Mr HALL (deceased), of the Rectory

Mrs PEACHBODY (deceased), of Broomfields

Eileen – (deceased), Wendy TREVOR's sister

Doris –, of New Zealand, Gerald TREVOR's sister
Laura, her daughter

THE VILLAGE

CHAPTER ONE

The night the war ended, both Mrs Trevor and Mrs Wilson went on duty at the Red Cross Post as usual.

There was, of course, no need in the world to go. Since the King had spoken on the nine o'clock and the village had poured spontaneously into the streets to celebrate, they had passed and repassed each other a dozen times, each time smiling shyly, tentatively, both unconsciously shrinking from the full greeting in which it might have been natural and necessary to agree that of course there'd be no point in going on duty tonight, no, nor never again, now that the war was safely over.

So at nine o'clock they had, like everyone else, wandered into the streets just to see what was happening, had stumbled round the Green in the fitful light from the flats above the Arcade shops on the southern side, had stood on the steps of the War Memorial when Mr Jenkins, the schoolmaster, had touched off the bonfire that the children had been amassing all day on the messy bit by the pond. They'd watched Jim Waters at the Master-At-Arms doing something complicated with wires round the windows, until a loud-speaker blared out dance-music, and suddenly people were dancing on the

1

cobbles in the forecourt, dancing right out in the village street. They were no longer in the Priory Dean they had stumbled about in the dark for the past six years; the air was warm, the houses and trees were strange and unknown in the angles they revealed to the fire constantly re-fed by the soon demoniac children, the music was wild and irresistible and who ever heard of dancing in the streets of Priory Dean? Gradually more and more people wandered along and danced or stood by watching, according to their age and station, but few of the older people said more to each other than 'Well, that's over now' or, with a nod towards the Master-At-Arms, 'I don't know how Mr Waters could fix it in the time.' They had no phrases ready for this intent and dignified dance, no attitude for the end of the war they had lived with so long. Only when two of the boys from Station Cottages came purposefully with axes towards the siren on the Green, George Bruce instinctively stepped forward to intervene. 'Leave that thing alone,' he said with the authority of a Head Warden, even though he wasn't in his uniform. 'That's Government property, and we none of us know when we mightn't be wanting it again,' and in the smoky firelight the elder heads round the War Memorial nodded agreement.

By eleven o'clock the dancing was going on as strong as ever, but the bonfire was dying away as more and more tired children slunk or were dragged to bed. Occasionally a shower of sparks would spurt up on the smoky air when some daring child kicked the charred brands into the semblance of a heap again, but the spirit had gone out of it and no one felt like bringing any more rubbish along to keep it going. The older people had started to say, 'Well, I must be getting along now,' and to nod farewells to the friends they could recognise now that the window lights were going out all along the street. By half-past eleven the Green was empty except for the little bit of road in front of the Master-At-Arms where the village boys and girls still danced sedately to the grinding gramophone.

But long before half-past eleven Mrs Trevor and Mrs Wilson had slipped away from the crowd and gone home to change into their thick navy serge trousers and tunics, change the scarves they wore over their heads (Mrs Wilson's in a turban, Mrs Trevor's knotted under the chin) for the smart little Red Cross caps, picked up the one the bottle of milk and the twist of sugar, the other the biscuits she'd baked that morning. Down the hill from Wood View, Priory Hill came Wendy Trevor and up the hill from 15 Station Road came Edith Wilson to meet in the porch of the Village Hall.

Some surprise but not too much was appropriate. 'I'm glad you decided to turn up,' Mrs Trevor said as she opened the door and, reaching out an arm, switched on the light in the little room off the main hall. 'I was in two minds whether to come or not,' said Mrs Wilson, 'but then I said to myself, well, there's been no orders come along to make any difference, I said, and with those Germans you can never be quite sure. It would be just like them to have a last raid, just for spite, knowing we was thinking it was all over and done with.'

'Yes, it would be funny if the only casualties we had in Priory Dean were on the very night the war ended,' Mrs Trevor agreed; and now both women had justified their presence, they comfortably relaxed. Mrs Trevor threw her little haversack down on one of the camp-beds against the wall, and Mrs Wilson said, 'I'll just get the sukey going, and then we'll have a nice cup of tea.' She lit the rusty gas-ring that stood on the draining-board of the stained old sink, filled the kettle and put it on. 'Here you are,' said Mrs Trevor, rummaging in her haversack for the sugar and tea. She added, 'I wonder how much longer we'll have to go on with the rationing now that it's over?'

'It was a good two-three years last time, as far as I can remember,' Mrs Wilson said. 'Mind you, we went much shorter then than we ever did this time.'

'I don't really remember much about it.' Mrs Trevor pulled a crumpled packet of Weights out of the breast pocket of her tunic, and both women lit cigarettes. 'I was in my last year at school when it ended. I remember we made a bonfire on the netball ground, just like we did tonight.'

'I'd just got my first place as cook with Sir Edward up at the Grange,' said Mrs Wilson. 'I remember him coming into the kitchen with two bottles of champagne under his arms. "That's for the staff, Mrs Haynes," he said (of course, I wasn't really Mrs, but it was a courtesy, like, in those days). "That's for the staff," he said. There were six of us in the hall then, and we made short work of that champagne. I don't suppose there's much champagne drunk up at the Grange these days, now all those railway clerks have taken it over.'

I don't suppose there's anyone left in the village who'll open champagne for the end of the war, thought Wendy Trevor in sudden surprise; no one will even think of it. 'There's the kettle boiling,' she said, and Mrs Wilson made the tea and then they both sat down on their camp-beds and sipped it out of thick white Utility cups.

'Funny how the village has changed since those days,' Mrs Wilson said thoughtfully. 'Twenty miles from London was right in the country then, what with no buses and a half-mile walk to the station and scarcely any of the trains stopping as it was. Why, I remember it being all fields on the south side of the Green where the Arcade is.'

'They were just putting up the shops in 1925 when we came here,' Mrs Trevor said, 'and the first bus was just about a year later.'

'Well, we didn't really need them before all the building started,' said Mrs Wilson. 'When I first married and left service, I don't suppose I went into Walbridge over once a month for a bit of shopping. And as for the people in the big houses, they'd all got their own cars. Why, old Mr Graham at the Hall, Miss Evadne's father, he kept his horse and trap until well after the end of the last war.'

'The Hall's the last of the big houses that's still lived in,' Mrs Trevor said. She pulled a bundle of striped yellow and green knitting from her bag and began working busily. 'Sir Edward was still here when we came, but he died the year after, and I think the railway company took over the Grange as soon as it came onto the market.'

'That's right,' Mrs Wilson agreed, 'and then there's the Convent at the Manor House, and Broomfields falling to rack and ruin and the garden no better than a mass of weeds. My Edie wants to go back into service when she gets her release from the factory – live at home and go out by the day's her

5

idea – but there just aren't the good situations around here any more.'

Mrs Trevor suddenly endured a moment's piercing agony. To hear of a good maid going begging and be unable to do anything about it was real mental distress. If I cut down smoking, she thought wildly, if – but there was nothing else left to cut down on. It only made things far worse, that moment of stupid imagining when she'd heard herself say, 'Now, Edie, you get the washing done this morning and then there's just the Major's and my lunch to get ready.' Unconsciously she looked down at her hands, as red and rough as Mrs Wilson's own, and Mrs Wilson, following her glance, said, 'That's a pretty pattern you're following. Is it a jumper for Miss Margaret or for Miss Sheila?'

'It's for Sheila,' Mrs Trevor said with a sigh, and politely held it up to be admired. 'I could do with another cup,' she added. 'Do you think there's any more in the teapot?'

'I'll just boil the kettle up again,' said Mrs Wilson. 'It'll be ready in two shakes of a lamb's tail.' She busied herself with the gas-ring, and Wendy Trevor got up and looked out of the window.

'The fire seems as if it's dying down now,' she commented. 'It must be getting on for midnight.' This was the time when both women usually lay down on their camp-beds and settled themselves for sleep, so as to be fresh for any emergencies the night might bring. So they had done every Friday night for the past six years, but now Edith Wilson said, 'Funny, I don't feel a bit sleepy tonight, though goodness knows it's been an exciting day.' 'Well, we needn't settle down till we feel like it,' agreed Wendy. 'After all, it's not as if anything's really likely to happen.'

Having both admitted, as plainly as they could, that they were here for the indulgence of each other's company, they could now settle down in happy ease for the second of the cups of tea that would keep them going through the night. 'I can't get used to not having to bother with the black-out,' said Wendy. 'In fact, I don't think I'll ever be able to call it drawing the curtains again; it'll be black-out with me to the end of my days.'

'Did you ever have a funny feeling when you went to American pictures?' asked Edith. 'All those people sitting in front of open windows with the lights just streaming out, and you wanted to scream at them either to do the black-out or put out the lights, one thing or the other.'

'A lot of things are going to seem funny,' said Wendy thoughtfully. 'I expect we'll see a good many changes. For one thing, I suppose we'll have a General Election now, though there can't be any doubt about who'll get in.'

Edith said surprisingly, 'I'm not so sure.' 'You don't mean you'd vote *Socialist*, do you, Edith?' said Wendy, shocked, and Edith obstinately replied, 'Well, I know I didn't ought to say such things, Mrs Trevor, but I can't see that the Conservatives have ever done anything for us working people. This war's been the first time in our married life we've been quite sure we're going to make out all right and save a little bit to put by. I'm not saying anything against the Conservatives, mind you, but it wasn't very nice me having to go out to work when Mr Wilson was stood off, and him staying at home to keep an eye on the children. It wasn't right.' Wendy made an uneasy gesture of protest, and Edith added hurriedly, 'Mind you, I was ever so happy working for you, Mrs Trevor, and no one could ever have been nicer to me than you and the Major. And I'll never forget the time when young Roy broke his arm and you let me bring him up with me to play with Miss Margaret.'

'She loved having a boy to play with,' said Wendy, gratefully turning the talk into safer channels than politics had proved to be. 'What's he going to do when he comes out of the Army? He ought to be out pretty early, shouldn't he be?'

'He certainly ought to be,' said Edith proudly, 'since he was in from the very day it started, like all the Territorials. He'll be all right, I'm thankful to say. He'd all but finished his apprenticeship when he went in, and there's always good money to be earned in printing. From what his father tells me now, he ought to be able to make his ten pounds a week easy, and, of course, there's his old job in Thatcher's waiting for him.'

Ten pounds a week for a boy of twenty-five, thought Wendy hopelessly, more than we've got to live on put together. 'That's very good news,' she said warmly, and her thoughts went back to the early nineteen-thirties, before the girls' schooling had eaten up her tiny capital and when Edith Wilson had come along every morning and sometimes back in the evening again if they'd had people to dinner. I've not been to a dinner-party since the war started, she thought. How can people manage them these days with no staff and all the rationing? I never imagined for a minute that Edith felt bad about coming

8

to me. 'Mrs Wilson's a thoroughly nice woman,' she often said to Daisy Bruce. 'I look on her as a real friend,' and there was wrung out of her, 'Edith, did you really hate coming to work for me?'

'There you are,' said Edith distressed, 'it's like Dad says, there's always trouble if you start talking politics. Of course I didn't hate coming to you, Mrs Trevor, and don't you think it for a minute. I was just talking in a general kind of way. In fact, if you was ever in any kind of trouble and wanted a helping hand, I'd be back again before you could say "knife."'

'Edith, you *are* nice,' said Wendy impulsively and came across the room to lay her red hand on Edith's. Immediately both women were acutely embarrassed, and when a loud knock sounded at the door Wendy was glad to be able to swing round and call out, 'Who's there?'

'What's going on in there?' shouted a loud voice, and Edith said hurriedly, 'It's Mr Timms,' and got up and opened the door to let the village policeman come through.

'Well now, I didn't expect to see you ladies here tonight,' he said. 'I saw the light in the window and I said to myself, you'd better go and see what's going on, I said.' He looked enquiringly at them and it was Wendy's not Edith's business to explain that there having been no orders to the contrary and not being able to be quite sure – 'Tell you the truth, I thought it was some of the children that'd got in here and were knocking things about,' Mr Timms explained. He took off his helmet and brushed back his thick fair hair. It was now for Wendy to say, as she'd so often said, 'Won't you have a cup of tea with us, Mr Timms, now you're here?' and before he'd answered, as he always did, 'Well, I can't deny it would come very welcome,' Edith was already refilling the kettle, bustling round the gas-ring, getting out another of the thick chipped cups.

'Well, I suppose there's nothing to stop the evacuee children going back home now,' Wendy said. For years it had been, 'It'll be a good thing when the war's over and those children go back to their own parents.'

'Good riddance to bad rubbish,' Mr Timms said fiercely. 'I've never seen anything like the way those children carry on. More like hooligans than children they are.'

'Talking of hooligans,' said Edith, 'have you heard there's a whole lot of Irish labour coming down this way to build the new paper-mills at Bentworth?'

'No, I'd not heard that,' said Wendy, surprised. Mr Timms could not admit to not having heard anything that might affect Priory Dean, and Edith went on, 'It was Edie's Jim that told me, him having been working there till he was called up. They say they've got priority to build the mills or something, but you'd think they could find enough of our own people to do it without bringing strangers into the place.'

'Well, I hope they manage to house them all at Bentworth,' Wendy said. 'Goodness knows there's no accommodation to spare in Priory Dean.'

'Ah,' said Mr Timms solemnly. Now he could come into his own. 'I've heard tell – mind you, I don't say what truth there is in it – that they're going to put up a whole lot of those pre-fabs down in the field beyond the churchyard.'

'Oh no!' exclaimed Wendy. The field beyond the church-yard was on the same side of the village as Priory Hill, the side that was still real country. Edith said angrily, 'Well, if they do put up any of those things up here, it's to be hoped our own people get first pick of them. I'm sure Jim that's been through the war has as much right to a home so's he and Edie can get married as any Irish labourers.'

'As to that, I can't say,' said Mr Timms. He drained his cup, rinsed it under the tap and set it down beside the sink. 'Thank you kindly, ladies, I'll be on my way now.' He put on his helmet again and the door closed behind him.

'When's Edie hoping to get married?' Wendy asked with interest.

'Just as soon as she can get a house, or even a couple of rooms,' said Edith. 'She's twenty-two now, and it's three years come August they'll have been engaged. I don't care what people say, it's not good for young people to have to go on hanging about like this. Mind you, there's some of them getting married these days and going on living at home, but I don't hold with it. Young people ought to start out on their own as is right and proper, but even supposing they wanted it, with the best will in the world we haven't got the room. What with Gran having to have her room to herself and young Maureen got to have somewhere she can do her homework in peace if she's to pass her exams and now Roy coming home, there's just nowhere I could fit them in even if I wanted to.'

Wendy asked politely, 'I suppose Roy's not thinking of getting married yet?'

'He's not said anything to me,' his mother answered. 'No, I don't think there's anything of that sort with Roy, though, mind you, he'll make some girl a real good husband one of these days. He's ever so handy about the house, and though I shouldn't be the one to say it, he's got the sweetest temper of any boy I've ever had dealings with.'

'He always did have,' said Wendy, remembering the stocky black-haired boy playing with Margaret. 'Maureen was always the spitfire of your family, wasn't she? How's she making out now?'

'Sobered down a bit, I'm thankful to say,' Edith replied. 'She's got her matric to do next month, and they say at the grammar-school she's likely to be able to get a scholarship to the University. Oh, she's the clever one of the family and no mistake, though a bit of a Miss Knowall, as Dad's always telling her. Still, I suppose it's only natural.'

'She's really rather like my Sheila,' said Wendy laughing. Then she thought, it would be funny if Maureen got the University scholarship and Sheila didn't. But Sheila *must* get her scholarship, she thought fiercely, and suddenly she found herself saying to Edith what she had never put into words before, could never have discussed with her own friends or imagined she could mention to someone like Mrs Wilson – 'Edith, I'm so worried about Margaret.'

The rhythm of the dance-music still hammered at the window. Edith was silent for a minute, looking down at her hands. Still not raising her eyes she said quietly, 'I've always thought Miss Margaret one of the sweetest-natured girls it's ever been my good fortune to have come across.'

Wendy said almost apologetically, 'I know you always used to think I was too impatient with her. I'll admit I'm quick-tempered but I don't see any point in mooning over a thing when you can get it done in half the time if you only put your back into it.'

'But Miss Margaret was always very thorough in everything she undertook,' Edith said.

'But what did she undertake?' Wendy demanded. 'I know she'd spend hours arranging her dolls' house or pinking the edges of a bit of pastry until I could have screamed. I'll admit she's sweet-tempered and all that, but now she's failed her matric, and where's her sweet temper going to take her next?'

'Miss Sheila was always your favourite though, wasn't she?' Edith said, and now she accepted the demands of the conversation and looked at Wendy's face.

'It wasn't exactly that,' Wendy said helplessly. 'Margaret was the sweetest baby anyone could have wanted, it's only – well, look, Edith, you know how we're placed. Now the chicken-farm's gone down the drain and the Major's almost an invalid and can't do anything but potter about in the open air –' She couldn't bring herself to particularise too closely about their financial straits; already she was saying more than she felt she ought to say, more than it was proper to say to anyone. She started again. 'We'd always agreed,' she said, 'that we'd put what we'd got in giving the girls a good education so that they'd be able to have decent careers. Now with Sheila we could see from the start that she'd justify it. She's had scholarships all the way through and Miss Latimer says there's no doubt that she's really brilliant. But I always worried about

Margaret. I mean, it was always clear she wasn't really good at lessons, and there was all that money being spent on her, and yet I don't see what else we could have done, do you?'

Edith said comfortably, 'I think you're worrying about nothing, if you ask me. After all, we can't all be scholars. I've always thought that what Miss Margaret would do would be to get married and make some man a really good wife.'

'Who?' Wendy demanded. 'Who? What young men are there in Priory Dean that she could marry?'

Neither woman thought for a moment of the crowd of young men now dancing earnestly outside the pub, the young men who had swarmed round Mrs Wilson's Edie till she'd made her choice of Jim at the paper-mills, the young sons of the tradespeople who'd go into their fathers' shops and be sure of a good living as far ahead as anyone could see. Instead their thoughts scanned the Hall, the dereliction of Broomfields, the villas up Priory Hill. 'There's Mr Roger,' Edith offered tentatively.

'Roger's the young son,' said Wendy, looking facts in the face. 'Giles is already qualified and is coming into the practice next year and he'll take over when his father retires. It'll be five years before Roger is even a doctor and he's still got to establish himself after that. And who else is there?'

There wasn't anyone else. 'Mind you, there's a lot of those Londoners will be going back to town now the war's over,' Edith suggested. 'You don't know who we'll be getting in their place.'

'That's possible, I suppose,' Wendy conceded. Then she leant forward and said earnestly, 'but there are so many other difficulties these days. Take clothes. Now she's seventeen she ought to be able to start dressing like an adult and not a schoolgirl. But you can't get a girl a new outfit with the rationing, let alone what it would cost.'

Edith Wilson had plenty of coupons and she wasn't short of money, not these days. It crossed her mind, not as a formulated thought, only as an incoherent impulse, that there was nothing would please her better than to buy Miss Margaret a real nice grown-up outfit in which she could hold up her head with the best. But it was inconceivable that any such offer could possibly be made, as it could, say, by Miss Porteous or Miss Evadne Graham, even if either of them could run to such a thing any better than could Mrs Trevor herself, who was now saying wistfully, 'I don't suppose they'll be calling up the girls any more now. It seems wicked to say so, but I'd always had it at the back of my mind that if Margaret went into the Services, it might solve the problem of clothes *and* a job *and* a husband, all at once.'

It *was* difficult, Edith could see that. In the ordinary way you'd expect someone like Miss Margaret to stay at home and go to tennis-parties and things until Mr Right came along and she could make a home of her own. But if you couldn't afford to keep a girl at home and there weren't any young men to meet at tennis-parties, what *did* you do? She asked, 'Haven't you and the Major got any nice relatives where Miss Margaret could go and stay for a bit and meet some really nice young people?'

'We haven't really,' Wendy answered. 'We seem to be very short of relations. The only one with a young family is my husband's sister in New Zealand, and that's not much use.'

'Perhaps Miss Margaret will have some ideas of her own,' Edith suggested, and Wendy said hopelessly and yet contemptuously, 'I don't think that's very likely,' and then, almost frantically, 'If only she was *pretty* –'

'Now you're not to say that,' protested Edith, really shocked. 'I'd say Miss Margaret was a thoroughly nice-looking girl.'

'But she's not noticeable,' Wendy insisted. 'Thousands of girls have got brown hair and brown eyes and a nice expression and all that. You've got to stand out in some way nowadays if you want to be noticed.' She added, almost as if talking to herself, 'You know, Edith, I was really very pretty when I was younger. When I first met the Major, after he came back from Germany, I was really pretty, and the Major was good-looking too. And I was – well – cheerful, if you know what I mean. I was always ready to chat with people and have a good time with them, but Margaret can never say more than yes or no to strangers, and how can you ever get to know people if you don't talk to them?'

'She's shy, that's all,' said Edith firmly. 'She'll grow out of it, you see if she don't.' She looked pityingly at Margaret's mother, at the greying fair hair, and the faded blue eyes, the cheeks now reddened and rough and the pale chapped lips. This is the sort of thing it's best not to say in so many words, she said to herself, and though she'd never before regarded it as her place to initiate the suggestion, she got up and said, 'I think it's time for another cuppa,' and as she was busying herself with the kettle she said, 'I've always meant to ask you,

Mrs Trevor, what made you and the Major decide to settle in Priory Dean?'

Wendy was still back in the past when she had been that pretty fair vivacious Rendell girl and Gerald had been so gay and cheerful and such a good sport. 'We went to Kenya, you know, just after we were married,' she said. 'That was in 1922 when the Major was demobbed. The doctors had just discovered about the gas destroying his lung and they said he'd got to lead an open-air life. He had a bit of money and his gratuity and so we went out there and bought a little farm near Nairobi.'

'And did you like it there?' asked Edith.

'Well, I did and I didn't,' Wendy answered with a sigh. 'I liked the social life and all the jollity, people always dropping in for drinks and parties going on all the time. But – oh well, we didn't seem able to make a go of the farm and there was all our money just oozing away and nothing to show for it. So we thought we'd get out while we still could and try our luck back home. It was sheer chance we came to Priory Dean. Wood View just happened to be the best house at our price with the field for the chicken-farm. But I always liked it here. People were very friendly, and being so high up it suited Gerald's health.' She paused, and then said tonelessly, 'There was something else, Edith. I've never told anyone here before. We had a baby in Kenya, a boy. We called him Stanley. He was really a beautiful baby, everyone said he was. He died when he was three months. He'd just started to smile –' Suddenly she collapsed, her face in her hands, choking with noisy ugly sobs.

Edith came beside her, put her arm round her shoulders. 'It's all right,' she said. 'It's all right now, my dearie. I've got you. Everything's all right now.' She went on murmuring meaningless comforting little phrases, holding the other woman tightly to her, until Wendy's sobs slackened and she began to grope in her pockets for her handkerchief. Then Edith moved away and silently started pouring out the tea.

Wendy said with a half-laugh, half-sob, 'Listen, the dance music's stopped. Edith,' she said, mopping her eyes, twisting her handkerchief in her hands, 'I don't know how to apologise. I don't know what came over me, making an exhibition of myself like that.'

'There's nothing to apologise for at all,' said Edith. 'We're all of us that tired and overwrought these days anyway, and if you can't have a good cry here tonight I don't know when you can.' She added almost casually, her face half-turned away, 'I lost a baby too, you know. A little girl, mine was. It was my first, too.' She sat down beside Wendy, and again the two women sipped their tea, talking now in soft relaxed voices of the children when young, of their husbands, their parents, remembering the little things that had made up their lives, made them what they were. Neither had ever talked like this to anyone before and never would again.

At last Wendy glanced up at the window and it was light. On a single impulse they both got up and went to the door, looking out at the village in the early morning light, at the Norman church and Dr Gregory's long Georgian house on the north side of the Green, the dark cedars that spread over the wall from Miss Evadne's garden on the short side, at the ugly new shops flanking the village hall and closing the triangle round the Green. The air was cool and sweet and no one was about. It was the first day after the war.

At last they moved back into the stuffy little room, smoothed the camp-beds, washed out the cups and the teapot for the last time, repacked their haversacks and slung them over their shoulders. Wendy locked the door behind them and hung the key in the not very secret place inside the porch, but still they lingered, unwilling finally to end this night and the years behind it.

'There's a lot of us will miss it,' Edith said. 'We've all of us felt at times, you know, how nice it was, like you and me being able to be together and friendly, just as if we were the same sort, if you know what I mean.'

'I'll miss it a lot too,' Wendy said. There was no point in her saying that it could go on now, the friendliness and the companionship and the simple human liking of one woman for another. Both knew that this breaking down of social barriers was just one of the things you got out of the war, but it couldn't go on.

Edith said, 'I wonder if the Doctor will keep the weekly dances going. They were a real nice get-together if anything was.'

The barriers were rising. It was Wendy and her friends, not Edith and hers, to whom the Doctor had said, when the black-out had started, that it was everyone's duty to support the dances, to ensure that those people had a bit of entertainment and didn't sit brooding in their houses. There would be no point in the dances now, and she couldn't explain to Edith why. She said, 'Goodbye, Edith,' and Edith said, 'Goodbye, Mrs Trevor,' and gravely, almost sacramentally, for the first and last time in their lives, the two women embraced and kissed each other.

Then they parted, Mrs Trevor going up the road to Wood View on Priory Hill where the gentry lived and Mrs Wilson going downhill on the other side, down Station Road among the working-classes.

CHAPTER TWO

But Doctor Gregory did arrange one more get-together at the village hall and this was, as it said on Miss Porteous's hand-drawn posters in nearly all the village shops, the Grand Victory Ball with Old Fashioned Dances, Ted Pickering's Rhythm Ragamuffins, Refreshments, and Entrance Fee One Shilling, Double Tickets 1/6d.

There was a committee meeting as usual before the dance, and it was Miss Evadne's turn to hold it at the Hall. Doctor Gregory as Chairman was there, of course, and Mr Robinson the new Rector, and George Bruce who lived next door to the Trevors; then there was Miss Evadne in her own right as Treasurer, and Miss Porteous's companion, Miss Trixie Beltram who was such a useful Secretary, and then there was Wendy Trevor and Mrs Green, the wife of Mr Green of the Ironmongery who had been invited at the start when the Doctor had said, 'And we'd better have one of them on it or they'll not take the same interest.' The Doctor had lived in the village since he was a boy and remembered when the Hunt used to meet at the Grange, but he never bothered to distinguish between the tradespeople and the people from Station Road way. True, he'd said, at the same time, 'I suppose we'd better have someone from among the farming folk,' but he was getting a bit forgetful at times, and he hadn't taken it at all amiss when discussion revealed that as most of the big farms had been cut up into smallholdings, there weren't really any proper farmers left to ask any more.

Everyone always enjoyed the meetings at the Hall. For one thing the drawing-room was big enough for everyone to sit down comfortably without a lot of squashing and carrying extra chairs, even if the floral linen on the sofa was worn into patches here and there that clearly showed the blue rep beneath. Then Miss Evadne had still got old Talbot who'd been with her for donkey's years, and you could say what you liked, it was nice to see the coffee and biscuits brought in by a maid in uniform instead of everyone feeling bound to jump up and offer to carry things to and from the kitchen. And then, best of all, Miss Evadne often had one of her fine modern jokes ready for them. No one remembered now when they had started, except Miss Evadne herself, who could never forget the day Miss Beltram had come into the drawing-room unannounced and found Miss Evadne dozing with the *Oxford Book of Modern Verse* on her lap. 'That sort of muck ought to be burnt,' Miss Evadne had woken to hear the flat ugly voice saying, and, as she woke, in instinctive defence she had said, 'Oh, I don't know –' and had read aloud from the page open on her lap some lines about dry bones in a desert. And Miss Evadne, in her position, would hardly have been wrong about a thing like poetry, so Miss Beltram had quickly realised that it was funny and had laughed out loud, and Miss Evadne – for there was nothing else to do – had laughed with her. Now people often said what a good sport Miss Evadne was and really it was amazing how she could remember such reams of that stuff when it didn't even make sense, but still, it was good for a laugh. But this evening, when they pressed her for one of her gems, she said she didn't seem to be in the mood somehow, and quietly closed the thin book that was lying on the sofa beside her. Miss Beltram inquisitively picked it up and said in her forthright way, 'Fancy spending ten shillings and sixpence on muck like that. I wonder they let it be published.'

Miss Evadne hesitated a moment and then said quickly, 'It's a cheap price to pay for a good laugh,' and she took the volume from Miss Beltram, pushing it hurriedly into the bookcase where it stood shoulder to shoulder with many more; you could see what fun she got out of them, actually buying all that lot, when everyone knew she'd hardly got a penny left to bless herself with.

'We'd better get down to business,' said Doctor Gregory briskly. 'I'm expecting to be called out any minute to Mrs Timms's latest.'

So they settled themselves comfortably while the Doctor issued his orders and everyone prepared to obey without comment except for Miss Beltram who was always ready to suggest an economy, a penny to be saved here and there. Usually some concessions were made to her point of view, particularly since she always backed up her suggestions by saying that making-do was patriotic, but tonight she found no supporters. This was the last dance, the Grand Victory Ball, and there was going to be a spotlight and prizes and paper streamers if Mrs Green, who was going into Walbridge next day, could find any such things, and no one, for once, com-plained of the four guineas that Ted Pickering was now asking for his Ragamuffins, though at the beginning he'd come for two and glad to.

So they got through the business in record time, and it was only half-past nine when Wendy and Mrs Green had agreed that they'd organise the refreshments as usual, and Miss Evadne had pressed the bell for Talbot to bring in the coffee-tray. Usually, as soon as this was over, everyone had shuffled off quickly to ARP duties or to get an early night for once, but tonight there were no duties waiting for anyone except the Doctor and his call hadn't come through yet. So they fell to chatting and it was Mrs Green ('These people know everything as soon as we do ourselves') who contributed the most surprising piece of news.

'Have you heard,' she asked, 'that Green Lawns has changed hands?'

Now this was of interest to everyone, for Green Lawns was the biggest and most modern of the new houses in Priory Hill. In fact it had been completed only just before the war, and the first people to occupy its red and white splendour in three acres of garden had been a London insurance company who'd been evacuated there and kept themselves to themselves, no asset to the village at all.

'Who's taken it, do you know?' the new Rector asked, and the sound of his faintly Cockney voice aroused, as usual, a contemptuous distaste in everyone present.

'I don't know the name,' Mrs Green admitted, 'but I did hear he was manager of some big motor works. Someone said he'd just come back from America, though what he was there for I didn't quite make out.' You had to be careful, when you were in trade; it wasn't wise to run down people who might turn out to be good customers, and she left it to Miss Beltram to snap, 'If I had my way, all those people who ran away to America during the war would be put up against a wall and shot.'

'He may have been there on business,' Wendy suggested mildly. She would have been shocked if anyone had suggested that she hated Miss Beltram, but she did, and so did everyone else there. But you can't afford to hate people openly if you live in a small community, and the most anyone ever said against Miss Beltram was that they couldn't understand how Miss Porteous put up with her.

The Rector said, 'Whoever he is, he must be pretty well-off to take Green Lawns. I hear they were asking seven thousand for it,' and though everyone immediately thought that the Rector shouldn't be thinking about such things, they all, except for Miss Evadne, fell to wondering what sort of difference someone well-off at Green Lawns would make to the village. George Bruce hoped they'd play bridge amiably at not more than a penny a hundred. Doctor Gregory and Mrs Green were simply hoping that they'd prove profitable patients and customers. Miss Beltram immediately feared that they might try to get friendly, too friendly, with Miss Porteous who wouldn't see that it was just for what they could get out of her. The Rector imagined a couple before whom he could appear as conventional, reverend, long-established, a model of a country rector. And Wendy Trevor just hoped that they'd have a nice young son who might do for Margaret.

Indirectly, it was thinking of the new people coming to Green Lawns that made Wendy decide to take Margaret to the dance. She had been cutting sandwiches all afternoon. She was hot and untidy and tired, and then the girls came in from school and Margaret said casually, 'Why don't you cut them in diamond shapes for a change?'

Wendy couldn't help it, she just lost her temper and flew out. She shouted, 'I slave and slave from morning to night and all you can do is to stand there and criticise.' She looked at Margaret to find fresh fuel for her temper. There she stood, mild, gentle and innocuous in her school tunic, her soft brown hair caught back with a slide from her sweet but oh, so uninteresting face. Wendy's anger turned to a pitying shame. She said, 'I'll just make tea and we'll have it on a tray in the drawing-room for a change. It'll do me good to get out of the kitchen for a few minutes.'

'I can make the tea,' Margaret offered eagerly, but Wendy said curtly, 'No, thanks, I'd sooner do it myself,' and Margaret stood by anxiously, not knowing what to do with her hands until the tea was made and carried on a tray into the drawing-room.

But it wasn't such a good idea having tea in the drawing-room after all, because the very act of doing such a thing roused Wendy to angry thoughts of the contrast between the life she had once known and the one she was living now. From where she sat she could see on the mantelpiece the silver-framed photograph of her elder sister Eileen in the white satin she had worn when she was presented at Court on her marriage. For years Wendy had had it in the back of her mind that when the girls grew up Eileen would present them too and perhaps even give them a season in London since she had no children of her own. But Eileen had died in a motor accident in 1938 and her husband had bought an estate in Jamaica and showed no interest at all in the family of his deceased wife's sister. But looking at the photograph reminded her that Margaret was now seventeen, the very age at which she'd always imagined her being presented, being miraculously transformed into that polished and promising creature, a debutante, and here sat Margaret, a schoolgirl, with no polish on her at all. Somehow it was her duty to transform Margaret into the embryo adult who might attract the young man at Green Lawns (always supposing there *was* a young man at Green Lawns) and it was with the simple idea of making a start with what happened to be available that she suddenly said, 'Margaret, would you like to come to the dance with us tonight?'

Sheila looked up excitedly and cried, 'Oh, Mummy, me too! Mummy, you wouldn't be so mean as to take Margaret and leave me out of it!'

'You're too young,' Wendy said firmly, seeing herself, for the moment, as the mother of Edwardian high society, the younger daughter in the schoolroom, the elder about to blossom forth. 'Well, Margaret,' she asked impatiently, 'it's you I'm asking, not Sheila. Don't you want to come?'

Margaret said uneasily, 'Honestly, Mummy, I'd sooner you took Sheila, if you don't mind. I don't terribly want to go.'

'Why not?' Wendy demanded; once again Margaret was failing to measure up to the demands of her mother's mental picture.

'Well, I wouldn't know anyone,' Margaret muttered, looking down at the floor. 'And anyway I haven't got anything to wear that would do.'

'Don't be silly,' Wendy said, 'you know everyone I know, and as for something to wear, you've got your beige silk.'

'But it's so babyish,' Margaret protested. 'All the other girls there would be wearing proper grown-up frocks.'

'And who do you mean,' questioned Wendy, 'by "the other girls there?"'

'Oh, you know,' Margaret muttered, 'Edie Wilson and Rosemary Green and – well, everyone.'

'You are not going to tell me,' said Wendy majestically, 'that we have now got to take people like Edie Wilson and Rosemary Green for our models of what's proper for us to wear?'

There was no answer to that. Margaret knew she'd been a fool as soon as she'd spoken. It was a mistake she and Sheila had made for years, suggesting that because Poor People's children had things, they'd a right to them too. Both she and Sheila knew perfectly well that Poor People's children stayed up late only because their parents didn't understand about the importance of sleep, ate lots of sweets because Poor People didn't care about their teeth, had oceans of pocket-money because Poor People didn't understand the value of money. It was always a tactical error of the first magnitude to hold up Poor People as an example to follow. The trouble was that there weren't any Nice Girls of her own age to hold up instead. So she said miserably, 'Honestly, Mummy, I'd sooner not go. Besides, I've got tons of homework to do.'

Wendy knew perfectly well that the beige silk dress was the last garment she herself would have chosen to wear for her first dance, even a dance in a village hall. It had come, like so many of the girls' clothes, in a parcel from their aunt in New Zealand, and, like all the clothes Doris's Laura wore, was of good quality and dowdy to a degree. But as soon as Margaret mentioned Edie Wilson and Rosemary Green, Wendy's defence mechanism began to work. The beige silk dress became the perfectly suitable ladylike garment it was proper that *her* daughter should wear in contra-distinction to the gaudy vulgar fashions flaunted by the village girls.

It was at this moment that Gerald came in from the field where he'd been fixing up the new chicken wire he'd at last managed to wangle out of Mr Green. 'What's going on in here?' he asked jovially. 'Why so grand, all of a sudden?'

'I just thought it would be nice to live like gentlefolk for once,' Wendy said wearily. The good idea had gone thoroughly stale on her; Gerald should have come in in tweeds, the gun stacked away in the gun-room, the partridges – no, it was the wrong time of year – the rabbits hung in the larder, and instead he stood there in his old flannel trousers and tweed jacket, his feet in the bedroom-shoes for which he'd changed his rubber-boots, his little fair moustache as perky as ever on his small round face. She poured him out a cup of tea and said, 'Margaret, you'd better go up and have a quick bath,' thinking how lucky it was that they'd got the boiler going today and what it would cost when there was enough coke to have the boiler lit every day and economy in fuel was no longer a virtue.

'Margaret being sent off to bed early?' Gerald asked in mild interest.

'No,' said Wendy. 'I thought we'd take her to the dance with us tonight for a treat.'

Gerald looked startled, wondering whatever had come over Wendy, suddenly realising with a shock that Margaret was nearly grown-up, that he was the father of a nearly grown-up daughter. He looked at her, then looked quickly at Sheila's strong dark face and curly brown hair and said quickly, 'And what about *my* girl? Don't tell me she's being left behind.'

Long ago, when the girls were small, Gerald had started calling Sheila his girl. 'Where's Daddy's girl?' he would demand when he came into the house, and Sheila would rush into his arms, while Wendy, sorry for the shy Margaret standing awkwardly in the background, would counter by saying that Margaret was Mummy's girl and drawing her quickly to her. But 'Mummy's girl' was a phrase that had long slipped out of family usage, while 'Daddy's girl' was still on Gerald's lips when he proudly called his clever vivacious Sheila. Now Wendy said firmly, 'Sheila's too young to be thinking about dances yet, and besides, she's got her homework to do.' 'I've got homework too,' Margaret said hopefully, but Margaret's homework didn't matter, wouldn't enable her to pass exams, win scholarships, make a career. Her future must be sought in other directions, and Wendy said with finality, 'You go upstairs right away, or you'll be keeping Daddy and me out of the bathroom.'

Daisy and George Bruce came from next door to fetch the Trevors just as they were finishing the meal that Wendy still despairingly called dinner but was really no more than a high tea, taken at half-past six so as to be over and done with and the washing-up finished before she could sit down and relax. This evening Sheila had risen splendidly to the occasion and offered, quite spontaneously, not only to wash up but to set the breakfast-table and put in the bottles, then to put herself to bed at half-past nine and not a minute later. Not that Wendy liked leaving her alone in the house, but there wasn't really any choice about it, and now that she was fifteen and so long as she didn't open the door to strangers, everything surely ought to be all right.

It was different for the Bruces whose Christopher was only five. It wasn't often they could get out together, but tonight old Mrs Wilkins, who came to Daisy three times a week and once to Wendy for the rough, had agreed to oblige so long as it wasn't after eleven. Daisy, as usual, looked extremely nice, fair hair lying in smooth finger-waves against her face and under her musquash coat a pre-war black lace frock with an imitation pink carnation at the neck. Everyone always admired Daisy immensely for always looking so pretty and keeping so gay when they all knew that George couldn't make anything worth speaking of as a junior partner in Stalybridge, Son & Bruce, Solicitors, in Walbridge. She made nearly all her own clothes and knitted so beautifully for little Christopher, and was always ready to listen to anyone's troubles and give a helping hand. But lately Margaret had begun to feel that perhaps Daisy was just a little bit *too* sweet and nice. It didn't seem natural to like everybody, even Miss Beltram, and then she would stifle the thought as disloyal when Daisy showed her yet another kindness, again took the trouble to do something nice especially for Margaret.

Now she came in and said admiringly, 'How smart you're all looking! I feel quite dowdy beside you.'

'You look enchanting as always,' said Gerald, falling happily into the role that pleased him best, the gallant young officer with an eye for the ladies. 'Do sit down,' Wendy said, 'I've just got to clear away,' but Sheila put in eagerly, 'No, Mummy, I'll do it all tonight. You and Margaret go up and get ready.'

'Why, is Margaret coming?' Daisy asked in surprise, and then, quickly, 'How very nice, dear. Won't you feel grown-up going to your first dance?'

There was no need to answer and Margaret found nothing to say. Daisy looked pitifully at the beige silk dress whose shapeless folds left Margaret colourless and unnoticeable, and turning to Wendy said gaily, 'Now I've got a real good idea and you're not to say no. If this girl of yours is old enough to be going to dances, don't you think she's old enough to try a bit of make-up for the first time?'

Wendy hesitated and Gerald said thankfully, 'Jolly good idea,' hoping that perhaps Daisy might, with her usual cleverness, achieve a miracle, produce the budding daughter he'd be proud to flaunt.

'Then that's settled,' Daisy said playfully. 'Margaret, we'll leave our elders and betters to get their coats on while we go upstairs and make ourselves look gay.'

There was an awkward silence after the two of them had left the room. The unspeakable thought – that they each hoped to goodness Daisy could bring it off – was almost audible. At last, with visible effort, George said, 'What do you think of this proposal to bring us under Walbridge Urban?' 'Well, I suppose it might mean some street-lighting,' Gerald answered, 'but if it means we've got to pay rates at fifteen-and-six in the pound – ' They carefully talked about the Urban District Council until ten minutes had passed and Daisy and Margaret came downstairs again.

The miracle had happened – for Margaret. All the adults tried hard not to meet each other's disappointed eyes, to avoid the common admission that the too-pale powder, the too-pink lipstick seemed not to belong to the face that wore them, the smooth dull face they all knew so well. But Margaret to herself was transformed. Some magic had worked in her while Daisy was wrapping the towel round her shoulders, saying, 'Now just stretch your lips – look, like this.' She was gay and grown-up and beautiful and sophisticated and longing to go to the dance.

Walking down the hill past the neat detached houses, past the thick box hedges and the white painted gates, Wendy managed to whisper to George, 'You will try to see she has a good time, won't you?' And George, desperately keeping up the pretence, whispered back, 'You don't have to worry about Margaret – she'll do fine. Just you wait and see,' and they both knew that he'd do his utmost to see that she had partners, didn't stand around neglected, gave every appearance of being in the swing.

In her new-found assurance Margaret was able to enjoy the exclamations of surprise her mother's friends all gave when she came into the little ante-room. At dances, the ante-room was officially reserved for the preparation of refreshments, but it was an understood thing that members of the committee and their friends were able to leave their coats there and, if necessary, to change their shoes as well, though Mrs Green never presumed, but hung her coat in the passage where everyone else did.

Miss Beltram and Miss Evadne were already setting out the sandwiches on plates and the tea-urn was boiling up in the corner. Miss Evadne said in her loud jocular voice, 'Well, it's nice to see the younger generation making an appearance on the stage,' and Miss Beltram put in acidly, 'Someone's grown-up and using lipstick all of a sudden,' and Margaret smiled gratefully at them both, glad they were welcoming her and appreciating the change in her, not knowing what words to use to reply to them.

In the big hall, behind the matchwood partition, the Rhythm Ragamuffins were starting off with an old-fashioned waltz. Wendy was getting into her flowered overall and looked helplessly for someone to take charge of Margaret and usher her into the world. Then Doctor Gregory came in with George at his elbow and said, 'Delighted to see you honouring our festivities, young lady. May I ask your permission to take you out for the first dance,' and Margaret smiled shyly and delightedly, and went into the big room on the Doctor's arm.

She had never seen the hall decorated for a dance, and indeed, for none of the wartime dances had the shabby wooden hall been bedizened as it was tonight. Everyone had contributed what they could find from their old stocks of party and Christmas decorations and everything in splendid confusion was tacked to the walls, to the platform, to the beams in the ceiling. Ted Pickering, who, having been invalided out of the Army after Dunkirk, worked at his Dad's electrical shop when he wasn't conducting his Ragamuffins, had managed to fix up the coloured electric lights that Mr Waters had dug out for Victory night so that they dazzled and twinkled (except for two blue ones that wouldn't work) right above the heads of the band. Then there were Japanese lanterns and odds-and-ends of paper concertinas and little glittering glass Christmas-tree toys and lengths of tinsel and tacked-up laurel branches – everything, in fact, that Priory Dean could produce in the way of festive gaiety to bedeck the village hall on the night of the Victory Ball.

To Margaret, waltzing against the rigid arm of Doctor Gregory, it was all glamour and all delight. She forgot to wonder if the steps they'd practised at school on Wednesday afternoons in the Michaelmas term would work the same if you were being the lady and not the gentleman. As she twisted and twirled, she could see Edie Wilson with her fiancé, and looking even prettier than usual in a flowered frock that swirled out as she danced, but she only thought how nice Edie looked and didn't worry in the least that she herself was in the old beige that was much too babyish. Then the music stopped and everyone clapped lustily, and there was Mr Robinson coming up to ask for a dance and after him Mr Bruce and after Mr Bruce old Mr Pennyfeather who was a retired Civil Servant and lived in the thatched cottage next to the Master-At-Arms. It was easy enough to talk to people like that whom she'd known since she was a baby, all except for Mr Robinson who was a bit trying with his forced jocularity, but Margaret, knowing how fiercely her family and all their friends resented Mr Robinson, felt sorry for him, and pitying him, lost the shyness that usually devastated her with people she didn't know well. Then after Mr Pennyfeather's dance there was a tango, so she stood against the wall with him and watched her father tangoing, and very well too, with Daisy Bruce. And after that, Gerald actually came up to her and asked, 'Can you spare me a dance?' just as if she was a stranger, and ecstatic with happiness Margaret fox-trotted in her father's arms to the tune of 'Tea for Two'.

After that it was the tea-interval, and Gerald said, 'You'd better run along and give your mother a hand with the refreshments.' She'd been thinking, in a silly kind of way, that it would be fun to lean up against the wall like the other girls and have someone bring refreshments to *her*, but, of course, people like her had their responsibilities and so she went along to the little room and asked, 'Can I help?'

Miss Beltram, who never lost a chance to set someone to work, said quickly, 'We don't think the fruit cake's going to go round. You can take a knife and cut all the slices in half,' and Margaret dutifully cut the already small pieces of cake into even smaller morsels, getting hotter and hotter in the crowded little room and feeling her gaiety somehow ebb away among the hurrying bustling women.

The music started again and Margaret put down her knife and edged her way back to the hall, unwilling to lose a moment of this wonderful evening that was making such a rich and miraculous change in her life. It was an old-fashioned polka this time and everyone seemed to be dancing. Even the older women who usually sat against the wall gossiping had been drawn with coy giggles into their husbands' arms. The very young girls, like Mrs Wilson's Maureen, danced with each other, the older girls danced with young men, Mr Bruce and Mr Robinson and Gerald were all doing their duties with the wives of Mr Green at the Ironmongery and Mrs Pickering of the Electrical Shop and Mrs Waters, the peroxide blonde from the Master-At-Arms. Then she saw Doctor Gregory coming towards her with Roger, his younger son.

She thought that Roger's spotty face looked sulky but she was feeling too exalted to guess, as she might otherwise have done, that it was because Roger resented having his dancing-partners chosen for him by his father, who made matters worse by saying jovially, 'This young man wants to dance with you and is too shy to ask for himself.' 'Thank you,' Margaret said, and as she moved off in his arms the thought suddenly came to her that this was the first young man she'd danced with all evening.

With this thought came self-consciousness. She looked at the girls circling around her, all chattering gaily to their partners, and then found that she herself was completely tongue-tied. She glanced at the door and there was her mother watching her, obviously watching her anxiously, Miss Beltram and Daisy Bruce watching her, the only silent girl in the room. Roger might try too, she thought, but Roger was too angry, furious at being forced to dance with Margaret who looked so unattractive and dowdy when if he'd only been a second quicker he could have nipped in with Rosemary Green. Margaret tried out sentences in her mind, 'Are you liking it at Guy's?' 'Isn't it nice that the war's over?' but none of them seemed capable of provoking the gay badinage that everyone around her managed to indulge in without any effort at all.

So they gyrated in frozen embarrassed silence, and when the music ended Roger curtly said, 'Thank you,' and left her standing in the middle of the room, and quickly walked away towards Rosemary Green.

She edged her way to the wall, the farthest wall from where her mother stood in critical judgment. All her confidence, all her gaiety had gone. She perceived now, not, indeed, that all her parents' friends had set out to see that she was all right, but that none of the partners who had thronged round her earlier in the evening had been moved by the impulses that should drive a man to seek a girl for a partner. There was something that made Jim choose to dance with Edie and no one else until one day he had asked her to marry him, something that made Ted Pickering leave the band to Reg Summers so that he could snatch a dance with Rosemary Green. There was something wrong with herself that made Roger Gregory, the only young man of her own sort in the village, dance with her only as a duty and escape as quickly as he could.

Standing lonely against the wall, thinking hard, she saw her mother on the other side beckoning frantically to her to come across so that something could be arranged, something, if only conversation, that wouldn't leave her isolated in her failure. But she could not endure the prospect of sidling solitary, noticeably round the room towards the protective pity. She stood where she was, blinking harder and harder to stop the tears that welled in her eyes from falling.

Then at her side she heard someone say, 'May I have the honour?' and she turned round and saw a sergeant in battle-dress, a small smiling soldier only a few inches taller than herself, with shiny black hair brushed back from his face and brown eyes that shone as brightly as his hair. He was smiling – no, grinning – and suddenly she remembered that grin and asked, 'Aren't you Roy Wilson?'

'That's right,' he said, obviously delighted at her recognition, 'and you're Miss Margaret. I'd have known you anywhere.' They stood smiling at each other and with another quick grin he added, 'Care to dance?'

Margaret said, 'I'd love to,' not because this was the polite answer but meaning it. The memory of childhood pleasures coupled with the instinctive knowledge that this was an invitation different in kind from all those she had accepted earlier dissipated all trace of the distress she had just been feeling. She said, 'Do you remember our cave under the laurels?' and he replied, 'I should say I do. We had a real good time together, didn't we?'

That was the difference, she supposed, between Roy and Roger. She had no childhood memories of easy delights with Roger. It had always been assumed by the parents of both that Roger and Margaret liked to play together, to go and have tea with each other at least once a week. 'Why don't you run along and play with Roger – or Margaret?' had been on the parents' lips when the children showed signs of being bored, and obediently they ran along and the parents said smilingly to each other, 'You can't keep them out of each other's gardens.' The children had never consciously realised that they didn't like each other, had nothing in common, and never really enjoyed themselves together. Only now, dancing with Roy, Margaret contrasted the dreary bickering she'd endured with Roger with the lovely make-believe games she'd played for two happy months with Roy, and there burst from her spontaneously, 'Oh, it *was* such fun!'

Roy smiled sympathetically at her, and said, 'You know, you haven't really changed.'

'I've got make-up on,' Margaret said proudly; she couldn't resist pointing this out, just as she'd once have said, 'I've got some feathers for the Indian head-dress.'

'I like the way you put it on,' he said, 'just a bit of it, not all over your face like the other girls.' That was one of the things that had drawn him to ask her to dance, thinking how quiet and ladylike she looked. Those fancy bints you saw abroad were all very well, but he didn't like it at home, the way all the girls smeared on the muck so that even Alice Evans at the cake shop, whom he'd taken to the flicks once or twice on his leaves, really didn't look much better than a tart.

'Bit of luck for me, wasn't it,' he said, 'getting leave and running straight into the dance like this?'

Somebody nearly bumped into them, but he tightened his grip on her waist and drew her deftly away from the impending collision. She looked up at him and thought, in a confused kind of way, that he looked as if he'd always be able to manage things, grinning away in that cheerful confident way he had, as if he was still someone people could be all right in trusting. Then the music stopped and he clapped it very hard and seriously as if to show that he really wanted it to go on and when Ted Pickering started up again he said, as none of her previous partners had said, 'Let's carry on, shall we?'

So they went on dancing and asked each other questions about the eight-odd years that had passed since they'd met. It seemed funny they hadn't run into each other, they agreed, but that was what it was like in a village, sometimes you hardly saw your next-door neighbour for years, and then he'd been in Africa and Italy and France and now in Germany, and when he had been home on leave – well, it had just chanced that they'd never run into each other. And even if they had, though they didn't say this, there was nothing they could have done about it but say 'Hallo' and smile and pass on because though two children could play together in the garden, it was quite another story when you grew older and your parents were quite different sorts of people. 'It was awfully kind the way you used to play with me when I was so much younger than you,' Margaret said. 'You never made me feel a fool,' and Roy said firmly, 'Well, you weren't a fool, that's why. Besides, I liked that kind of make-up game we played, and Edie and Maureen never did like pretending things.' 'When do you come out of the Army?' Margaret asked, really wanting to know, and he grinned and answered, 'Just as soon as I can wangle it. I've had enough of being pushed around. I want to settle down and get on with my job. What about you?' he asked, and Margaret blushed and said, 'Well, I'm still at school, but I don't know what I'm going to do next.'

Again the music stopped and Margaret, glancing round the room, saw Wendy signalling to her with quick jerks of her head, saying plainly, 'Come here, I want you.' Without conscious intent to deceive, Margaret instantaneously let her eyes travel on round the room, not stopping long enough to respond to her mother's demanding stare. Then the music started and the lights went out. She felt Roy catch hold of her firmly and heard him say, 'It's a spot dance. Bet you we win.'

And they did. That was the astonishing thing. The bright pink spotlight shot across the room, flickering here and resting there, but when the dance ended it was firmly fixed on Roy Wilson and Margaret Trevor.

There was a burst of clapping, and people turned to slap Roy on the back and say, 'Well done, old sport. You go along and pick up the doings.' 'Will Mr Wilson and Miss Trevor come and receive their prizes,' shouted George Bruce from the platform, and in the first burst of acclamation she had ever received in her life, Margaret climbed on to the platform with Roy and was given a little package that turned out to contain an enamel powder-compact, while Roy received a packet of twenty Player's. Then they climbed down again and there was Wendy waiting for them on the floor.

She said pleasantly – no, graciously, 'Well, Roy, it's very nice to see you again after all these years. Your mother's been telling me how splendidly you've been doing,' and before he could answer her she added quickly, 'Come along now, Margaret, you've been keeping us waiting long enough. We're all nearly dead.' It was clumsily done, but it was not a situation of which Wendy had any previous experience.

'Goodbye, Roy,' Margaret said, her mother's hand on her arm pulling her away, and Roy grinned at her again and said, 'Goodbye, Miss Margaret.' The 'miss' obscurely reassured Wendy, but she couldn't help saying, in what she hoped was a light contemptuous voice, 'That young man's getting a bit too big for his boots. A pity, because his mother's such a decent woman.'

'Oh, I don't think he's a bit stuck-up,' said Margaret. They were getting on their coats now, and Wendy was able to say with the obvious approval of her friends around her, 'Well, it was a bit of a cheek dancing with you like that.'

Margaret faltered and mumbled, 'I thought it was all right. I mean, Daddy danced with Mrs Waters –' she was trying to draw an exact parallel in social etiquette.

Wendy said impatiently, 'Of course I don't mean you should have been rude. But after the first dance you should have just excused yourself politely. Still, I suppose you couldn't have known.' But her tone added that this was one of those things that any daughter of hers should have known instinctively.

43

'Would it have been all right if I'd gone on dancing three times with Roger?' Margaret asked. She knew she was a fool to pursue the subject, but felt some deep need to justify the behaviour that had given her so much pleasure.

'That's obviously very different, isn't it?' Wendy said coldly. 'Come along now, you're keeping Daddy waiting.'

CHAPTER THREE

Miss Porteous had decided to give a party to celebrate the General Election. It seemed to her, as, indeed, it seemed to the people who received her invitations, rather a debonair and sophisticated thing to do, just the sort of unusual gesture proper to maintain Miss Porteous's position as the cultural leader of Priory Dean society.

Two newspapers were delivered daily at Kelmscott, the red-brick house Miss Porteous had built for herself when she retired from her position as Senior English Mistress at a very expensive girls' boarding-school in the right part of Sussex. These newspapers were the *Daily Telegraph* and the *Daily Graphic*, the former for Miss Porteous herself, the latter for Miss Beltram. Officially Miss Porteous never looked at the *Daily Graphic*, but it had come to be tacitly understood that it should be lying on the carved oak coffee-table in the drawing-room for Miss Porteous to pick up and flick over idly while she waited for Miss Beltram to come out of the kitchen and tell her that dinner was ready. It was thus that she learned that Lord Rothermere was giving a General Election party and, transcribed into terms of her own special social position in the village, the idea seemed to her an admirable one.

It was an understood thing that whenever any of Miss Porteous's ideas involved manual labour, such work was carried out by Miss Beltram. So for days before the party she had been busy polishing up the wheelback chairs, the water-lily tiles in the fire-place, the repoussé brass proclaiming that Beauty and Truth were synonymous under the drawing-room mantel. She had beaten the Morris chintz on the sofa and armchairs and reluctantly – for she herself was no smoker – put out the little glazed clay ash-trays that Miss Porteous had picked up on her last pre-war holiday at St. Ives. It had also been Miss Beltram's job to go and see Mr Waters at the Master-At-Arms – out of hours, of course, she couldn't be seen going into an inn when people were drinking there – and persuade him to supply her with four bottles of sherry 'for Miss Porteous's party,' she was careful to add. And then she had the invitations to send out, for neither she nor Miss Porteous would ever have invited people to a party the casual modern way, just ringing them up on the telephone. But there was no difficulty about *that* job, because parties among the Priory Hill set always involved asking exactly the same people: Major and Mrs Trevor and Mr and Mrs Bruce, Miss Graham, Dr and Mrs Gregory (though Mrs Gregory, of course, never came) and two or three other couples all equally well known to each other. The present Rector was, by tacit understanding, invited only when the occasion was a semi-official one, like talking about how they were going to raise funds for the new organ. It was true that on this occasion Miss Porteous had suggested asking Margaret with the Trevors but Miss Beltram, who had lately been a little jealous of Margaret, had said that she was sure it would only be boring for Margaret without any other young people. Besides, though she didn't admit this to herself, if anyone as young as Margaret came to the party, her own position as Miss Porteous's permanent Young Person would be jeopardised.

Many people during the past twenty years had wondered what link bound Miss Porteous and Miss Beltram together. Miss Porteous was so quiet, so dignified, so cultured – was she not the author of a charming book of children's poems, *Silver Bells and Cockle Shells*? – and Miss Beltram was so crude, possessive, noisy and utterly unlettered. True, Miss Beltram had once been one of Miss Porteous's pupils, but even so, what bond could possibly hold them together? No one hit on the truth, which was that, for Miss Porteous, Trixie Beltram was the eternal prototype of the adoring schoolgirl, the pupil with a crush who would fetch and carry, wash and mend, give unstinting doglike devotion; while Miss Beltram herself was able to forget the passing years, the unsatisfied spinsterhood in the assurance that to Miss Porteous she would always be included in the phrase 'you young gels'. No, emphatically Margaret Trevor must not come to the party.

All the Priory Hill people looked forward to the party and the General Election with about equal anticipation. Both would make a pleasant break, a fitting mark of the end of the war and beginning of the peace, the opening of a new era in which things quickly got back to normal with people like those Trixie always referred to as 'that Bevin' put firmly in their place and Mr Churchill unassailably established in the seat of power.

Now that the war was over, the Priory Hill housewives seldom listened to the radio news except for the nine o'clock before bedtime. They were so sure of the Election result that they hadn't bothered to change their habits, and, since they seldom went out in the afternoons and consequently heard nothing from the village people who normally had their radios on all day, the first impact of the news broke upon them when the husbands returned from work. At first they just couldn't take it in. It wasn't true, it couldn't be possible. Hurriedly they sought to minimise it, there were still results to come in, it would all be reversed, it just simply couldn't be true. Now they turned their radios on, kept them blaring while they prepared the dinner, sausage-meat cakes with boiled potatoes and beetroot and the remains of the cold shape, but by half-past eight, when they all set off for the party, there had been no consolation.

'It's the ingratitude!' everybody kept saying as they sipped their sherry in Miss Porteous's drawing-room, making it last as long as they could, 'It's the rank ingratitude! When you think of all Mr Churchill has done for us, then just throwing him away like an old glove. What they're going to think of us abroad, I shudder to think.'

'It's the end of everything,' somebody said, and Miss Beltram chipped in, 'To think of being ruled by Communists like that Bevin. I'd like to string him up with my own hands.' 'Well, I suppose it's the end of people like us,' George Bruce said sadly, and Doctor Gregory snorted and agreed, 'Yes, we'll just have to get used to being ruled by a lot of piddling little clerks without an aitch to their names.' 'They'll get on with nationalising medicine now,' someone suggested, half-jovially, half-sardonically, and Doctor Gregory straightened himself and said with real fury, 'They can try till they're blue in the face, as far as I'm concerned. Think I'm going to be told what to do by some tuppenny-ha'penny jack-in-office who can't tell one end of a thermometer from another!'

Miss Porteous and Miss Evadne Graham were just as distressed as the others, but both instinctively felt that it wasn't quite nice to make all this fuss about it. Marie Antoinette hadn't fussed about going to the guillotine, and if things were going to be as bad as they were obviously going to be, well, the thing to do was to pull oneself together and greet them with calm dignity. Miss Evadne tried to smooth the gathering with a weak, 'Well, after all, it is a *British* government – I mean, they're all *Britishers*,' but Miss Porteous was far more successful in providing a diversion with her simultaneous remark, 'The new people next door moved in this afternoon.'

Immediately two or three people murmured, 'Well, I *did* think I saw some vans coming up the road, and I *did* wonder –' Doctor Gregory, whose function was to be forthright and bluff, barked, 'And what are they like?'

'They've got some very good things,' Miss Porteous said, taking and offering reassurance from the fact, 'not exactly – well, *heirlooms*, if you know what I mean, but nothing vulgar.'

'I'd like to know how they found the coupons for all the velvet curtains I saw going in,' Trixie Beltram snapped, but everyone was used to her automatic innuendoes, and Daisy Bruce took her remark as an excuse to murmur soothingly,

'Perhaps they brought them back from America,' and to follow this with 'You didn't happen to see them, I suppose?'

'Well, I did as it happens,' Miss Porteous admitted. 'That is to say, I saw a lady who, from the directions she seemed to be giving, I assumed was the mistress of the house. She didn't look at all like one's idea of an American, not in the least smart or – if I may use the word – "flashy."'

'What *was* she like?' someone asked anxiously.

Miss Porteous seemed at a loss to explain. 'Perfectly – well, ordinary,' she said at last. 'A tall woman in a tweed suit and flat-heeled shoes and wavy black hair.'

It occurred irreverently to Wendy that the only place in Kelmscott from which the ladies could possibly have seen over the high laurel hedge dividing them from Green Lawns was the bathroom window, and that was certainly only wide enough for one lady to see out of at a time. Did they quite openly take turns, she wondered, or was the whole thing done surreptitiously under quite another pretext? At present she herself had only one interest in the newcomers. 'Any children?' she asked.

'Unfortunately yes,' said Miss Porteous with a sigh. 'I need hardly tell you that I, of all people, have no aversion from children as such, but when I think of all the incidental annoyances that their presence, so near to our little retreat, may entail, I must confess my heart sinks.'

Then they must be small, thought Wendy. Her disappointment was greater than she had anticipated. Unconsciously she had been staking all her hopes on the possibility that the new people at Green Lawns would include a husband for

Margaret. My head aches, she said to herself, I can't stand all this noise.

'I suppose one ought to call?' suggested little Mrs Winterton, the war widow from the Rowans.

'I think we should,' agreed Miss Evadne warmly, 'particularly as she's an American. I've always heard that they're very warm and friendly themselves, and we wouldn't want her to think we're stand-offish.'

'Still, one wants to be discreet,' said Mrs Paynter-Smith, the wife of the retired clergyman. 'I've always heard that it's very hard to disengage oneself from Americans once one has made their acquaintance. And, after all, we don't know anything about them. They may not be our sort at all.'

'But a call doesn't do any harm,' said Daisy encouragingly. 'You call on them, they return the call, and if you don't like them it can all end there.' She herself was determined to be one of the first to walk up the drive of Green Lawns with her visiting-cards. Enthusiastic curiosity coupled with a total inability to dislike anyone richer than herself would spur her on. 'You'll come with me, Wendy?' she added.

'If I feel up to it,' Wendy said heavily. The headache was very real now, a piercing stab that left little lights dancing before her eyes.

'You look all in,' said Doctor Gregory bluntly. 'Been doing too much, that's what it is. Why don't you shoot off home now, and I'll come along and have a look at you in the morning.'

'I'm all right,' Wendy said irritably; no need to have a doctor until one was actually ill, and that one couldn't afford

51

to be. Gerald had broken off his chat with Mrs Winterton and had come to her side, saying, 'Better be getting off now, old lady, if all these good people will excuse us,' and they said their goodbyes and left the party, every step up the hill a hammer blow on to Wendy's aching forehead.

Daisy Bruce, dropping in next morning to borrow the steriliser to bottle some peas, was shocked at Wendy's appearance. 'Why don't you take the day in bed?' she asked solicitously. 'Gerald can come and eat with us and I'll pop round with a tasty morsel for you. It's silly to overdo things and knock yourself up.'

But Wendy was beyond good advice. Her overwrought irritability drove her on and on. 'There are a thousand things to do,' she had protested to Daisy, and to justify herself innumerable odd jobs were started, mostly pointless and futile like hacking off the fur inside the kettle, unravelling an old jumper that was too far gone ever to be knitted up into something new, each job, in any case, discarded before it was finished as Wendy thought of another one and forgot the first. She knew perfectly well at the back of her mind what it was she was trying to evade, but it couldn't be put off for ever, and just before the girls came home she rang up St Friedeswyth's School in Walbridge and made an appointment to see Miss Latimer to talk over Margaret's future.

Though Miss Latimer was, as everyone agreed, a very nice woman, a very intelligent and conscientious woman, it was beyond human possibility that she should be able to devote the same amount of attention to the future of each of her seven hundred pupils. She had, of course, the knack which every good headmistress must possess, of being able to convince the parent she was speaking to that *her* child was her most especial interest, but while discussing Margaret with her mother, a part of Miss Latimer's mind was reminding her that it was the other Trevor girl who was the clever one and that it didn't matter much what Margaret did, she'd never amount to much. In Miss Latimer's opinion, clever girls had careers and girls who weren't clever did something or other until they got married, and what it was they did didn't really matter very much.

'I wondered,' said Wendy, 'if perhaps she'd shown some special talent for something, perhaps something we at home wouldn't have noticed?' She has a genius for organisation, drawing, hockey – she imagined, but Miss Latimer said, 'Of course, I haven't had to teach Margaret myself, as she's not passed beyond the matric class. But I've had very full reports on her from her form-mistress, who tells me that although she is an extremely nice girl, a very good type indeed, she really has no special talents we can lay our fingers on.'

'You see, she's nearly eighteen,' Wendy said hesitantly, 'and we'd wondered – well, whether she oughtn't to spend this next year being trained for something. I thought you might be able to advise me –' Her voice trailed away.

Miss Latimer remembered something. 'You will forgive me if I speak frankly,' she said, 'but I believe you told me, when the girls first entered school, that you and your husband had decided that it was your intention to, as it were, invest in your daughters' education rather than provide them with – er – I suppose one could say a dowry when they grew up.'

Wendy nodded. 'A wise decision,' Miss Latimer continued, 'and one that one could wish more parents would make.' She hesitated, not quite sure how to go on. It was obvious that the Trevors were as poor as church mice, but one still had more or less to abide by the convention that one was never prevented from doing the best for one's children for lack of money. 'In these times,' she went on smoothly, hoping that her pause had not been too long, 'I feel we must all of us consider very carefully whether the old way of doing things is the one that will best benefit our children. Before the war, Mrs Trevor, I should have had no hesitation in advising you to leave Margaret with us for still another year. Even though, in her case, there would have been no question of a university, there are still a great many corners to be rubbed off in the last year at school, while the responsibility of being a prefect is, for most girls, an excellent preparation for adult life. But now, Mrs Trevor, we can none of us see what the future may bring. And though' – she gave a little laugh – 'I suppose I shouldn't let the Governors hear me saying it, you may well feel that Margaret could more profitably pass the coming year in doing some definite training rather than remain at school.'

'What training?' asked Wendy abruptly.

Miss Latimer smiled largely, at a loss for words. 'Nowadays,' she said, 'there are so many splendid opportunities for girls. The trouble, I fear, is that for most of the more interesting careers, the minimum educational requirement is the matriculation certificate and that, unfortunately, was beyond Margaret's capacity. Personally, I think a girl can never go far wrong if she takes a course in shorthand-typing. There are always interesting jobs available for the *better* class of girl, private secretarial jobs and so on.'

'Of course,' said Wendy with relief. Of course there were all those jobs one had always heard about, the secretary to the author, the MP, the society hostess, *nice* jobs that took one among interesting people and led to something. She didn't realise that Miss Latimer, in fact, knew nothing about the opportunities for shorthand-typists; was simply voicing the same belief in jobs for well-bred girls that Wendy held herself. Miss Latimer's information on the subject of jobs for university graduates could hardly be bettered; if a definite career needing poorer qualifications was called for, Miss Latimer's secretary knew where to find the appropriate booklet for the enquiring parent; for the rest, as now, Miss Latimer recommended shorthand-typing.

'I'm so very much obliged to you for your advice,' said Wendy, standing up, slipping her hands into the old but still good hogskin gloves, easier in her mind now that something was, as she saw it, settled. 'We have high hopes of Sheila,' said Miss Latimer, graciously standing too. 'I don't think there can be much doubt, Mrs Trevor, that a distinguished mathematical career lies before her.' 'You do still think she'll get a University scholarship?' Wendy asked anxiously at the door, remembering again that they'd only worked out the money until the girls were eighteen, and Miss Latimer again assured her that there was no doubt, no doubt at all. 'And don't worry about Margaret,' she added. 'I'm sure she'll find a very satis-factory niche for herself somewhere.'

Back home, Wendy found the family having tea. They seemed to be having a good time, judging by the shrieks of laughter that greeted her as she came in at the door. 'What's the joke?' she said, and then, without waiting for an answer, 'Don't you think it would have been a little more polite if you'd waited till I came in?'

Sheila ignored this and went on eating. Margaret looked imploringly at her father, but he kept his eyes on his plate and it was left to her to say pleadingly, 'Daddy came in and Sheila wanted to get on with her homework, so I thought you wouldn't mind –'

'Oh, all right then,' said Wendy grudgingly, sinking on to one of the kitchen chairs. Then a new cause of offence caught her eye and she exploded, 'Haven't I told you before that I won't have your finickety ways in my house? What's the idea, cutting sandwiches in those fancy shapes when you know we've been asked to save bread?'

'Sorry, Mummy,' Margaret said miserably. It had been awful this last week. She never seemed to be able to do any-thing right and Mummy lost her temper all the time. 'I'd better be off and do my homework,' said Sheila rising, secure in the knowledge that now that Margaret had got herself into trouble, she wouldn't remind Sheila that it was her turn to wash up. Besides, Sheila said to herself, not wanting to behave badly but needing some justification, my homework really matters and it's not as if Margaret's got anything else to do.

Wendy drank her tea and felt a little better. 'Don't clear for the moment,' she said to Margaret, 'I want to have a little talk with you.' 'You won't want me, will you?' asked Gerald, thinking there'd just be time to get down to the village and try for a packet of Weights before the shops shut. 'I thought we might discuss Margaret's future,' Wendy said coldly, some of her irritability returning, 'but if that's not a subject that interests you, you might as well be off to your cronies.'

'All right, I'll stay,' Gerald muttered and sat down again. Margaret found her fingers and toes slowly bunching up and slowly straightening again as she waited uneasily.

'I've just come back from seeing Miss Latimer,' Wendy said, 'but before I tell you her suggestions, I'd like to know, Margaret, if you've got any of your own.'

Goodness knows Margaret had thought about it enough. You couldn't not think about your future when at home everyone was worrying about money all the time and at school nearly all her contemporaries were talking excitedly about being grown-up. Every night in her striped flannel pyjamas Margaret thought about the future, but none of the things she knew she wanted of it could be expressed in words as an acceptable intention.

'I don't really know,' she said miserably at last, 'I mean, I'm not really any good at anything.'

'That's not very helpful, is it?' Wendy commented. There was really no reason for the approach she had chosen since she had already accepted Miss Latimer's suggestion, but some obscure groping for justice made her willing to impose it only after Margaret had been shown to have no clear wishes of her own. She went on impatiently, 'But you must have some kind of an idea of what you want. What do you see yourself doing when you grow up?'

'Being married,' Margaret said immediately. She had no intention in the world of allowing this to slip out. It was simply an unconscious response to the way Wendy had framed her question; every night, before she went to sleep, Margaret saw herself as married, saw herself in a kitchen cooking, in a living-room knitting, in the streets with her ration-books, pushing a pram.

Gerald said unexpectedly, 'I think the girl's right. She'd make someone a first-class wife. Look how good she is round the house.'

Wendy herself was thoroughly bad around the house and knew it. Loathing everything to do with housework, constantly resentful of the circumstances that against all her reasonable expectations had forced her to do it, she did it incompetently and with a very bad grace. To have sat down every week and polished the silver, to have read the recipe-books and produced appetising meals for her family would have meant, to her, willing acceptance of the servitude to which she was so unwillingly bound. Margaret's obvious longing to be allowed to do the job her mother most loathed struck at Wendy's belief that her own attitude was the right and proper one and so criticised, not only her methods but the attitude itself. That she'd run her own house in her own way had increasingly become her stock response to Margaret's longing offers to help.

Now she said coldly, 'Are you trying to break it to us, Margaret, that you've become engaged? I didn't think that in

58

these days any girl would look on marriage as a way to get out of taking a job.'

Margaret blushed a fiery scarlet. Her fingers went on clenching and unclenching themselves. She said nothing.

Wendy went on with mounting fury, 'I suppose you'd like me to be the one to go out and take a job while you run my home for me.'

It would be marvellous, sprang into Margaret's mind. Mummy's often said how bored she is – how she'd like to get away – does she really mean it? Almost instantaneously she realised that Wendy was speaking not seriously but in angry derision, but an idea had presented itself to her. She said, 'Mummy, do you think I could take a job as a cook?'

Wendy said, 'You must be mad.' Then she said, 'What do you think you mean?'

Margaret said eagerly, 'Mummy, listen, Mummy, I can cook, you know I can, it's a thing I'm really good at. Mummy, everyone wants cooks and I heard you say to Mrs Bruce only the other day that cooks get at least three pounds a week and they live in so it's all pocket-money and I'm sure I couldn't get as much as that at anything else.'

Wendy said in icy anger, 'Do you realise what you're proposing? You're suggesting that you – my daughter – go and live in somebody else's house as a servant at everyone's beck and call, sleeping in a maid's room, walking out with the butcher's boy, mixing with low common –' Her anger, her disgust choked her.

Margaret was devastated. What a fool, what a fool she'd been. It was just like her to think of something that was impossible.

Gerald was moved by her obvious distress. He said, 'Buck up, Wendy, I'm sure that isn't what the girl really meant. She just hadn't thought.'

It's true she'd make a good cook, Wendy thought irrationally, if she wasn't my daughter, I mean, if she was someone like Edie Wilson, I'd be glad to employ her. An idea came into her head and she said gently, 'Look, Margaret, if you'd really like to cook there are other ways of doing it than going and standing over someone else's stove. I believe there are all sorts of openings for dieticians in hospitals and schools and places, if one's properly trained.' I don't suppose it would cost any more than the shorthand-typing, she thought, and it's a perfectly respectable kind of work.

Margaret shook her head. 'I don't think I'd like that,' she said dully. It was the idea of cooking for a home, pleasing a family that appealed to her. Working out diets after taking a training had no relation to what Margaret meant by cooking.

'Then what it comes down to,' Wendy said in tones of martyred patience, 'is that since you don't really want to do anything within the realms of possibility, it doesn't much matter what you do.'

There was nothing for Margaret to say.

Wendy went on, 'So I'd better tell you Miss Latimer's extremely sensible suggestion, which is that you should take a shorthand-typing course with an eye to getting a good secretarial job. How does that appeal to your ladyship?'

'It's all right,' Margaret muttered, trying hard not to let the tears springing into her eyes grow large enough to fall.

'I hope it *will* be all right,' Wendy said coldly. 'Daddy and I can hardly afford to spend money on expensive courses for you unless you're prepared to make a real effort to see that it will be all right.'

'I'll do my best,' Margaret said in a choked voice and then the tears wouldn't hold back any longer. With a strangled sob she turned round and left the room. They heard her slowly, heavily, going up the steep narrow stairs to her bedroom, and Wendy and Gerald were left staring at each other across the cluttered kitchen table.

Gerald stretched out his legs, his hands in his pockets. 'I suppose it's the best thing,' he said uneasily, 'but I can't really say I like it. Damn it, it's not what we used to hope for for the girl.'

'I know,' said Wendy. There was a pause. Both thought back over the many hopes and plans they'd had, remembered them too vividly, with too much mutual comprehension to need any words.

'It doesn't seem fair, does it?' Gerald said gently, softly. 'You didn't have to work. Your sister didn't have to work. My sister Doris didn't have to work. Nobody thought it wrong that you all just stayed at home till you married. That bitch Trixie Beltram never even married, but because she's got a private income no one ever expected her to go out and take a job.'

'But it's different nowadays,' Wendy said pleadingly. 'Most girls do want to take jobs. Even if they've got money, lots of them work just the same.'

'But some of them don't,' said Gerald, 'and Margaret's

one of the ones that doesn't want to. Well, I don't know, but it does seem hard.'

Wendy's momentary calm cracked and she cried, 'My God, what else can we do? We're not going to live for ever. Suppose she doesn't marry, suppose she never marries, there isn't a penny in the world for her except what she can earn for herself. There isn't a penny in the world for our children.'

Her face twisted in a sudden contortion of despair, then fell on her arms stretched out over the kitchen table as she sobbed and sobbed over the dirty tea-cups.

CHAPTER FOUR

Mrs Green of the Ironmongery was entertaining Mrs
Pickering of the Electrical Shop in the lounge of her little flat
over the shop in the Arcade. Both husbands had been sent,
not in the least unwillingly, to the Master-At-Arms for an hour
or so while the ladies settled the details of the coming alliance
between their two families.

'I didn't want to say it in front of Albert,' said Edna
Pickering, 'he's that particular about gossip, being People's
Warden and all, but I was wondering if you'd heard any
rumour about Miss Moodie?'

'Rumours don't often come my way,' said Mrs Green in a
slightly superior tone, though everyone knew there wasn't
a thing happened she wasn't the first to cotton on to. 'But if
people keep themselves to themselves like Miss Moodie's been
doing lately, they can't be surprised if people wonder if there
isn't something to talk about.'

'Well, I did hear,' said Mrs Pickering, leaning towards her
hostess across the rayon-damask couch of the three-piece
suite, 'that Miss Moodie's been thinking of giving up the
Drapery and retiring for good.'

'Well now, it's funny you should be saying that,' said Mrs

Green graciously, 'because just that very story did come to my ears – let me see – it must be a good week ago now. And I said to myself when I heard it, well, I said, if there's any truth in it, I said, that's the very thing for Ted and Rosemary.'

'There's a little gold mine in that shop,' Mrs Pickering said. 'Mind you, I'm not saying it ought to be run like Miss Moodie's been running it. She's not kept up with the times, to my way of thinking. But if someone took it that felt like branching out a bit, say, with some pretty little kiddies' clothes and some really dainty lingerie, there's a lot could be done with it. If Ted kept on with his father, now, it would be the very thing for Rosemary, and put a nice little something in their pockets. There's not another drapery store between here and Walbridge, and in these times people would sooner go to someone they know who'll keep back a bit of something for them than try where they're no better than strangers. There's no doubt about it, you don't get anything these days unless you know the right people.'

'You don't happen to know what she's asking for it, do you?' enquired Mrs Green, keeping firmly to the point.

'It oughtn't to be too hard to find out,' said Mrs Pickering. 'It'll be a packet, I'll be bound. Miss Moodie's not one to let anything go cheap.'

Mrs Green said idly, 'I wonder what she'll do now. That sister of hers in Eastbourne died last Easter, didn't she?'

'Last Whitsun,' corrected Mrs Pickering, and then, 'You don't think she'd have some idea of just letting the shop and keeping on with the flat, do you? That wouldn't be a mite of use to our young people. After all, they want somewhere to live as well as a business.'

'Well, we'll just have to see,' said Mrs Green with decision. 'But if it did come off, and I don't see why it shouldn't, then we could get them married, say, just before Christmas. I'll have a talk with the Rector as soon as we know anything definite.'

'It's a pity old Mr Hall died,' said Mrs Pickering with a sigh. 'Somehow I can't seem to take to this new man. He's a bit too – well, he's not really a gentleman, if you know what I mean.'

'And that wife of his,' agreed Mrs Green, 'she doesn't seem to have the faintest idea of how a Rector's wife is supposed to behave. I saw her pushing that baby of theirs along to the Clinic last Wednesday, no hat, bare legs, and the baby not the least bit dainty. Do you know, for the moment, I didn't recognise her. I thought she was one of those Station Road women. Well, I suppose it's not surprising, considering what she was before she married.'

'It's a marvel to me how you get to know these things,' said Mrs Pickering, generously attentive.

'An elementary school-teacher, that's what she was,' said Mrs Green with relish. 'An elementary school-teacher at an LCC school somewhere in Paddington. Well, it just shows, I mean, it's hardly what one expects of a Rector's wife.'

Mrs Pickering's daughter Eileen was an elementary school-mistress and thought to have done nicely for herself, but both ladies agreed with complete sincerity that it wasn't the background they liked to see in their Rector's wife.

'They've not been taken up by the Priory Hill people,' said Mrs Pickering maliciously.

'That lot,' said Mrs Green with contempt, 'there's not one of them I'd give you a thank-you for, except, perhaps, Miss Graham. Now she's a real lady, even if she hasn't got two pennies to rub together. But the rest of the gentry – well, you can have them as far as I'm concerned. It's not them that's going to make our fortunes, as you know very well. I reckon there isn't one of them that we couldn't buy up with one hand tied behind our backs, as the saying goes. To tell you the truth, Edna, and I don't mind who hears me say it, there's more business done these days with the Station Road people than with the Priory Hill lot.'

'Just what Mr Parker was saying to my hubby only the other day,' Mrs Pickering agreed. 'I don't get a mite less meat in, he said, even with the rationing, than I used to do before the war. The difference, he said, is that before the war the Station Road people didn't buy meat not more than once in a blue moon, and now they take up their full ration every week, and offal too whenever it's going.'

'Mind you, it's shocking the way they throw their money about,' Mrs Green said in virtuous indignation. 'Some of those kiddies, now, there seems to be no limit to what they've got to spend. Mrs Brotherton said to me, only the other day, she said, there's some of them come into the shop two and three times a day and buy anything that takes their fancy, comics and sherbet powder and even things like quite expensive toys. There's any number of them, she said, that get ten shillings a week and more to put in their pockets.'

'It can't go on like that, you mark my words,' said Mrs Pickering. 'You wait till the war-spending's over and they've got to come to their senses. It stands to reason that they can't go on making money the way they've been doing.'

'My hubby says that's when *we're* going to feel the pinch,' Mrs Green said with a sigh. 'There'll be a few more years of it, he says, what with gratuities and then everyone wanting the goods coming back into the shops. And after that, he says, that's when we're going to feel the draught, what with the Priory Hill people, who used to be steady spenders, looking twice at every penny.'

'What about these new people though?' said Mrs Pickering hopefully. 'These Americans or whatever they are who've taken Green Lawns. That must have cost them a pretty penny, I shouldn't wonder.'

'Funny you should mention them,' exclaimed Mrs Green. 'That's just what I said to my hubby. There'll be new people coming in, I said, like those Wetheralls, I said, who've got a bit of money to spend, and so long as they find they can get what they want in the village, I said, we all of us might be able to build up a really high-class trade again.'

'Wetherall?' repeated Mrs Pickering. 'That's an English enough name. Why, I used to know some Wetheralls at Harrow when I was a girl.'

'It's only her that's American,' Mrs Green explained. 'It seems he's the London manager of one of the big motor firms. Bill Cotterell, he's going to be their gardener, and he heard it all from the Nanny they brought with them. They're looking for a good maid, he said, and I thought of recommending Edie Wilson if I got the chance. Mrs Wilson was in the shop yesterday and she said Edie's getting her release from the factory any day now. She's a good reliable girl, too, not like some of them nowadays that think themselves too good to go into service. Why, now –' she broke off, hearing footsteps on the stairs, 'if it isn't those men back again and me so busy gossiping I forgot to put the kettle on.' She reared her large bulk from the deep armchair and bustled into the kitchen as the men came in.

'You ladies got everything cut and dried and settled?' asked Mr Green, settling himself and motioning Mr Pickering to do likewise.

'As near as makes no difference,' Mrs Pickering replied, wondering whether to mention the rumour about Miss Moodie, and then deciding that it was one of those projects best hinted at privately in bed.

'Well, Mr Pickering and I have been cogitating on weighty affairs of state,' said Mr Green jovially. 'Isn't that so, Mr Pickering?'

'Meaning what, may I ask?' said Mrs Pickering archly.

'Meaning the street-lighting,' Mr Pickering said seriously as befitted a man who was not only People's Warden but Chairman of the Parish Council as well.

'You talking about the street-lighting?' asked Mrs Green, coming in with a tray. 'Well, we could do with it and no mistake. Mr Pickering, what do you say to a nice cup of tea?'

'I don't mind if I do,' said Mr Pickering conventionally. 'Yes, we've done without it too long if you ask me. Every meeting we've had where it's been brought up, it's been the

Priory Hill people put a spoke in the wheel. Last time it was Mr Bruce saying it would destroy the old-world character of the village, but if you ask me, it's something extra on the rates *they're* frightened of.'

'As to the old-world character or whatever it is,' said Mr Green, 'there's not so much of it left now, and with the pre-fabs on the field back of the churchyard and the new Housing Estate they say the Walbridge Rural is going to put down at the bottom of Archery Lane, there'll be less still. And what I say is, not having the street-lighting is going to take trade away from the village. People like a bit of cheerfulness on winter evenings, and if they don't get it here, well, they're just going to take the bus into Walbridge and do their bit of shopping there.'

'And there's another thing,' put in Mrs Green, busy dispensing tea and handing round the sliced slab cake, 'if what they say is true and it's Irish they're going to put into the pre-fabs, well, it won't be safe to have the place unlit at night. It's all right when it's just our own folks, but Mr Timms can't be everywhere at once, and if the Irish are anything like what they say they are, it just won't be safe for our girls to go out alone without the streets are properly lit.'

'I hadn't heard about the Housing Estate,' said Mr Pickering who liked to take things in slowly. 'That'll make a bit of difference to the place, won't it?'

'Be all to the good, if you ask me,' said Mr Green firmly. 'There'll be no excuse for not having the lighting if there's going to be a lot of expansion. Anyway the Priory Hill people don't really cut no ice any more. If we set about it properly, we should get a resolution through about the lighting at the next Parish Council meeting.'

'Which reminds me,' said Mrs Green, 'Dad, you were going to have a word with Mr Pickering about the television, weren't you?'

'That's right,' said Mr Green. 'The wife and I were thinking it's going to be a bit lonely in the evenings when Rosemary goes off – not that we see much of her as it is. So we were thinking, when you get those television sets in, we'd ask you to put one aside for us.'

'The very first that comes in,' promised Mr Pickering grandly, 'shall be yours. And the second,' he added, 'Mother and I are going to keep for ourselves. Seems to me there's going to be quite a run on television sets.'

'Well, it's been very nice,' said Mrs Pickering, getting up. 'Come on now, Albert, we must be getting home. Goodbye, dear,' she said to Mrs Green, and a glance between the two ladies confirmed that the rumour about Miss Moodie and the Drapery would be relentlessly pursued.

The calls on the new people at Green Lawns were duly made. Every afternoon at twenty-past three – for prior discussion had arranged just who went when – one or other of the Priory Hill ladies had walked between the laurel-hedges up the neat gravel drive, up the red brick steps to the porch with its round copper lantern dangling overhead, rung the bell that sounded in the hall with such melodious chimes. The first lady to call, Mrs Paynter-Smith, had reported that Mrs Wetherall didn't seem to have much experience of callers, had assumed it was an informal visit and had pressed her to stay to tea. But of course Mrs Paynter-Smith had not allowed this warm-hearted American hospitality to deflect her from her duty, and, when twenty minutes had gone by, rose and took her leave, depositing, as she went, three visiting-cards on the table. Miss Beltram, the next caller, reported that Mrs Wetherall had evidently now been instructed in the niceties of calling, for she was allowed, at the end of her twenty minutes, to take her leave without demur and found a round silver tray waiting for her single card on the hall-table.

The general opinion of the newcomers was distinctly favourable. All allowances were made for Mrs Wetherall's origins and it was agreed that you really got used to her accent quite quickly and it wasn't in the least displeasing, not a bit like the films. 'There's evidently plenty of money there,' the ladies agreed, as they told their husbands about the big radiogram and the fitted carpets and the new paint that shone resplendent everywhere, even though the official amount allowed to be spent on houses was only ten pounds a year. But this wasn't a regulation that public opinion had accepted as moral, and finding a builder who would break it was perfectly all right and not in the least like buying meat on the black market.

Daisy Bruce was determined to foster her acquaintance with the Wetheralls. For one thing it had come out in conversation that Martha Wetherall's elder child, David, was just the same age as her Christopher and in a village where the gentry were sparse and tended to be barren, a possible new acquaintance for any child was a prize of the highest order, to say nothing of the incidental advantages that might accrue from knowing a household with a Nanny who might, if won over, sometimes be persuaded to take Christopher and relieve his mother from her otherwise unremitting vigil. And then (though Daisy wouldn't have liked to put such a thing into words, even to herself) there had come with the Wetheralls a breath of a more spacious world in which people dined out in London and wore nylons and tailor-made clothes and rang the bell for maids to bring this and clear that. It wasn't, no, not even for a minute, that Daisy would have dreamt of asking or suggesting or even hinting that such a thing as a pair of nylons might ever be offered to her, but the mere coming into contact with such things after so many years of privation seemed to suggest a richer more promising life opening before her.

So a couple of days after she'd made her call, Daisy, running into Mrs Wetherall outside the grocer, said, 'Now I wonder if you'll mind if I'm frightfully informal and ask you if you and your husband will come in and have coffee with us after dinner tomorrow. I'm sure you've got an awful lot to do without returning calls, and if you'll just come in and take us as you find us, it would be perfectly delightful.'

'Why, that would be just lovely,' said Martha Wetherall. 'To tell you the truth, I haven't got any English cards printed as yet, and wherever I go to try to get them done, there seems to be some kind of a regulation against it. So I'd certainly be relieved not to have to make a proper call without the right equipment. Would nine o'clock be about right?'

'Well –' said Daisy hesitating. 'Say – half-past eight, if that isn't too early for you.' She'd really meant to say eight o'clock, which had become the regular Priory Hill time for evening parties now that everyone had their evening meal at seven or earlier, but evidently the Wetheralls dined formally at the usual time and Daisy didn't like to confess that her own habits were less conventional than theirs.

'Half-past eight will be lovely,' said Mrs Wetherall heartily. 'We'll look forward to it,' and Daisy went back up the hill, dropping in on Wendy on her way home.

Wendy was, as usual, in the kitchen, angrily thumping some pastry. 'Come and sit down,' she said. 'I'm trying to get something done for tomorrow as usual, but it never seems to work out, and tomorrow I'll be doing something for the day after.'

'I've asked the Wetheralls in tomorrow evening,' Daisy explained, 'and I was thinking it would be nice if you and Gerald would come along too.'

'Goodness, I haven't even called yet,' Wendy exclaimed in dismay. 'I meant to, and then there seemed to be so many other things to do.'

'Never mind, do come,' Daisy urged. 'She really seems very nice, not a bit like an American.'

'How old is she?' Wendy asked, thumping the pastry on to the board and leaning heavily on to the rolling pin.

'Thirty-ish,' Daisy said. 'Quite good-looking if you like the sort. You know, tall and dark and very alive-looking. If the husband's presentable too, they might be quite an asset. It'll do us good to have some new people around.'

'I'm not sure that I feel up to meeting new people,' Wendy said doubtfully. 'I've had such a headache this past week, and as soon as I've got the dinner washed up, I've just dropped into bed.'

'Why don't you see if Doctor Gregory can do something about it?' Daisy suggested, but Wendy said hurriedly, 'Oh, it's not bad enough for that,' and then, 'All right, we'll come. Perhaps it will do me good to get out.'

'Well, I won't keep you now,' said Daisy, having gained her point. At the kitchen door she turned and suggested, 'Why don't you bring Margaret too? You know they've got a tennis court at Green Lawns, and if they put it in order again, they might ask her down to play.' Across both minds flitted a vision, a remembrance of earlier summer afternoons back in their own girlhoods, the young people in trim white, the gaudy awnings over the swing-couch, the assiduous young men handing glasses of tart lemonade. 'I'd like to, if she's home in good time,' said Wendy. 'She's going to tea with that friend of hers, Jill Morton.' Picking up the disapproval in Wendy's voice, Daisy obediently said, 'Somehow I can never take to that girl; I don't know why it is.'

'I suppose they're bound to get all sorts at a school like St Friedeswyth's,' Wendy said reluctantly, 'though I must say I wish Margaret had shown a bit more discrimination. It's a pity we couldn't manage to send her to Wycombe Abbey, as we'd hoped.'

'Her father's got a shop or something, hasn't he?' Daisy asked sympathetically.

'Yes, a cheap clothing-shop or something with branches

all over the City,' Wendy said. 'I believe they're Jews, though naturally I've never liked to ask. Mind you, I've nothing against Jews as such, but they do tend to be a bit – well, you know.'

'I know,' Daisy agreed. 'I must say, I always thought the girl rather over-dressed whenever I've seen her. I wouldn't be surprised if you weren't right. Where do they live, anyway?'

'The other side of Walbridge,' said Wendy. 'I believe it's quite a nice house, from what I can drag out of Margaret, you know, one of those new ones round the Common. Really, it's lucky it's so far away; at least they can't be running in and out of each other's homes every minute.'

'It's a pity there aren't any girls of her age round here,' said Daisy for the hundredth time. 'Well, I must be running along now or Mrs Wilkins'll be off and there'll be Christopher all alone. They won't stay a minute beyond their time, these days. As soon as it's twelve o'clock she's off, even if it means leaving something half done.'

'Well, we'll be along,' Wendy called after her, 'and I'll bring Margaret if she's back in time.'

Though it was a fine sunny day, Margaret and Jill Morton found Jill's bed-sitting room far more conducive to confidential discussion than the trim tended garden. Life at St Friedeswyth's was deliberately organised so as to leave no time for leisurely – and therefore, by definition subversive – talks between the girls, and Jill and Margaret's friendship flourished on the meagre diet of a going-out-to-tea about once a month. This was their first meeting since Margaret's future had been decided, and at about the same time Jill's future had been decided too.

'So Daddy spoke to the Advertising Manager,' Jill was saying, 'and *he* spoke to the Editor and *she* said that she'd take me on to try. I went to see her last week and she was awfully friendly, not a bit frightening, and she said that if I worked hard and didn't mind what I did to start with, I'd have a good chance of becoming a real journalist. Mind you, I don't want to stay on a magazine like that all my life. What I really want is to get on to *Vogue*, but I didn't like to say that to her, of course. But Daddy says if I get experience, then I ought to be able to go where I want later on.'

'What's *Meg's Magazine* like?' Margaret asked. 'I've seen it in Brotherton's, but I've never looked at it.'

'It's really a servant-girls' magazine,' Jill said contemptuously. 'You know the sort of thing – letters to Nurse Madge and how to knit the most godawful striped pullovers. I bet I can pep it up a lot.'

'I'm sure you can,' Margaret agreed admiringly. She added, 'But won't you get awfully tired going up to London every day? Everyone says the trains are horribly crowded now, and it'd take you a good hour each way.'

'I'm not going every day,' Jill said loftily. 'Mummy's going to arrange for me to have a room with some friends of hers who've got a boarding-house in Hampstead, and I'll only come home for weekends. Won't it be marvellous, being absolutely free and on one's own?' An idea struck her, and she turned eagerly to Margaret. 'Look here, Meggie, why don't you persuade your people to send you to a secretarial school in London, and then you could come too? Just think what fun it would be, just the two of us, able to do whatever we liked. I bet we'd have a marvellous time.'

'It *would* be awfully nice,' Margaret said. 'Perhaps we could have a room with a gas-ring and cook our own food.'

'Oh, we don't want to bother with anything like *that*,' Jill said loftily. 'These people are Austrians and Mummy says they're frightfully good cooks. I can't see why anyone wants to bother with cooking unless they have to.'

'But I like cooking,' Margaret protested. Jill looked at her searchingly and said, 'You know, Margaret Trevor, what you ought to be is a wife, not a secretary. You seem to like all the things that bore me stiff. I bet you'd be happy in a little house somewhere, counting the laundry and washing out the nappies.'

'I should,' said Margaret with a sigh. Jill said, 'Well, I'm not going to marry a poor man and work like that. The man I marry's got to have enough money for me never to do any housework.'

'Then I'll come and be your maid,' Margaret offered with a laugh. Jill laughed too, and then said, 'But since neither of us is going to get married just at present, what do you think of my idea?'

'I think I'd rather like it,' Margaret said hesitantly. 'I mean, what I'd really like best of all is to stay at home and help Mummy. She works much too hard and then she gets bad-tempered with me and I'm sure it's just tiredness. But I seem to get on her nerves all the time and Sheila never does, and perhaps if I did go away she'd be pleased to see me when I came back.'

'I don't know how anyone could get annoyed with you,' Jill said tenderly; Margaret's humble admiration had been for the last few years the mainstay of her own self-confidence. And the knowledge that to Jill she would be welcome led Margaret to promise, 'I will ask them. I think I'd like it very much if they said "Yes."'

But there was no chance to ask anything when Margaret got home, for she was only just in time to be hurried into the beige silk dress and snatch a mouthful of curried beef and lettuce before they must all go down the crazy-paving path out of Wood View and up the crazy-paving path to Ridgeways, next door.

From the coffee-and-biscuits at eight-thirty to the tea-and-home-made-madeira-cake at ten, the evening went off swimmingly. Ralph Wetherall turned out to be a trim plump man of about forty with gleaming iron-grey hair and a softly-tended ruddy complexion. He seemed anxious to learn all the other men could tell him about village personalities and affairs, and while not crudely pushing himself forward showed that he would be ready gradually to take in such matters the proper part of the owner of Green Lawns. Meanwhile the three ladies chatted together, Margaret listening interestedly on the outskirts of the group, appreciating though seldom profiting by the kindly efforts Mrs Wetherall made to drag her in to the conversation.

'What made you decide to come and settle in Priory Dean?' asked George Bruce over the tea-cups, when the conversation conventionally became general between the sexes.

'Pure chance,' Mr Wetherall replied. 'We wanted to be some little way out of London for the sake of the children, but not so far that I couldn't get in every day. We'd started looking south of the river and couldn't find anything that took our fancy, and then one day I ran into a man at the club – but you must know him, young Alan Thatcher of Thatcher and Son?'

'I've met him once or twice,' said Gerald, a little uneasily. The Thatchers of Bentworth Park with their Rolls-Royce and their herd of pedigree Jerseys were simultaneously admired for their wealth and position and despised for being of the new urban aristocracy who kept themselves to themselves and played no part in the life of the countryside.

Mr Wetherall went on, 'Well, it was he who suggested we should try Priory Dean. "It's one of the few unspoilt villages within twenty miles of London," he said to me, and by Jove he was right. Martha and I fell in love with it as soon as we saw it. Those houses round the village green now, they're real gems. Martha fell for that big Georgian one in the middle – the doctor's house, isn't it? – but I said to her, better to have some modern conveniences and keep the others for looking at.' He laughed heartily and the ladies fell to praising Green Lawns, its admirable modernity, the ease with which it could be run.

'But we don't know how much longer the village will stay unspoilt,' said George Bruce with a sigh. 'They've only put up those ugly shops along the Arcade in the past twenty years, and now we hear there's some talk of a new Housing Estate along Archery Lane. I'm afraid the character of the village is changing, there's no doubt about that.'

'I don't know that there's any harm in it,' said Ralph Wetherall, 'so long as they don't over-build. There seems to be no doubt that the overflow from London's got to go somewhere, and all these people should bring money into the village.'

'We've always rather prided ourselves on not just being a London dormitory,' said Gerald with dignity. 'Most of the people living here work locally, and we've rather felt it will destroy the character of the place if we get a lot of people whose interests lie outside.' It occurred to him that perhaps he was being a little rude, and he hurriedly added, 'Anyway, it's very good news that you and Mrs Wetherall propose taking an interest in our little local politics. We'll all be glad of some new blood.'

The Wetheralls murmured polite gratification and then Martha said, 'I'm afraid I'll be tied to my own home for a while until I've got it all straight. I've got a very pleasant girl Mrs Green kindly recommended to me, but it's going to take her some time to get used to my outlandish ways. When I told her to open a can of peaches to put with the sausages this evening, she looked at me as if I were mad.'

Daisy and Wendy had considerable difficulty themselves in preventing their faces from showing shocked incredulity instead of sympathetic understanding. Only Margaret for the first time that evening spoke spontaneously. 'Is that nice?' she asked eagerly.

'It's delicious,' Mrs Wetherall said firmly. 'You interested in cooking?' 'Ever so much,' said Margaret and Mrs Wetherall said, 'I'll tell you what. You come along to me one afternoon and I'll show you some American cooking. I've got Ralph's young step-brother coming on leave soon, and perhaps you'll come along then and help me to entertain him.'

'I'd love to come,' said Margaret, 'to learn about the cooking, I mean,' she hurriedly added, but Wendy, unwilling to let the topic die, asked, 'Is your brother-in-law in the Army?'

'No, the Navy,' said Martha, 'he's a regular. We're expecting him sometime after Christmas, and then I expect I'll have to set to and give some parties for him. He's a very gay young man.'

So it was with a newly-raised spirit of hopefulness that Wendy said her goodbyes and took her family home again, and it was the worst possible moment for Margaret to ask, as she did as soon as they got inside the door, 'Mummy, do you think I could go to a secretarial school in London?'

'Why, whatever for?' asked Wendy in astonishment. 'What's the point of going all that way and spending all that money on fares when there's a perfectly good school in Walbridge?'

'I hadn't meant wasting money on fares,' Margaret explained. 'What I really wondered was whether you'd let me go and live in London with Jill and just come home at weekends?'

Wendy exploded. 'I've never heard such nonsense,' she cried. 'In the first place, do you think I'd ever let a daughter of mine go off and live in London, completely unchaperoned, with a girl like Jill Morton? And secondly, where do you think the money's coming from? Daddy and I have all we can do to find the money for your fees at Walbridge, without keeping your ladyship in the lap of luxury in London while we work our fingers to the bone here.' On and on she went, lashing herself into a greater and greater frenzy of objurgation till at last she burst into tears and stood leaning against the stair-rail, shaking with spasmodic sobs.

Gerald said tentatively, 'Steady, old lady,' and then, as the sobs went on, 'I say, Wendy, you don't want to take it like that.'

Margaret stared at her mother in dismay. Never before had she seen her break down completely. Never had she seen anything like this dry, soundless sobbing she seemed totally unable to control. 'You must come to bed,' Gerald urged in a voice growing panicky, but he was unable to move Wendy and at last he called to Margaret in a voice angry with fear, 'For God's sake, don't stand there doing nothing. Get Daisy, she'll know what to do.' Margaret turned and fled out of the door, found herself explaining to Daisy that something was wrong with Mummy, was terribly, frighteningly wrong.

Daisy had started to train as a nurse before she married, and for all her little ways was consolingly competent in an emergency. She came quickly back with Margaret and without showing dismay persuaded the still sobbing Wendy to go up to bed, to swallow a couple of aspirins, to try to get to sleep. Then she came down again to where Gerald and Margaret had been waiting silently in the hall, and said, 'I think you'd better get Doctor Gregory to come and have a look at her in the morning,' and Gerald turned to Margaret and said with hysterical anger, 'She's ill now, she's going to be ill and it's all your fault.'

CHAPTER FIVE

When Doctor Gregory came next morning he diagnosed complete nervous exhaustion. 'I've seen it coming on for some time,' he said to Gerald, pacing up and down the muddy field at the back of the house, 'but there was nothing anyone could have done about it. These women are all the same, they go on working till they drop, and the only surprise is that the drop doesn't come sooner than it does.'

'But what's the *cause*?' asked Gerald desperately. 'She's never been ill before, except for flu and ordinary things like that.'

'Be much better if she had been,' said the Doctor firmly. 'Forced her to have spent a few days in bed occasionally. There isn't any cause except consistent overwork and too much nervous strain. All our women have been working like navvies since the beginning of the war, and now that the worst of that's over and some of the strain's been removed, they just pack up. Personally, I shan't be surprised if we see a lot of it now.' He pulled out his old silver turnip-watch, looked at it admonishingly and continued, 'There's no cure for a nervous breakdown but rest, good food and complete absence from worry. Now, how are you going to manage?'

He looked round at the dilapidated chicken-houses, the

rotting wire, the notice-board that had once been put up so hopefully, painted so gaily, and now sagged on its wooden posts, barely able still to convey the information that this was the Wood View Chicken Farm supplying pedigree birds and new-laid eggs at Competitive Prices. He thought: the little man's never had the guts to make a go of anything; it's that wife of his has been the moving spirit in everything and with her laid up he'll be sunk. Then quickly he modified his uncharitable criticism. He's only got one lung, he told himself, you can't expect – but still he was irritated and disappointed to hear Gerald saying plaintively, 'I really don't know how we'll manage. There's all the cooking and the housework –' His voice trailed dispiritedly away.

Doctor Gregory was used to organising the households in his parish. He snapped the watch to, slipped it into his waistcoat pocket again and said firmly, 'That elder girl of yours, Margaret. Can't you keep her at home for a bit and let her get on with the cooking?'

'I suppose so,' Gerald said miserably, 'but I don't think Wendy would like it. Besides, Margaret was supposed to be going to the secretarial school in Walbridge next term.'

'Put it off for a bit,' said the Doctor impatiently. 'The secretarial school won't run away. Mrs Trevor's got to have a good three months in bed and another three months taking it easy. Girl ought to be glad of the chance to do something for her mother. And surely you can find a woman to help with the rough?'

'There's old Mrs Wilkins,' said Gerald, 'she comes to us every Saturday.'

'Well, make her come a bit more often,' said the Doctor impatiently, 'and don't skimp on the food. I know what these women have been doing all through the war, going short themselves and giving their rations to the rest of the family. You tell Margaret from me that her mother's got to be fed up.' He turned his face away and said to the chicken-houses, 'You don't have to worry about my fees. There's no hurry about *them*. You put all you've got into Mrs Trevor's stomach. Yes, and put in a few bottles of port, *and* some champagne if she fancies it. Coddle the woman a bit.' Then he was gone and Gerald was left to review his financial position and wonder what the devil could be done.

All that was left of the capital he had started with was earmarked for finishing the girls' education. It was unthinkable that Sheila's share of it should be touched. If the cost of living went up any more, if the chicken-farm finally failed, if his health gave out, there was no hope for the future but Sheila's putative ability to earn and her willingness to help her parents in their old age. To help Wendy at Sheila's expense would simply be cutting off their noses to spite their faces.

But Margaret – Margaret, thought Gerald desperately, was a different proposition. Margaret was never going to be able to earn more than would barely keep herself and though, if they used the money put aside for her training, there wouldn't be any money for her training, surely something, something would turn up. She'd marry or – well, surely she would marry, and anyway the money had got to come from somewhere and Wendy's health was the first consideration. Besides, if you looked at it one way it was mostly Margaret's fault that Wendy was ill, being so worrying and difficult lately. It wasn't – no, it wasn't too unfair that she should pay for it. Of course it wasn't a happy solution, but a happy solution wasn't available. Miserably Gerald went indoors to tell Margaret that she must take over the cooking and the nursing and the housekeeping, and that whatever she could find in the way of nice food for Wendy must be bought, regardless of expense.

It wouldn't have been so bad, Margaret thought as the days went by, if only Mummy would seem *pleased* about it. But the first few weeks Wendy was unable to feel pleased about anything. Each time Margaret came up with a tray, a hot-water bottle, a nice cool drink, Wendy would raise herself for an irritated interrogation. How many loaves had Margaret taken? Had she remembered to send for the sweep? How much had she paid for the sole, and didn't she know that sole cost too much, much too much? It's all part of her being ill, Margaret told herself resolutely, she can't help it, and gradually she learnt to put on an expression of placid willingness, to assent to all Wendy's demands in theory and in practice to make out the best she could.

Gerald was no help at all. He carried on with the household tasks that were conventionally his, the stoking of the boiler, the boiling up the scraps for the chickens. He was, in fact, neat and tidy, almost finickety in his ways, and undoubtedly could, if encouraged, have done a great deal more in the house, but the girls had had it so firmly impressed on them that Daddy was delicate and must be looked after that

Margaret never thought of asking for his help, and simply added the cosseting of her father to her other labours.

It was impossible to look for much help from Sheila, who must be left in peace to get on with her schooling and the coming examinations. She changed Wendy's books for her at the Public Library, did her fair share of the washing-up and the cleaning at the weekends, and all one could say was that at least she didn't make much extra work. It had proved impossible to get Mrs Wilkins for any more time; her week-day mornings were all pledged to Daisy or to little Mrs Winterton at the Rowans and nothing was thought worse of in the village than seducing someone else's char.

The neighbours, of course, helped all they could. Hardly a day passed without someone dropping in, Mrs Paynter-Smith with some old magazines that Wendy might like to read, Miss Evadne with one of Talbot's special caramel custards. Margaret welcomed them all thankfully, not so much for what they brought but for their company for Wendy in the sick-room, the small local tittle-tattle that momentarily, at least, seemed to rouse her out of her depression.

Edith Wilson had heard about Wendy's illness, and worried herself sick, not knowing what to do for the best. 'I always did say I'd go back if it ever happened that she needed me,' she said for the umpteenth time, 'but I can't hardly go to her and say I'd come for nothing, now can I?'

'You stop worrying about it, Mum,' said Maureen, raising her head from her homework. 'I bet Mrs Trevor's not the sort to worry about you if it was you that was ill.'

'That's all you know about it, Miss,' said Edith sharply, 'that time I had the bronchitis when I was working for her she was along next day to see if there was anything I fancied she could get for me.'

'Oh, I'm not denying they'd spend their money if they'd got it,' Maureen said contemptuously, 'but I don't see Mrs Trevor coming along with an apron and scrubbing out the kitchen which is what you're longing to go and do for her.'

'And it's not proper that she should,' Edith said. 'Everybody helps the best way they can and that's all you can ask of anybody. I tell you straight, Maureen, I get real fed up with all your communist notions, from first thing at morning till last thing at night. If you can't find something nice to say, you'd do better to keep your mouth shut.'

'Oh, all right,' Maureen muttered and turned again to her work, her face in her hands, her lips moving automatically as she struggled to learn the prepositions on her page. Mrs Wilson at last made up her mind. 'There's an hour before Dad and Roy get back,' she said. 'I've made a nice stew and it's in the saucepan on the back of the stove. You put it on the gas in half an hour if I'm not back. I'm just going out to get a breath of air.'

Margaret, sitting down for the first time that day, heard the ring of the back door bell. 'Oh bother,' she said, struggling to her feet, thinking that Miss Beltram hadn't been for a couple of days, feeling that if it was Miss Beltram she'd scream. Most of the Priory Hill people had taken to dropping in at the back door since the war had driven them from their drawing-rooms into their kitchens. True, this meant that the housewife could, to some extent, get on with her work while she chatted (though only in so far as her work didn't entail leaving the kitchen and starting on the bedrooms) but it did prevent her ever being 'Not at Home' to inopportune guests.

So it was with positive pleasure that Margaret found she had opened the door not to Miss Beltram, but to Mrs Wilson, of whom all her memories were kind and warm. It was Mrs Wilson who had first taught her to cook; Mrs Wilson who always had a smile and an encouraging word for her whenever she had come into the kitchen; Mrs Wilson whose presence in the house had been the outward sign of the period of prosperity in which Wendy, comparatively free from care, had been consistently loving, good-tempered and gay; and more, Mrs Wilson had provided Roy, with whom the happiest memories of her childhood were linked. So she said spontaneously, 'Oh, Mrs Wilson, how nice to see you. Won't you come in?'

'I won't stay a minute,' said Mrs Wilson. 'I just happened to be passing and I thought I'd like to drop in and ask how Mrs Trevor was getting along. I was ever so sorry when I heard she was laid up.'

'Well, do come in just for a minute,' Margaret urged, and at last persuaded Mrs Wilson over the threshold and into the kitchen.

'It must make a lot of work for you,' she said, looking round. 'You want to be careful you don't go and knock yourself up too.'

'Oh, I'm all right,' Margaret said awkwardly. It wasn't quite true. She was feeling painfully tired all the time now and there was an ache in her back that wouldn't go away.

Edith Wilson took her courage in both hands. 'Your mother did a lot for me in the old days,' she said, 'and now she's laid up and can't see to everything herself, I'd like to be a bit of help. What I want you to let me do, Miss Margaret, is the wash. It's much too heavy work for you, and I've got young Edie to help me with mine after she gets back from Mrs Wetherall. She could come along every week and collect it, and we've got so much already your little bit won't make a mite of difference.'

'Oh, I couldn't,' Margaret said instantly. To be rid of the heavy wash would be the biggest boon imaginable. Laundries were getting more and more expensive and the fact that they'd lately been calling only about once a month had given Wendy a convenient excuse for doing everything at home. With inadequate equipment it was a back-breaking, infinitely tiring job – but one didn't accept favours from Poor People. She added quickly, 'But it's simply sweet of you to think of it.'

Looking at Margaret's tired face and the languor of her movements, Edith's courage grew. 'I'm not going to take no for an answer,' she said firmly. 'Turn and turn about's my motto, and it's not likely I'd ever forget all your mother did for me. If you think it would worry her to know about it now she's ill, you just say nothing about it till she's up and about again. Mind you, I'm not saying it's right to deceive her, but when people aren't well, you've often got to keep things from them for their own good.' She saw that Margaret was wavering and went on with kind finality, 'Now don't you think twice about it, Miss Margaret. You'd be doing me a real favour if you let me do it. I'll send young Edie along on Saturday evening to collect your bundle on her way back from Mrs Wetherall's.'

'It would be marvellous,' said Margaret with a sudden rush of relief. 'You don't know what a difference it would make. I can't tell you how grateful I am.'

'That's all right,' said Edith awkwardly. 'It's me that's grateful for the chance to do something to help. Well, I must be running along now. There's Dad and Roy's supper to get and though I've left it all ready, Maureen's that forgetful when she's got her nose in a book, I know she'll forget to put the gas on if I'm not there to chivvy her. I always say, joking like, she's one that would forget her own head if it was loose.'

'Is Roy out of the Army now?' Margaret asked.

'Been out this past month,' said Edith proudly. 'He's back at Thatcher's now and doing real well. He finishes his apprenticeship this spring and then he'll be well on the way. And I hope the Major and Miss Sheila are keeping well?'

As always, the parting courtesies were prolonged. But it was with real thankfulness that Margaret at last shut the door on Edith, and it was with less apprehension than usual that she was able to respond to Wendy's inevitable cry, 'Margaret, Margaret, who was that at the door?'

'It was Mrs Wilson,' said Margaret, running up to the bedroom. 'She said she was just passing by, and she looked in to see how you were. She sent her best wishes.'

'How very, very kind of her,' said Wendy with genuine pleasure. 'What an extremely nice woman she is. I do hope you were thoroughly polite to her.'

'Of course I was,' said Margaret, but she said it without irritation, with the studied calm she had schooled herself to adopt. Wendy looked at her daughter. She was gradually beginning to feel rested and relaxed and now, for the first time, could turn her thoughts away from herself to Margaret's tired face. 'I do hope it's not all being too much for you,' she said anxiously. 'I wish we could manage to have Edith in for a bit and take some of the work off your hands.'

'I'm doing all right,' said Margaret with forced cheerfulness. 'You don't have to worry at all. All you've got to do is to lie there and get well.'

'Thank you,' said Wendy faintly. Gratitude suddenly stirred in her, and she added, 'You're managing splendidly. I don't know what we'd do without you.'

Nearly all the Priory Hill people had now had the Wetheralls in to coffee after dinner and had been invited to meet them at coffee after dinner in other people's houses. It was generally agreed that the impression they had made was a good one. 'Of course he's clearly a self-made man,' Miss Porteous said with kindly contempt by Wendy's bedside. 'But she's a lady, as far as one can tell with Americans, and they're not pushing. Besides, these days one must be broad-minded about people.'

So when Mrs Wetherall rang up everyone to say that she hoped they'd come to a little party she was giving, everyone was delighted to accept. 'Half-past eight,' she said, having learnt Priory Hill ways by now, and in speaking to Gerald on the phone she had particularly asked if Margaret could come. 'I suppose there's no hope of seeing Mrs Trevor yet?' she asked, and Gerald said no, not yet, but soon, he hoped; Doctor Gregory was very satisfied on his last visit.

Wendy was insistent that Margaret should go. Her concern for the girl continued and deepened with her returning health. Surely it wasn't natural, she said to Doctor Gregory, that a girl of eighteen should look so run-down after doing a bit of housework, and the doctor had said it was the poor diet, same for most of the young people nowadays, not getting enough to eat and outgrowing their strength. 'Get her out in the fresh air as much as you can,' he said, and now Wendy insisted that Margaret take a walk every afternoon, out in the fields at the end of Priory Hill on the side of the village that was still real country. Still, it was a dull life for a girl, and the Wetherall party would make a pleasant change, particularly as the beige silk frock could at last be discarded for a really not-too-bad navy blue wool that had come in the last parcel from New Zealand.

So at half-past eight exactly – 'it'll take us five minutes and we don't want to be there on the dot' – Gerald and Margaret walked down the hill to Green Lawns leaving Wendy with the wireless and a nice book eagerly awaiting their return.

'Well, what was it like?' she cried as they came in at eleven, creeping quietly until they saw the light under her door and knew she was still awake. 'It was awfully well done,' Margaret said excitedly. 'They'd got a proper buffet with all sorts of exciting little cakes and something called Coca-Cola, a sort of fizzy brown drink and –' she ran on happily, but behind her Gerald shook his head meaningly at Wendy. 'What was wrong?' she said to Gerald, ignoring Margaret's enthusiastic prattle.

'It was showy,' Gerald said with pontifical gloom. 'They'd put themselves out a bit too much, if you know what I mean. There was any amount of stuff to drink – whisky and gin galore – and Wetherall went round pressing all the men to take cigars. It wasn't necessary, that's what I felt, and the Bruces felt just the same.'

'What a pity,' Wendy agreed, and it was a pity. You couldn't ask people in to coffee and biscuits followed by a cup of tea or perhaps occasionally a glass of beer if they were going to reciprocate with whisky and cigars. Priory Hill hospitality had been empirically scaled down to a universally possible level, and anything higher would mean that hospitality soared out of range.

'There were some awfully nice cheese straws,' Margaret broke in, unaware of the regrets passing over her head. 'And Mrs Wetherall hadn't forgotten about showing me American cooking. She asked me if I'd go to tea on Wednesday, but I said I'd have to ask you.' She looked pleadingly at her mother. 'I'd leave your tray all ready, if Daddy wouldn't mind just making the tea and taking it up.'

Wendy was in a dilemma. If the Wetheralls were going to do things in a big way, then they weren't going to fit in; but equally, if the Wetheralls were going to do things in a big way, the chances she had hoped they could open for Margaret might still be available. To gain time she asked Gerald, 'Who was there?'

'Very mixed,' said Gerald dolefully, 'very mixed indeed. They'd got the Thatchers, and there were some rather smart-looking friends of theirs from London who are apparently looking for a house round here. Something to do with engin-eering, I gather. I mentioned Broomfields to them and they seemed quite interested.'

'It needs a lot doing to it,' Wendy said thoughtfully. 'It's been empty for years.'

'I told them so,' Gerald said, 'but that didn't seem to worry them. These business people, you know, they don't mind how they spend their money.'

'But who from the village?' Wendy pursued.

'The usual people,' said Gerald. 'I suppose they couldn't very well get out of asking Robinson, though I must say I was surprised to see Jenkins and his wife. I wondered where the devil they picked *them* up.'

'Perhaps through the Robinsons,' Wendy suggested. 'I believe Mrs Robinson and Mrs Jenkins are friendly. After all, it seems Mrs Robinson was a schoolmistress before she married, so I suppose they've got something in common. Though I must say I'm rather surprised at Mrs Wetherall; one would have expected her to be a bit more discriminating, somehow. Still, I suppose that's American democracy.'

Margaret broke in eagerly, 'Mrs Jenkins is really awfully nice, Mummy. I often talk to her in the village and she's got a sweet baby, a little girl called Jennifer Ann.'

This settled Wendy's mind about the Wednesday invitation. If it was a choice between Margaret hobnobbing with the schoolmaster's wife or the *nouveaux riches*, the Wetheralls had it every time. 'I'm sure we'll manage all right on Wednesday,' she said kindly, 'and why don't you take Mrs Wetherall a pot of your crab-apple jelly and show her what you can do? We don't want all time favours to be on her side, do we?'

'We'd need to get up a committee like they did,' said Mr Brotherton anxiously. 'We want to do everything decently and in order.'

'Of course we'll have a committee,' agreed Mr Green firmly. 'There's us three to start with, anyway.' He looked round at his prospective colleagues gathered in the lounge, himself, Mr Brotherton from the Stationery and Mr Pickering. 'The first thing we've got to decide is, are we going to make it a regular Conservative dance or just a friendly get-together, as you might say?' He had already made up his own mind, but knew that Committees liked to be consulted.

'Personally,' said Mr Pickering judicially, 'I'm in favour of doing it for the Association all open and above-board. After all, we're all supporters of Mr Churchill and don't mind who knows it, eh? And we can't deny the Association needs a helping hand. I'm not saying that Priory Dean would ever help to put a Socialist in, but that Labour Party woman got a deal too many votes for my liking.'

'It's the Bentworth votes that do it,' Mr Brotherton said gloomily. 'Those men at the paper works, they're all Reds, if you ask me.'

'Well, we can't hope to influence Bentworth,' said Mr Green bluffly. 'But there's quite a lot of good we can be doing a bit nearer home. Those new people down on the Housing Estate, now, I'd say there's many of them would be glad of a regular weekly dance, and we don't want to leave them to the Socialists to get hold of.'

'Then who else shall we have on the committee?' Mr Brotherton asked. 'Do you think we ought to have any of the Priory Hill people? They're all good Tories, that I know for a fact.'

'No call that I can see,' said Mr Green in his capacity as the local Treasurer of the Association, 'it's not official after all, or if it was we'd have to have Doctor Gregory, he being President. As it is, it's just that we offer the proceeds to the Association, as a generous gesture, like. But if you once get one of that lot on, they'd be running the whole show in no time.'

There was general agreement. 'We want one or two of the ladies,' suggested Mr Pickering. 'What about your good wife, Mr Brotherton?'

After some amicable bickering, it was finally agreed that Mrs Brotherton and Mrs Pickering should be asked to serve, Mr Green undertaking that Mrs Green would willingly stand down in favour of Rosemary, now Mrs Ted Pickering, as representative of the younger generation.

'Then we can be sure of young Ted's band,' finished Mr Green, 'which I'm told by them as knows is quite as good as professionals. Now, what do you say to Fridays? After all, Friday's pay-day when all's said and done.'

Friday was unanimously agreed on, and just at the right moment, as if she'd been listening outside the door, in came Mrs Green with bottles of beer and glasses on a plated tray. 'Here's to your very good health,' said everyone to everyone else, and Mrs Green, when pressed, agreed that she'd take a glass too, just this once, so's to be matey.

'The young people still out, eh?' said Mr Green to his wife, and Mr Brotherton commented, 'So you've still got them with you. I did hear some rumour as how they were going to take over the Drapery when Miss Moodie gives up.'

'Well, it's hardly a secret any more, is it?' said Mrs Green with a gracious smile. 'Yes, she's going out on March quarter-day and then as soon as we can get a bit of work done, our young people are going to move in. But what *is* a secret, Mr Brotherton, though I'll tell you confidentially, is where Miss Moodie is going when she *does* move.' And in a jocular stage whisper she imparted the priceless, the savoury little bit of information.

Mr Brotherton was so taken aback he nearly choked and had to put his glass down quickly on the embroidered table-runner. 'You don't say,' he exclaimed, 'you don't say,' and then, with delighted relish, 'Well, what do you know about that!'

CHAPTER SIX

❧⊹✿⊹❧

Although news about the gentry was all round the village before you could say 'knife', it wasn't till halfway through March that Priory Road first heard Mrs Green's secret. Wendy had been coming down to dinner in her dressing-gown for quite a time now; today, for the first time, she was up and dressed for tea. Margaret had made a sponge-cake with some of that clever cream you did by mixing powdered milk and margarine so long as you could spare the sugar. Daisy Bruce had just begun to establish a tentative visiting relationship between her Christopher and David Wetherall, though she sometimes uneasily thought that two invitations came from her side to one of theirs. Still, today Christopher was safely away in the Wetherall nursery and Daisy had been invited to come to tea and so make a real party of the occasion.

She hadn't meant to break the bad news until after tea was over, but when the opportunity arose she just couldn't keep her mouth shut. 'Those Tremletts next door moved out today,' Wendy remarked. 'They've got a house in London again at last, I hear. I wonder who we'll get at Fernlea now.'

Daisy tried, but it was no use. 'I can tell you who we're

going to get,' she said in a voice heavy with doom, 'but you won't believe me.'

'Who?' Wendy asked uneasily. She could tell from Daisy's voice that something was very wrong – but how –?

'The new person who's coming to live at Fernlea,' said Daisy, 'is Miss Moodie.' She paused. There was satisfactory stupefaction on every face. 'There now,' she said, 'what do you think of that?'

'It's a bloody impertinence,' shouted Gerald angrily. 'Who the devil does she think she is, just because she's made a bit of money in that shop of hers?' A jumble of confused apprehensions assailed him, the pre-fabs going up on the field only a hundred yards away, the tradespeople moving in and the street going down.

Wendy had had a moment to think and the new-found calm of her returning health determined her attitude. 'Well, I'm sorry for the poor woman,' she said coolly. 'I'm afraid she'll find it a very foolish thing to have done, and very lonely, too.'

'She's quite nice,' Margaret said timidly. 'I mean, she's not nosy and always asking questions like Mrs Green.'

'Oh, I quite agree,' said Wendy, 'and that's why I'm so sorry about it. Poor creature, she'd be so much happier down in the village with her friends to chat to. I really can't think what she was about.'

How sensible Wendy was, Daisy thought gratefully. How much more dignified and – yes, how much more discouraging and ladylike her cool aloofness than Daisy's own immediate urge to do something about it. Aloud she said, gathering encouragement, 'Quite possibly, you know, she bought it as an investment and is only going to live there till she finds something more suitable.'

That was probably it, they all agreed with relief. After all, house property was always a very popular investment with people like that and it was funny they hadn't thought of it right away. 'Have you heard if those friends of the Wetheralls are going to take Broomfields?' Wendy asked, but the last thing Daisy had heard was that they still hadn't made up their mind: it wanted a couple of thousand spending on it, and they – the Council – were being so sticky about licences and it wasn't really safe to spend as much as that, you'd never get away with it.

Doctor Gregory walked in just as they were finishing tea. It was a nuisance, not knowing just when he was going to call so that you could be all ready for him. But Wendy said, 'You'll have a cup of tea, won't you?' wondering, as everyone in the village did, just how well he was looked after at home with Mrs Smith having to be housekeeper and nurse to Mrs Gregory and, some people whispered, more of a comfort to the doctor than she should be as well. 'Thank you,' said the Doctor. 'I've come at a good time, haven't I? Glad to see you following instructions and getting up and about.'

'I'll be off to fetch Christopher now,' said Daisy, getting up. 'It takes so long to tear him away from David Wetherall. Those two are getting to be such buddies they can't bear to be parted.' She paused at the door to ask, 'Doctor, can you suggest anything I could put on Christopher's gums? He seems to be cutting some back teeth, and he keeps complaining of them.'

But Doctor Gregory knew Daisy too well, was too much of an old hand to let a free consultation be slipped in over the tea-cups. 'I'll be over to have a look at him in the morning,' he said firmly, and Daisy had to add hurriedly, 'Oh no, don't bother. It's not as important as all that. I just wondered, that was all. Well, goodbye, Wendy dear, it was lovely to see you up again. And what a delicious cake, Margaret.'

'See Daisy out,' whispered Wendy to Margaret, who dutifully went into the hall to help Daisy into her musquash coat and wonder again why she couldn't like Daisy as much as Daisy seemed to like her.

Back in the drawing-room Doctor Gregory was saying, 'If you keep on like this, I'll be able to discharge you in a few more weeks. So if you want to send that girl of yours off for her training, I don't see why she shouldn't start for the summer term.'

Gerald and Wendy looked awkwardly at each other, looked at the doctor and away again. There was an uncomfortable silence. At last Gerald said, 'I was telling Wendy last night, doctor – we'll have to think of something else for Margaret – I suppose you wouldn't know of anything?'

'I see,' said the doctor sharply. So Mrs Trevor had only been able to have her sole and port wine at the expense of Margaret's training. Then he said slowly, 'Matter of fact, I do know of something that might fill the bill. Only this morning Matron at the hospital asked me if I knew of a girl to work in the X-ray department. Might be the very thing.'

'But Margaret doesn't know anything about X-rays,' Gerald objected.

'She doesn't have to,' said the doctor impatiently. 'It's a clerking job.'

'Sort of secretarial?' asked Wendy hopefully.

'If you like,' said the doctor a little testily; he preferred to call things by their proper names. 'It's a question of filling in the slips for the patients, keeping the files in order and so on. She'd have to be able to do a bit of typing. Does she know anything about it?'

'Not proper typing,' said Wendy. 'We've got an old portable we used to use for the farm correspondence and both the girls have picked up a bit. But she can't do touch-typing or anything like that.'

'Well, she'd better go along and see what Matron wants,' said the doctor with finality, getting up to go. 'I'll have a word with Matron about it, and she can ring up and make an appointment.'

When he had gone and Margaret was in the kitchen cooking supper, Gerald and Wendy discussed the suggestion. It wasn't, they came to think, such a bad idea. If there really wasn't a lot of typing needed, then Margaret could earn while she learnt, so to speak, and since she wouldn't be starting for a month, it would give her a chance to practise on the old machine at home. And she could learn shorthand from a book in the evenings. Of course, it wouldn't be for a permanency, they agreed, just for something to be going on with so that they had time to look around, and she might well meet some nice people at the hospital, doctors and so on, not like going into a government office, say, with a lot of clerks. After supper they put it to Margaret and obediently she agreed that it sounded quite a good idea. So the next day Wendy rang up the Matron at the Walbridge General and made an appointment and in due course Margaret went to see her and was given the job at two pounds ten shillings a week to start in a month's time in the middle of April.

Miss Evadne was wondering what had happened. Here it was already the end of March and still the Rector hadn't been to see her about the arrangements for the Church Fête. Ever since the Grange had changed hands, the Church Fête had been held every year at the beginning of June in the gardens of Priory Hall, and it was more than time for the annual consultation about ordering the marquee and what to have for the side-shows. She'd had a discreet word with Miss Porteous, who was President of the Church Organ Fund, but Mr Robinson hadn't been to see *her* either and she, too, was beginning to think that it was time someone reminded him that they'd have to get on with it soon if there was to be anything at all on the stalls. So one day Miss Evadne pulled her old felt hat over her sandy hair and picking out a stout cherrywood walking stick which had belonged to her father went off to pay a call on the Rectory.

The whole place looked sadly different, she mused, as she went up the drive, from the days of old Mr Hall. There were weeds everywhere, the laurels hadn't been clipped, and the paintwork round the beautiful Georgian window-frames was grey and cracking. Of course he couldn't afford to spend anything on it, she conceded, but he might at least clear away the dirty paper, and she poked irritably with her stick at a scrap of sodden newspaper here, an old ice-cream carton there, remembering the days when people seemed to be naturally orderly and neat and wouldn't dream of leaving their debris around, let alone allow it to blow into the Rector's drive. She pulled the old bell on the front door and waited a long time before Mrs Robinson came to the door in a flowered overall. 'I'm so sorry to have kept you waiting,' she apologised. 'I was in the kitchen and I had to put Sally somewhere safe. Won't you come in?'

'Is the Rector at home?' Miss Evadne asked.

'Yes, he's in his den,' said Mrs Robinson. 'Do come in and I'll tell him you're here.'

Miss Evadne stepped into the hall, trying not to wrinkle up her nose at the smell of stale cabbage, stale washing, stale fustiness that greeted her. 'It smells like a slum,' she thought distastefully, but her natural kindness made her quickly remember that the Robinsons had no maid, that it was a grossly big inconvenient house to run single-handed. 'Do you find it very cold in winter here?' she asked, following Mrs Robinson along the uncarpeted passage, and Mrs Robinson said, 'It's like a tomb, I can tell you. At Dagenham we had such a nice little modern house, and I'm missing it all the time.' She opened the door of what used to be the morning-room, and stood aside for Miss Evadne to go in.

It used to be such a delightful room, Miss Evadne remembered regretfully, with Mrs Hall's delicate satinwood furniture against the pine-panelled walls, her heavy brocade curtains framing the view over the walled back garden, her pretty

Dresden china on the mantelpiece. Now it drooped with the makeshifts of poverty. The curtains were of that rust-coloured sacking you could buy without coupons, the sagging sofa covered in blue casement-cloth had obviously been picked up cheap at a sale and the only picture was a cheap reproduction of the Raphael Madonna. 'I'll just go and tell the Rector,' Mrs Robinson said, and went, leaving Miss Evadne to stare distastefully at the broken toys on the floor, the empty flower-vases, the unemptied ash-trays. She had wondered once, when she'd heard that Mrs Robinson had been a school-mistress, if it mightn't have been a good idea to have her to tea and to share a laugh – or perhaps even to share something other than a laugh – over the slim volumes of modern poetry that thronged the rosewood bookcase in her drawing-room. But shyness had held her back and now she could realise quite clearly that it wouldn't have done at all.

The Rector seemed to be a long time coming. It was a good five minutes by the oak clock on the mantelpiece before he came into the room and Miss Evadne could see straight away that he looked embarrassed, though she automatically put that down to the untidy room, the stuffy house, the gap between what surely must have been his intentions and the performance that was possible.

'I thought I'd better come and see you about the fête,' she said, plunging, as was her way, straight into the business in hand. 'We'll have to get a move on if we're to have it all ready by the beginning of June.'

The Rector tried to start a sentence, choked over it, fumbled, started another. 'I thought –' he began, 'that's to say,

106

I thought – well, that Mrs Wetherall would have had a word with you.'

'What's she got to do with it?' asked Miss Evadne. 'Does she want to come on to the committee?'

'No, no,' said the Rector. 'It's – it's that she very kindly offered – one day I happened to be speaking about the fête – and seeing what a mess we made of your beautiful garden last year,' he finished with a rush, finding nothing else to say.

Miss Evadne's garden wasn't beautiful and she knew it. With a weak heart and sciatica, with only one gardener now, and that old Birch, who still managed to turn up most mornings, nobody could keep a garden beautiful. But the fête had always been held in the gardens of the Hall.

'I see,' she said. She added, though she knew it was uncharitable, 'I suppose Mr Wetherall is giving a large subscription to the Organ Fund?'

'It's not that at all,' said Mr Robinson very quickly. 'I thought you'd be pleased to be spared the trouble – Mrs Wetherall's got a regular gardener to give a hand and tidy up afterwards – and the villagers, you know, curiosity brings them when it's somewhere new.'

'I see,' said Miss Evadne again. She could indeed see that it was true that the new people coming into the village would far more readily snuff round the Wetherall garden with its trim flower-beds, its pergolas, its gravel paths than saunter on her own patchy lawn under the old cedars. She wanted to say to Mr Robinson that he should have had the courage to tell her himself, but discovered that the kind of hurt she was feeling was not one she could in any way bare to the Rector.

'Good afternoon,' she said curtly, and turned and went out of the room, out of the fusty house.

All the village heard about Miss Evadne's discomfiture with an unhappy sense of guilt. 'I don't like to see her belittled,' Mrs Green said to her husband. 'It isn't right, you know, after all these years. But you can't deny,' she said with uncomfortable honesty, 'that it'll be more of a do at the Wetheralls. If I know them, they'll put themselves out to do things in style, and I suppose it's the Church we ought to be thinking about rather than Miss Evadne's feelings.'

Up Priory Hill too, people admitted in the end that there was no doubt that the fête would be far more successful at Green Lawns than at the Hall, but the admission did not enhance the Wetheralls' popularity. After their party the Priory Hill people had tended to shrink away from them. The jolly bridge evenings George Bruce had hoped for never seemed to materialise, and nobody felt that the Wetheralls would really enjoy being asked a second time to coffee and biscuits. 'I hear they're for ever running round with the Thatchers,' Wendy said to Daisy, who'd brought her mending over for the afternoon while Christopher played in the field among the chicken-houses. 'Well, we can't keep up with their kind of life, and it's no good pretending that we can.'

'I hadn't told you before, Wendy,' said Daisy, realising that this was the occasion when telling the story would enhance not diminish her prestige, 'but I had rather a nasty snub from the Wetheralls last week. I rang her up, just like I might have done anyone, and asked her if she'd mind having Christopher for the afternoon because I wanted to go to Walbridge to see if I could pick up a new suit. Well, she was as sweet as pie, said she was awfully sorry it wasn't possible, wished she'd known earlier and all that sort of thing, but that David and Caroline were already fixed up that afternoon. Naturally, I took her at her word. I didn't go to Walbridge and I didn't think twice about the matter. Then I took Chris for a walk after tea and we were just passing Green Lawns when we saw the Thatchers' Rolls come out of the drive with their two children and the governess inside. You can imagine how I felt. 'Course, it wasn't for myself I minded, but for Chris. After all, he saw it too. It's not very pleasant for one's child to feel he isn't good enough to be invited with the Thatchers.'

Wendy agreed that it wasn't nice, not nice at all. 'I'm afraid money's all that matters to people like that,' she said with a sigh, 'though I'll admit,' she added, 'that Martha Wetherall is extremely amiable to Margaret. She quite often asks her down there to tea, and only last week she gave her a lovely cashmere twin-set, practically new. It'll be the very thing for the hospital. Mind you, I don't like her to accept presents from them, but one can't very well send it back, can one?'

'But I can't bear to feel that people like that have it in their power to hurt poor Miss Evadne,' said Daisy with renewed indignation. 'When I first heard about it, the thing I wanted to do was to go straight down to the Hall and say how sorry I was, but then Miss Evadne's not really the kind of person you can do that sort of thing to, is she?'

Wendy, too, had wanted to go and say something comforting to Miss Evadne, and if the snub had been administered to any other of her friends, that's what she'd have gone and done without a moment's thought. But it would have been truer to say that the Priory Hill people were accepted by Miss Evadne than that she was a member of their set. Miss Evadne was, apart from the Doctor, the only one among the local gentlefolk who belonged to the village by birth and not by infiltration. Her father, after all, had really been the squire, and though, of course, it was all nonsense and nobody thought anything of such things nowadays, both Wendy and Daisy were uncomfortably aware that a Kensington doctor and the headmaster of a not very well-known preparatory school weren't quite the same thing as a Squire Graham; not that they felt that Miss Evadne thought for a minute about things like that, but they did themselves, and so Miss Evadne went uncomforted.

Margaret had taken Mrs Wilson's advice and kept from her mother the fact that every Saturday evening Edie had called at Wood View to pick up the washing, every Tuesday evening bringing it back. But now that Wendy was practically all right again she would have to be told if the visits went on, and even with her new-found good temper Margaret wasn't prepared to face a possible explosion about putting oneself under an obligation to people like that. So after she'd got the tea washed up she slipped out on the pretext of a walk and went down to the semi-detached red-brick house in Station Road where the Wilsons lived.

She was surprised and a little disconcerted to have the door opened to her by Maureen, who had rather a fearsome reputation in the village. As a small child during the war she had been universally known as a young devil, a leader in all the gangs the evacuee children formed, an inveterate breaker of windows, shouter of rude remarks. Now she was said to be clever and a bit of a Bolshie as well – an unusual reputation for a sixteen-year-old girl in Priory Dean. 'Ugly as sin, too,' people had said, but Margaret, looking at the little pointed face with its straight black fringe and its twisted sardonic smile, didn't think Maureen looked ugly. In fact she thought she looked rather nice and smiled too as she said, 'Is Mrs Wilson in?'

Maureen leant towards her and whispered, 'She's gone to the pub with Roy, but I daren't say it out loud for fear Gran should hear. She's got ears like a fox, and she carries on like mad if poor Mum ever has a drop of anything. Decent women didn't go to pubs in her young days, she says, and when she gets an idea in her head there's no shifting her. But come in and wait, won't you? Mum won't be long.'

'Thanks awfully,' Margaret said and followed Maureen into the narrow linoleum-covered hall. There was nothing to stop her leaving her message and her thanks and going, but in the moment of the whispered confidence she had discovered that she liked Maureen and besides it would be only polite to wait and say thank you to Mrs Wilson and perhaps hallo to Roy. 'You don't mind the kitchen, do you?' said Maureen, going ahead. 'I'm in the middle of making a treacle tart – I don't much care for it myself, but Dad and Roy fair leap at it.'

'I wonder you've got time to cook with your exam coming

on,' said Margaret, following Maureen into the little crowded kitchen. 'We never dare ask Sheila to do anything.'

'Perhaps she needs to work harder than I do,' said Maureen with a wicked grin, winking at Margaret, who was astonished to find that she too could laugh light-heartedly at Sheila's earnestness instead of respectfully deferring to her capacity. 'Do sit down,' Maureen said, and Margaret sat down and leant her elbows on the oilcloth cover of the table where Maureen was pouring the treacle over the breadcrumbs in her tart.

'I can't tell you what a help it was your mother doing our washing,' she said earnestly. 'Not having to do that bit extra made all the difference, but what I came to say was that we can manage again now all right. I'm going to be earning next week,' she said proudly, 'and we'll be able to afford to send the heavy stuff to the laundry again.' Her mother would have said that she should be ashamed not proud to talk about what they could and couldn't afford to someone like Maureen Wilson, but Maureen replied with equal sincerity, 'Well, you must be glad to be able to help. But you mustn't think your bit of wash made a mite of difference. We all muck in together and the jobs get done in no time. Even Roy's not too proud to turn the mangle, though if Gran sees him as much as lifting a finger, she gives me and Mum what for. Boys are made to be waited on to her way of thinking, and you should hear how she creates when Dad brings up Mum's breakfast on a tray of a Sunday morning.' Both girls burst out laughing and they didn't hear the old lady coming down the stairs and along the passage. They stopped abruptly as she came in to say sharply,

'What d'you think you're about, my girl, asking a lady like Miss Margaret into the kitchen? What she'll think of us, that I don't know. You take her along to the parlour right away as you ought to have done at the start.'

The grin disappeared from Maureen's face and now, looking at her grimly closed lips, her furious eyes, Margaret could see the ugliness the village attributed to her. To her immense surprise Margaret found herself rising and saying firmly, 'It's extremely kind of you to think of it, Mrs Wilson, but I was enjoying myself chatting with Maureen in here. Goodbye, Maureen,' she said turning round. 'You'll give my message to your mother, won't you?'

'I'll see you to the gate,' Maureen said gravely, but her eyes were smiling again. Once outside the door she said, 'It was decent of you to speak up like you did. Roy always said you was nice.' They walked to the gate and as Maureen opened it she again gave her wicked wink, nudged Margaret in the ribs and said, 'The trouble with you, Miss Margaret, is that you've got no sense of class.'

CHAPTER SEVEN

Before Margaret went to work for the first time, Martha had asked her to drop in for a drink on her way home. 'You'll need something to cheer you up at the end of it,' she had said, and all through that long bewildering day Margaret had looked forward to the promised visit as the one visible pleasure ahead.

Wendy had lately begun saying that she couldn't understand what Margaret could see in the Wetheralls and complaining testily that Margaret spent more time at Green Lawns than she did in her own home. 'Oh, I rather like them,' Margaret would say deprecatingly, unwilling to explain the pleasure it gave her to be with Martha, who was always, somehow, so alive compared with her mother and her friends, and who never grumbled except vigorously, cheerfully and with obvious enjoyment. 'She's really rather vulgar,' Wendy had once said distastefully, seeing Martha in the village street in a lime-green raincoat and lipstick more vividly scarlet than any of the English gentry would dream of wearing, but vulgarity, so long as it implied vitality, always satisfied Margaret by compensating for her own lack of it. Everyone I really like is vulgar, she thought, Martha and Jill and lately Maureen, and sometimes she added Roy to the list. Vulgar people seemed to stand up to things better than refined people, to be able to take in their stride difficulties that at home would have been quite overwhelming. So Margaret would happily follow Martha round the house, to make an apple-dowdy in the kitchen, to watch Martha trying on new clothes in the bedroom, or just to relax on the big sofa in the living-room and listen to Martha telling her about life in America. She didn't talk much, because she never had and never could. But she knew that Martha liked her, just as she knew that the other vulgar people, Jill and Maureen and Roy, liked her – and if, as this evening, it was easier to go to Green Lawns without saying anything about it at home, well, she just went.

She was a little shy, when she got there, to find that Ralph Wetherall was already at home. She hadn't seen much of him and he always impressed her as very grand and sophisticated compared with the other men she knew. But he couldn't have been nicer than he was, saying she must sit down, she must be dead tired, and would she have a Martini or a Bronx.

Margaret gathered up her courage and said, 'I've never had a cocktail. Do you think it would make me drunk?' 'Ralph's cocktails would make anyone drunk,' Martha said. 'Darling, give Margaret a sherry. Now tell me what it was like.'

'It was all right, I suppose,' Margaret said dubiously. 'The Sister seemed quite nice, and there's another girl doing the same work as me and she showed me what to do. Anyway, it wasn't difficult; it was just typing slips when people come in, and learning where to find old Plates and things.'

'And did you like it?' Martha asked encouragingly.

'There wasn't really anything about it to like,' Margaret said sadly.

Ralph and his wife looked at each other and then he said jovially, 'Anyhow there must have been some handsome young doctors somewhere around the place.'

'Not in the X-ray department,' Margaret said. 'There's a woman – I suppose she's a doctor – and a foreigner of some kind, I think he's a German or an Austrian, but he wasn't young. Still,' she added, 'they did all try to be nice to me. I suppose it will be all right when I get used to it.'

When she had gone Martha poured herself another drink and said, 'I do feel sorry for that child. She's as sweet and wholesome as they come and she never seems to have had a really good time in the whole of her life. You'd think they'd have been able to find something better for her than that dreary dead-end job.'

'Of course they could have,' said Ralph vigorously. 'There are any number of things they could have found. But this one turned up and it was safe and respectable, and they just hadn't the guts or the sense to look any further.'

'They really are a pathetic bunch,' said Martha. 'They give you the impression all the time that they're scared stiff of anything happening that's the least bit different.'

'So they are,' said Ralph, 'and they've got plenty to be scared about. Most of them live on incomes that would send any self-respecting workman out on strike, and the only thing they've got to hang on to is that they belong to the so-called upper classes. And even that doesn't cut the ice it used to any more.'

'You know, I'd been wondering,' said Martha tentatively, 'if I couldn't possibly suggest that Margaret came here as a kind of nursery-governess to the children. They're really getting a bit old for Nanny, and Margaret's so gentle and kind, she'd be just what I want. Besides, I'm sure she'd follow their diet-sheets, which is a thing I can never get Nanny to do.'

'For God's sake don't suggest it,' said Ralph forcefully. 'I quite agree that the girl would be ideal, but the Trevors would never forgive you for even thinking of it.'

'But being a nursery-governess is perfectly respectable,' Martha objected. 'My sister worked as a nursery-governess one vacation and I thought that it was, to use a real English expression, a thoroughly ladylike occupation even over here.'

'Yes, it is,' said Ralph. 'But it wouldn't be for Margaret Trevor to come and work for us. Don't you see, it'd be putting her in an inferior position to us in their own village; it would be different if she went away to some other nasty rich people elsewhere.'

'But surely they don't feel like that about us?' asked Martha.

'They would if you suggested Margaret coming to work for us,' said Ralph grimly. 'At the moment they've got all the fun of looking down on us because we're in trade and they're real gentry, and anyway it's vulgar to have money. But if you once give them the idea that you're patronising them, they'll never forgive you.'

'All right, I won't then,' said Martha amiably, 'though it all sounds very silly to me. I thought that even in England all those old ideas about class were going by the board.'

'Officially they are,' said Ralph, 'but actually they're as strong as ever, and don't you forget it. Even if they never talk about it, class is still the most important thing in the world to people like the Trevors.'

'They don't get much fun out of it,' said Martha, 'but nobody seems to get much fun over here. There's absolutely nothing for the young people in the village, no swimming-pool, no corner drug-store, no movies, just nothing at all. What they do with themselves in the evenings I can't imagine. I suppose they go into Walbridge or just stay at home.'

'That's about it,' Ralph agreed. 'And talking of what to do in the evenings, Alan tells me that the new Country Club over the other side of Bentworth is going to be good. They've got tennis-courts and a swimming-pool, and he says they're going to have dances. I thought we might drive over after dinner and see if we think it's worth joining.'

'I'd like that,' Martha said. 'You're right, we need something for our own evenings too, though it'll be better if Freddie and Moira decide to settle here so that we can have a bit of company. Otherwise we'll soon find ourselves thrown back on to the local coffee-parties.'

They both laughed. 'Well, I must go and change if we're going out,' Martha said and added thoughtfully as she went to the door, 'I'd still like to try to do something for that poor child.'

At home Margaret said yes, thank you, it was very nice, everyone was very nice, she was sure she'd like it all right once she got used to it. Wendy went on asking for a few days, and for a week or two she'd remind Margaret that she ought to spend an hour or so on her shorthand, but it was easier to let Margaret quietly pile up the plates and get on with the washing-up, and gradually Margaret's job came to be accepted by the family as something inevitable and unalterable.

But to Margaret herself it never came to mean anything more than an active, ever-present and paralysing boredom. As she had said to the Wetheralls, there was nothing to like about it or to take an interest in; there wasn't even any social life to compensate for it, for the X-ray department lived in a hut apart from the main building and saw virtually nothing of the rest of the hospital. Even lunch in the canteen was taken at such variable hours as fitted in best with the day's work, and except for the odd word passed here and there, Margaret talked to no one and made no friends. Gradually she came to live more and more in a world of day-dreams. In the bus in the mornings she would pretend that she'd left behind her the little home of her own, that her shopping bag was in her hand, that she was just going into Walbridge to find something tasty for supper. And coming back again in the evening rush, having queued sometimes for half an hour before she could get on to a bus, she would imagine the little house waiting, waiting for her to come home and draw the curtains, turn on the gas, cook the delicious titbits she had bought for his – but for whose? – supper. Sometimes she would snatch her lunch extra quickly and then saunter along the High Street, critically examining the shop windows, deciding that she'd buy the little blue matinée jacket for Baby and the beaten pewter coal-hod for the living-room. She got no conscious satisfaction from these dreams; they merely became more real than the life she was leading.

Even outside the job her life seemed to have closed in. She had never dropped in on Green Lawns in the evenings when Martha would have Ralph and not need her, and at the weekends Wendy was apt to say that she liked to have her at home, they saw so little of her nowadays. Once or twice she'd met Jill in Walbridge on a Friday after work and they'd gone to the pictures together, but Jill's family, too, liked to see her at weekends, and such meetings were few and far between.

But one day, towards the end of May, Jill had phoned to say that she thought her family were going out to dinner the next Friday, and could Margaret be by the box-office of the Plaza at half-past six that evening, just on the off chance. 'If I'm not there by quarter to, you'll know I couldn't make it,' she said. 'But I'll do my damnedest. It'd be lovely to see you again – I've got so much to tell you.'

So Margaret told her family that she'd probably be going to the pictures with Jill and anyway not to wait supper, if Jill didn't turn up she'd have a sandwich and some cocoa when she got in. She dressed as nicely as she could to meet Jill who always looked so smart nowadays – the blue twin-set from America and the new grey Utility suit Wendy had bought her when she started the job. She was really feeling quite happy and excited by the time she closed her typewriter and could walk along to the big mock-marble cinema opposite the bus-station.

But Jill wasn't at the box-office when she got there, and as she waited on the thick patterned carpet surrounded by

huge glossy photographs of film stars, she slipped into her
dreaming again. 'It's the anniversary of our wedding-day,'
he'd said that morning at breakfast. 'Why don't you get Mrs
– Mrs –' her imagination fumbled for a name then let it slide,
'– to come in and keep an eye on Baby, and you could meet
me at the Plaza and we'd make an evening of it, just like old
times.' And so she was waiting for him dutifully outside the
box-office, and it didn't in the least interrupt her dream when
someone said 'Hallo' and she looked up and there was Roy
Wilson.

'Hallo,' she said, and he said 'Hallo' again, and then they
stood there smiling at each other.

He said, 'Have you been in or were you just going?'

'Well, actually I was waiting for someone,' Margaret said.
She glanced quickly at the rectangular clock over the doors.
'But she said she'd be here by quarter to if she could come and
it's ten to now, so I suppose she won't turn up.'

'Funny, that's what happened to me,' said Roy. 'I was waiting outside, that's why I didn't see you before, but I thought
I'd better slip in and see if my friend was here.' He heaved a
theatrical sigh and said, 'Looks as if we've both been let down,'
and Margaret laughed at his funny mock-tragic face.

'I suppose I'd better be getting home,' she said, and Roy
said, 'That's too bad, isn't it? They say it's a really good film
and it comes off tomorrow.' He hesitated and then suggested
very shyly, 'I suppose – seeing as how we've both been let down
– you wouldn't care to come in with me?'

Oh I couldn't, said Margaret's frightened mind. Oh I
couldn't, Mummy would never forgive me. She looked at him

and it was Roy Wilson who'd been so nice to her at the dance, so nice to her in the garden as a child, Roy Wilson who was always so nice and who'd told Maureen that she was nice too. 'I'd like to very much,' she said.

Roy's whole face wrinkled with sudden pleasure. 'You wait here half a jiffy and I'll get the tickets,' he said eagerly, and Margaret had to put her hand on his arm to stop him so that she could say, 'Oh no, Roy, do let me pay for my own.'

But Roy was feeling more confident now, and he wasn't having any. 'I wouldn't dream of it,' he said, and somehow Roy had never been a person you could argue with when he'd decided what he was going to do. So Margaret waited for him, not quite in her dream, not quite in reality, until he came back with the tickets and they went together up the marble stairs.

The main picture was a British film and it was about a village, not, indeed, such a village as Priory Dean, half rural, half suburban, but a real picturesque thatched roof and local dialect village in the depths of unspoilt countryside. But since every film village is inevitably stereotyped, this one could provide plenty of occasions for Roy and Margaret to giggle happily together, for one to whisper 'Isn't that just like Mr Green?' and the other 'Jim Waters 'ud give something to see that much beer being unloaded.' It was all friendly and familiar, and in sharing their recognitions, much of the shyness and strangeness of their being there together could melt away.

They sat through the cartoon and the news and the trailer and then there was no excuse for sitting there any longer. The lights went on as they stood up to go, and in the illumination both instinctively, apprehensively scanned the audience to see if anyone either of them knew could have seen them together.

In the passage outside, before Margaret could make any gesture of parting, Roy quickly suggested, 'What do you say to a bite before we set off on the homeward road?' 'It would be nice,' Margaret said hesitantly, thinking of the solitary sandwich and cocoa at home after the long dark walk up the hill. 'They do snacks in the café here,' Roy urged, 'there's hardly ever anyone there,' and Margaret knew that he had understood her hesitation and was telling her that this was as unlikely a place as any to meet anyone from Priory Dean.

Except for two elderly women whispering together over a table, the café was, indeed, empty. Without question they both made their way to the table most out of sight of the rest of the room, the one behind the screen in the corner by the door. 'What'll you have?' asked Roy, assuming an indisputable right to be host, and Margaret submissively accepted this and agreed that on the grease-spattered menu what looked tastiest would be fish-and-chips and some bread-and-butter and a pot of tea.

They both found it a bit difficult to get the talk going. Roy asked Margaret about her job, but he quickly saw that she didn't like it and hated even to remember it in conversation. Then she asked Roy about his, but though he liked his work very much, he wasn't used to talking about it outside, and anyway, it was hard to explain just what being a compositor was to someone who didn't know anything about printing. Then Margaret thought of saying something friendly about Maureen and that broke the ice, because Roy was very fond of

Maureen and very proud of her, and though a lot of people admired her cleverness, there weren't many who thought she was nice.

'The trouble with young Maureen is that she's lonely,' he said. 'There's no getting over the fact that she's a lot brighter than the rest of us and she's apt to be a bit cocky with it, as is only natural. If there was only someone she could talk to who'd give her as good as they got, it 'ud be much better for her, instead of Gran flying out every time Maureen starts an argument and then Dad ticking Maureen off so's to keep the peace.'

'Gran's your father's mother, isn't she,' asked Margaret, 'not your mother's?'

'That's right,' said Roy, 'and to tell you the truth we all loathe the sight of her, the cantankerous old devil. But there's no one else in the family'll put up with her, so I suppose we're landed with her till she passes on to a better world.'

'Isn't that Mrs Taylor down Archery Lane an aunt of yours?' said Margaret.

'She's Mum's sister,' Roy explained; ''s matter of fact, we did try to push Gran off on her once, but she wasn't having any and I don't blame her. She's got a lodger at the moment, that Miss Fairlie who teaches the infant class, and she's only got two bedrooms, so she's safe.'

It was easy and comfortable to go on talking about Roy's family, and both took for granted the sudden furtive glances with which each occasionally raked the room. She said interestedly, 'I wonder she didn't take Jim and Edie so that they could get married. They've been waiting ages, haven't they?'

'Well, it was suggested,' said Roy, 'but Jim wasn't having any and I don't blame him. A marriage never works out, he says, when it's a question of living with relations and I don't know that he's far wrong. Ted Pickering said to me in the Month-Of-May, only the other evening, he said, that if he and Rosemary had had to go on living with the in-laws, there'd have been a divorce in no time flat.'

'I saw they'd moved in over the Drapery,' said Margaret. 'I should think they'd do very well there.'

'And how's Miss Moodie settling down at Fernlea?' asked Roy. 'I should think she'd feel a bit lost at first, having nothing to do after all these years.'

'I quite often see her doing a bit of gardening,' said Margaret awkwardly; the presence of Miss Moodie next door was a constant source of irritation to the Trevors, and no acquaintance had yet been acknowledged.

'She's one of the real old village families,' Roy remarked. 'Her dad and his father before him were the village smiths as far back as anyone can remember. In that cottage behind the Master-At-Arms, the forge was, where old Mr Pennyfeather lives now. My grandfather used to work at Reardon's Farm, where the allotments are, and I remember him telling me how one of his jobs was to take the horses to Miss Moodie's father at the forge to be shod. It was him made those big gates up at the Grange.'

'Was it really?' said Margaret. 'I don't think I've ever seen a real forge, not working, that is.'

'There's one at Little Poulteney, ten miles the other side of Bentworth,' Roy said. 'We might go and look at it one day.' He stopped abruptly. The easy natural flow of talk had been broken. Margaret said with a little hope, a lot of embarrassment, 'That'd be simply lovely.' She looked quickly at the clock and said, 'My goodness, it's after ten! I must be getting back.'

On the stairs, just before they emerged into the brightly-lit splendour of the foyer, Roy said shyly, 'I did enjoy that,' and Margaret turned a glowing face to him and said, 'Oh, so did I. And thank you ever so much for taking me.' People were coming behind them, and they couldn't linger any longer. Not too noticeably but each impelled by the same knowledge of necessity, they moved a little apart as they walked across the spongy carpet, let the crowds come between them on the pavement outside, so that by the time they had crossed the road and taken their separate places in the bus queue, no one would ever have thought that Margaret Trevor and Roy Wilson standing there was a matter of more than the sheerest coincidence.

The little single-decker bus was, as usual, crowded out, and Roy and Margaret found themselves at opposite ends of it. So it was only natural that they should have nothing to do with each other, that Margaret should sit and stare at her own reflection in the black blind that hung behind the driver while Roy chatted with Reg Summers as they hung from the greasy straps by the door.

It was all-but dark when the bus drew up outside the Master-At-Arms, and as for Priory Hill, with hardly any lights showing through its trim exclusive hedges, you couldn't tell one person from another till you got right up to them. It was here that Roy caught up with her and said breathlessly, as if he'd only just thought of it, 'I say, could you come again with me next week?'

Once was an accident without forethought or consequence. Twice was a deliberated action, a step that might lead to another step, to steps in sequence. Once meant a few lies, but little lies, unimportant lies, lies that could hardly be avoided just to save people trouble. Twice meant premeditated lies which meant deceit. But once meant that there were only the day-dreams, the loneliness and the boredom. Margaret sighed, not knowing that she'd sighed, and pleaded with Roy to make up her mind for her. 'Will it be all right?' she asked.

'Yes, it'll be all right,' Roy said. The words could have meant that he promised not to seduce her or that he assured her that he wouldn't be inconvenienced, that next Friday would suit him perfectly. But they meant to him, as they did to her, that he understood as perfectly as she the razor's edge of discretion they must walk if they were to go to the pictures together again.

'I'd love to come then,' Margaret said, and he could perceive though he could not see the shy smile on her face, for the darkness came quickly now. 'I'll just see you up the hill,' he said gruffly, and he seized her arm and tucked it into his own, holding it there rigidly as they walked together in silence.

A light could be dimly seen from an upper window at Fernlea, and just before Miss Moodie's gate their footsteps slowed and stopped. He dropped her arm. 'Well, see you same place next Friday,' he said abruptly, waited, wondered. 'Good night, Roy,' said Margaret, suddenly tense, suddenly uncomprehendingly desirous. They both waited a moment in silent rigidity, then Margaret smiled tenderly in the dark, and walked past Fernlea and in at the gate of Wood View.

CHAPTER EIGHT

Margaret, like Sheila, had often practised the sort of passive deceit that is involved in not mentioning the things that would surely cause trouble if spoken of. But in deliberate deceit she was wholly unversed, and had no experience of the practical difficulties that this course entails. So it was an entirely unforeseen fright that gripped her when, the morning after she had been out with Roy, her father called to her from the sitting-room to say that Jill was on the phone and wanted to speak to her.

Apprehensively Margaret went to the telephone. Gerald was working out the chicken-feed rations at the desk, and it would never occur to him, any more than it would to Wendy, to leave the room so that Margaret could speak to her friend in private. Margaret gingerly picked up the receiver, asking silently whether by any ill-chance Jill had already said something casually revealing to her father.

'Hallo,' she said, and Jill said, or, so it seemed to Margaret, shouted, 'Hallo. I was awfully sorry about last night,' she boomed. 'I do hope it didn't put you out too frightfully.'

To Margaret the echo of the hollow voice seemed to fill the room. She glanced at Gerald, but he was still apparently unconcernedly counting coupons. She tried to half cover the ear-piece with her hand as she said, 'It was perfectly all right.'

Jill embarked on a long explanation, quack-quacking through the telephone. 'I see,' said Margaret, and again, 'I see,' trying hard to stem the remorseless flow of revealing noise. 'What about next week?' Jill suggested at last. 'I'm sure I can make it then.'

Margaret tried to think quickly about this new entanglement of problems. 'I'm not quite sure,' she said hesitantly. 'I think I can manage all right, but if you don't mind I'll ring you later and let you know.' 'Well, do try,' urged Jill, and then to Margaret's enormous relief rang off.

Gerald looked up from his papers and asked casually, 'How's she liking her new job?' 'Oh, very much,' said Margaret over-emphatically. 'She's frightfully keen on it and she seems to be having a lovely time.' She waited a moment but Gerald didn't appear to have anything to add, and Margaret went back to the kitchen where she was getting the lunch so as to save Wendy all she could when she was home.

As she whipped up the national dried milk for the semolina pudding, put the gooseberries on to stew with a saccharin to save the sugar, her brain went round and round in circles, wondering just how everything could be arranged. The most important thing, of course, was to get a chance to speak to Jill privately and explain things a bit, but to speak to Jill privately seemed insurmountably difficult to arrange. Even if no one else was in the sitting-room and you could be sure that no one could hear what the person at the other end was saying, the person who was talking from Wood View could be heard in the kitchen through the hatch. It was no good getting up early because Jill would be in bed and so she might be last thing at night, and Gerald and Wendy and Sheila were hardly ever all out of the house together, at least not at a time when Margaret would be in it. In fact, it didn't seem as if it would be possible to telephone from home at all.

It would be no use waiting till Monday and trying to telephone Jill at her office. The telephone at the hospital mustn't be used for private calls and to wait till the lunch-hour meant that Jill would be out to lunch too. Besides, Monday might be too late; Jill might easily have a bright idea and ring up again and say to whoever answered it something that made it absolutely clear that it wasn't her that Margaret was out with the night before.

Scraping the potatoes, shredding the cabbage according to *Food Hints*, Margaret considered the telephone-box in the village on the corner beside the Master-At-Arms. But that wasn't any help. Anybody who saw her in it would know she was doing something underhand if she was phoning there instead of at home, and it could even happen that Gerald might suddenly take it into his head to go to Brotherton's for a packet of Weights and actually see her there.

Surely lots of people must want to put through private calls. It couldn't be so difficult as it seemed. But the Bruces' telephone was in a little cubby-hole under the stairs where everyone could hear all that was said, and anyway what would people think if you suddenly walked into their house and said you wanted to make a call you couldn't make openly at home? You'd have to make some excuse and that meant more lies – but Margaret's conscience hurriedly brushed away the lies as if they were cobwebs that threatened to soil her. It wasn't her fault, said her conscience, that she had to tell these lies, not anybody's fault, just an inescapable necessity. There would have to be a lie to explain the use of someone else's telephone – and so after lunch Margaret walked down to Green Lawns and unnecessarily explained that there wasn't any real reason, just that she thought that she'd like to see Martha and after a while she was able to exclaim, as if she'd only just thought of it, that she'd promised to phone Jill and please could she possibly use the telephone.

The Wetherall telephone was the sort that had extensions and Margaret at last found privacy in the room that was called the library, though there weren't any books in it, only maga- zines on the tapestry bench in front of the fire. As she dialled the number she had a moment's fear lest Jill should be out, but her luck held and Jill answered.

Margaret said urgently, 'Jilly, are you alone?'

'Why, yes,' said Jill, puzzled. She'd often started a conver- sation like that with her other friends as they had with her, but somehow it wasn't a question she'd ever expected to hear from Margaret Trevor.

'Listen, Jill,' Margaret said. 'It's awfully difficult to know how to put it, but will you do something for me?'

'Of course I will if I can,' came Jill's voice impatiently. 'Why do you sound so funny?'

Margaret said hurriedly, 'It's just that I don't want anyone to hear. Listen, Jill, what I wanted to ask you was if you'd pretend you were coming to the pictures with me next Friday but not really come.'

'How do you mean, pretend?' Jill asked.

It was all being horribly difficult, more difficult than Margaret had anticipated. In trying to work her way through the obstacles that confronted her, she hadn't looked further than getting into private touch with Jill, after which everything would be all right.

She said, 'I can't quite exactly explain, but what I wanted you to do is not to mind not coming with me yourself, but not to ring up my home when we're supposed to be there and if ever you did see Mummy to pretend you'd been with me, if you don't mind most awfully. Oh, and not to let anyone know you weren't with me last night, either.'

'Margaret,' came Jill's voice, mock-minatory, 'don't tell me it's a man.'

Over the telephone she heard something she had never heard before, Margaret giggling with nervous delighted embarrassment.

'It *is* a man,' said Jill triumphantly. 'Come on, Margaret, come clean. Who is he?'

It was like when Jill used to tease her at school, flattering, exciting, and yet infinitely more flattering and exciting than ever before. Margaret found herself laughing, bubbling, confiding to Jill in a quick spurt of words, 'I can't tell you who he is, honestly I can't, but he's awfully nice. I mean, there isn't really anything in it, it's just that I do most awfully want to go out with him and I simply daren't say anything about it at home, so if you *would* help me, Jill, I'd be most frightfully grateful.'

'OK,' said Jill. 'I'll support you to the death. But I warn you, I shall expect to hear all about it.'

'There really isn't anything to tell, honestly there isn't,' repeated Margaret helplessly, 'but if there was, you know you'd be the first person I'd tell, really you would.'

'OK,' said Jill again. 'But look here, Meggy, if you're going to pretend to be seeing me when you're not, how are we actually going to meet?'

'I don't know,' said Margaret. That was another problem that hadn't yet occurred to her.

'Well, see how it goes,' said Jill encouragingly. She added with deliberate mystery, 'And if it goes well, who knows but what we mightn't get up a foursome one evening. You're not the only person with something to tell.'

Miss Porteous's links with the Westbourne Diocesan Home for Fallen Women were of long standing. This charity had always been, as she sometimes playfully remarked, one of the pets of her father, the Vicar of a respectable West London parish, and its peculiar nature had always particularly appealed to Miss Porteous as an admirable opportunity for showing that a calm broad-mindedness was the proper intellectual equipment for dealing with the less pleasant facts of life. As a schoolmistress, she had always prided herself on being able to correct the mispronunciation of 'womb' without a flicker of awareness that this word in any way differed from others (except, of course, in being rather difficult to pronounce). Now, in her retirement, something of the same pride could be derived from dispassionately discussing fallen women on every suitable doorstep in Priory Dean.

So once a year, when the weather looked as if it had really settled down for a bit, Miss Porteous would take her raffia satchel and her special notebook in its tooled leather cover, and set out on what she always called 'begging for alms'. The phrase sanctified the undertaking; in its resolute humility was something of an almost Assisi flavour which Miss Beltram's preliminary protests at the lowering nature of the task served enticingly to enhance.

Miss Porteous did not, of course, allow to all and sundry the privilege of an annual contribution. The smallholders around the village were never called on, and in Station Road her visits were confined to what she called 'the very best type of the old-fashioned village folk' which ultimately meant the Wilsons and Mrs Birch, the wife of Miss Evadne's old gardener.

The tradespeople she canvassed thoroughly. 'Now I've come begging again,' she would say gaily as she entered each shop, secure in the knowledge that being asked for contributions by Miss Porteous conferred its own prestige. Right along the Arcade she went, even into the Master-At-Arms ('Our Lord consorted with publicans,' she would murmur to herself as she went through the private entrance in the yard), though she left out the Month-Of-May in Station Road where the young tradespeople and working-class people went and never even considered the Station Hotel, right down at the bottom of the hill, which was no better than an ale-house for the old, old men.

In computing her demands, Miss Porteous worked on a very nice assessment of needs and abilities. 'What are other people giving?' Martha Wetherall asked, and Miss Porteous searched her little book and said dispassionately, 'Green Lawns always used to contribute a pound,' leaving it to Martha to make the inevitable calculation that the same would be mean and five would be showy, and finally to compromise on three.

Miss Porteous had no intention of dunning her own friends. Miss Evadne was told that she always gave five shillings while the Trevors and the Bruces were asked for half-a-crown each, a fair enough assessment of their relative places in the social and financial scale. The problem, this year, was whether or not to call at Fernlea.

All the time she was working up the rest of Priory Hill, Miss Porteous was trying to make up her mind. Last year it had been easy. Miss Moodie, unambitiously set in her Drapery Store, had been asked for and given her ten shillings like all the rest of the tradespeople. Not to call on her among the other inhabitants of Priory Hill, Miss Porteous felt, would be to make a definite gesture of rejection; conversely, did not calling imply acceptance? Curiosity drew her on, the niceties pulled her back, but at last, by equating the niceties with false pride and curiosity with putting the cause before all else, Miss Porteous saw clearly where her duty lay and rang the bell at the front door of Fernlea.

To Miss Porteous's immense surprise, Miss Moodie, when she came to the door, was seen to be wearing a tweed suit. Miss Porteous had never thought of it that way before, but tweed suits, in Priory Dean, were definitely gentry wear. In the past

Miss Moodie had always been seen in the unnoticeable stock-inette dress and cardigan of the respectable tradeswoman; she might, indeed, in these days even have worn a skirt and a hand-knitted jumper, but never, Miss Porteous obscurely felt, a tailored tweed jacket. Why, now, with her smooth grey hair in the neat bun above this unassailable uniform, she looked just like anyone else, not even very unlike Miss Porteous herself, and it was the confusion she was feeling that led her, without thinking, to cross the threshold when Miss Moodie said, 'Do please come in, there's really quite a nip in the air today. You'd hardly think it's really June,' and then to walk into the sitting-room when Miss Moodie turned the oxydised copper handle on the oak-grained door.

'How very attractive you've made it,' she said, unable to keep the surprise out of her voice, for really, Miss Moodie's sitting-room was not so very different from the sort of room she had chosen for herself. The walls had been distempered a nice warm cream; the curtains at the casement windows were of that charming mock-cross-stitch mock-Jacobean linen, and the furniture, instead of being the tightly stuffed elaborately veneered walnut that most of the tradespeople bought, consisted of what Miss Porteous immediately sized up as A Few Good Pieces – a small oak gate-leg table, a long rush-seated oak stool, a painted pine corner cupboard with what was surely some genuine old lustre china inside. 'It really is extremely attractive,' she repeated, and going up to the cupboard, 'I'm so interested to see that you have a lustre tea-pot; I've been searching for one for years, but the teapots seem to be extremely rare.'

'That one was my great-grandmother's,' Miss Moodie offered calmly. 'I've always been very fond of old things, and I've never liked to turn them out and buy the sort of things they make nowadays.'

'I do so agree with you,' said Miss Porteous, whose good pieces had mostly been acquired not by inheritance but by purchase. 'One doesn't find the quality now that one used to. I feel that we no longer have the craftsmen who will put the same devoted care into everything they undertake.'

'That's just what I always say,' Miss Moodie agreed. 'I really was shocked, Miss Porteous, last November at the Women's Institute meeting, when we were all asked to bring a piece of embroidery, at some of the things that came out. Why, there were chair-backs and tea-cosies that a child of nine would have been ashamed of in my young days.'

Miss Porteous, for ever decrying the decay of the graceful arts, had never before found a sympathiser in Priory Dean. Now, at Miss Moodie's invitation, she willingly laid down her satchel and notebook to view the eighteenth-century sampler that Miss Moodie, with effortless superiority, had taken to the meeting as a simple example of her maternal great-great-grandmother's work. She was easily led on to view the elaborately convoluted fire-irons wrought by her grandfather the smith, the lace that her great-aunt had crocheted round the linen tea-cloth. Soon, she didn't quite know how, she found herself upstairs in Miss Moodie's bedroom, exclaiming with refined delight at the patchwork quilts that each generation of Moodie women had added to the common store.

'People tell me they're getting quite fashionable again in London,' Miss Moodie said with a sniff. 'Many a time I've been told there's dealers would pay me pounds for such things, but I don't care to part with them.'

'You are indeed right,' said Miss Porteous. It did not occur to either woman that the hoarded quilts might well have served their original purpose on their owner's bed, which was covered, like all the Priory Hill beds, with a counterpane of rayon taffeta machine-embroidered with flowers. 'I have rather an interesting hand-knitted one that an old nurse made for my mother's trousseau,' Miss Porteous said as they went downstairs again. 'You must come and see it one day,' and Miss Moodie said quietly that she would like to, betraying no more pleasure than a lady should at receiving an expected invitation. When Miss Porteous left the house, Miss Moodie's name had been entered in the notebook for the regular half-crown subscription of the top end of Priory Hill. As far as Miss Porteous was concerned, Miss Moodie had arrived.

If during that week someone had said to Margaret, 'But how do you feel about all this? What do you expect?' the question would have been incomprehensible to her. To think about things had never been demanded of her. The Trevor way of life seldom involved taking a decision that had not, in fact, been unconsciously made before the problem apparently arose. Events inevitably succeeded each other, and, in so restricted a life as theirs, the normal margin for accidental influences to bring about changes was extremely small. Thus, no mechanism had ever been developed for the assimilation of the unexpected, and Margaret's inevitable response to something she did not know how to think about was not to think about it.

She did not, then, think guiltily about deceiving her parents because it was unthinkable that she had done so, as unthinkable as it would have been to have told them that she had been to the pictures with Roy Wilson and was going again next week. Nor did she, during that week, consciously remember the last Friday, anticipate the next. The only thing that happened was that her day-dreams suddenly stopped; they had come into touch with reality, and to continue them would have been to tempt providence, like, when awaiting examination results, to imagine success instead of failure. She still walked up and down the High Street in her lunch-hour but now, instead of focusing her mind on the visible symbols of her inventions, she was gripped with a taut uncomprehended excitement of expectancy.

The next Friday she again met Roy by the box-office of the Plaza. 'There you are,' he said, his voice gruff with attempted casualness, and like dancers perfecting a difficult routine they meticulously reshaped the evening of the week before. But they laughed less readily at the film, this time an American comedy, not only because it less naturally aroused their laughter but because each was conscious of the need to excite and then to share enjoyment. 'We'll go to the café again, shall we?' Roy said quickly as soon as it was over, and then at last, when he looked at her over the menu and demanded quickly, 'Same again?' their elaborate mimicry of their own week-old selves dissolved in slow hugely relieved smiles.

Roy sighed and said frankly, 'I was scared you wouldn't come.'

Margaret said, 'I never thought of not coming.'

'Well, I couldn't be sure,' Roy muttered. The subject had to be changed quickly. It wasn't right that a doubt so founded should become an initial part of their developing relationship. Margaret said, 'They do keep it nice and cool in here, don't they?'

Both fell eagerly on the weather – yes, it was warm, nice and warm, not too warm, just right for the time of year. The traditional English ritual carried them through the meal without any awkwardness or difficulty, building up phrases that slid easily from their minds and set a smooth comfortable background for the welcoming smiles in their eyes.

But at last the food was eaten, the bill was paid, it was time to go. 'Pity the buses don't run later,' Roy said as they stood up, and Margaret agreed, yes, it was a pity 'though there's nothing to do in Walbridge after half-past ten,' she said, and there wasn't, the cinemas over, the pubs closing their doors, the cafés and milk-bars all shut. 'In France you can sit at tables on the pavement and talk till all hours,' Roy said in the corridor, and then, 'We don't ever seem to get the chance to really talk, do we?'

They looked at each other with wistful yearning. No, there was nowhere to go, nowhere to talk and find out what there was to talk about. 'I'll pick you up on the hill like last time,' Roy said quickly, and then they came out into the public splendour of the hall.

Squeezed on to the seat of the bus Margaret found she was breathing quickly as though she'd been running, breathing quickly and twisting her mouth in funny quick little smiles. It wasn't like ordinary life, somehow, it was like – well, she didn't know what it was like except that there was something exciting and different, so that you wondered – no, not exactly wondered. . . . Under the trees where Priory Hill bent away from the Green, her footsteps lagged as she waited for Roy.

He took her arm as he had last time, took it right away and held it closely to him. 'Oh, Margaret,' he said, saying her name aloud to her for the first time, 'Roy,' she said softly, smiling again in the gathering dark, and then they walked slowly and silently up the hill.

When they got to Fernlea he said, 'Let's just go to the end and back.' There were only half a dozen more houses before the road tapered into the path through the fields, but they walked there slowly and then paused a moment, looking ahead to the dark trees at the top of the hill and above them the stars. They were still arm in arm, close to each other, looking steadfastly ahead for fear of looking in each other's faces.

'I must go now,' Margaret said at last, slowly and regretfully. 'I'll wait here till you're in,' said Roy, 'it might be better.' He loosed her arm, turned to face her, almost moved quickly towards her, and then turned away. 'OK for next week?' he said casually. 'OK,' Margaret replied, and quickly turned and went down the hill again.

CHAPTER NINE

❦

Seeing on the notice-board at the village hall an announcement of the Parish Council meeting the next Tuesday, Martha insisted to her husband that they should go. At first he was reluctant. Everyone knew that English Parish Councils were completely moribund, he told her, they had no real power, they got nothing done, but the more he said in their depreciation, the more he fired Martha's zeal. How could they be other than moribund, she asked, if intelligent people, the people who really ought to be leading, just stood apart and contributed nothing. Every village ought to be a real community, she maintained, and people like themselves had a positive duty to play their part and even, if it were asked of them, to take a lead. At last Ralph found himself agreeing that perhaps she was right, perhaps in these times those who had the advantages of a wider vision had something to offer, perhaps even, that in his position – after all, Green Lawns, if not the most venerable house, at least paid the highest rates in Priory Dean – the village might well expect to see him there. So Martha organised a scratch meal at the, to her, ungodly hour of seven o'clock, and at eight she and Ralph were sitting with some fifty other people in the larger of the two classrooms at the village school.

The Councillors were seated in an uneasy half-circle facing the audience. Some of them she knew, at least by sight – Mr Pickering, the Chairman, Mr Pennyfeather, George Bruce – but now the proceedings started and she tried hard to concentrate on listening with an intelligent interest.

The first subject that seemed to be troubling everyone was the refuse collection, and Martha was glad to hear it. It had long been an outrage to her hygienic mind that the dustbins were emptied only about once a month if you were lucky, and even then with no sort of regularity on which you could depend. 'It isn't really very nice,' said each speaker, more or less, and after each speaker had finished Mr Pickering got up to explain that refuse collection wasn't really the business of the Parish Council but of the Rural District which just hadn't got the drivers for the vans and that was all there was to it. But the fact that discussion of the matter here and now couldn't possibly have any remedial effect didn't prevent one person after another getting up to add his quota of discontent. Martha noticed that none of the women there seemed to have anything to say, though surely this inadequacy must affect them even more than the men. It was with the intention of offering just the kind of contribution she felt she was best fitted to make that, after one of Mr Pickering's interjected disclaimers of responsibility, she rose and began, in proper form, 'Mr Chairman, Ladies and Gentlemen –

'If the difficulty arises from the Rural District Council not having enough drivers,' she said firmly, 'surely, Mr Chairman,

we could as a village community fill that gap ourselves instead
of letting something go on that's a menace to our own and our
children's health. I myself would gladly volunteer to drive a
van round once a month and I'm sure that there are many
people here would say the same.' She paused a moment,
moved by the sense of the new world bringing a breath of
constructive social vigour to the worn-out old. 'Surely, Mr
Chairman, when outside agencies fail to fill the need, then
vigorous self-help is the only real democratic solution.' Then
she sat down, hopefully waiting for the fruition of her call to
parochial unity.

Mr Pickering slowly rose. 'If Mrs Wetherall will allow me
to say so,' he said pontifically, 'though we're delighted to
see her rise and have her say like the rest of us, she's not been
here very long and a lot of our ways are still probably strange
to her. What she suggests is very interesting and perhaps it
would work very well in America, but I'm afraid it isn't quite
the answer for Priory Dean. As I've said before, ladies and
gentlemen, the Rural District Council –' and he was repeating
his former explanation yet once again and no one seemed to
want to discuss Martha's suggestion at all.

They moved on to the question of the War Memorial next;
should there be a new plaque attached to the old one, should
a second memorial be set up at the other end of the Green or
should some altogether new method of commemoration be
tried like inscribed oak benches round the Green or a new
lich-gate for the churchyard? Martha felt she knew exactly
what ought to be done, but nothing was going to get her
to risk another public snub. Then, to her huge surprise, Mr

Pickering was turning to Ralph and saying with unctuous politeness, 'Perhaps Mr Wetherall, whom we're all delighted to welcome here for the first time with his good lady, has got a suggestion he'd like to make?'

So that's what I did wrong, she thought between laughter and humiliation; this is men's business and I shoved my oar in. But it wasn't that, because after Ralph had said a few sedate words, as she would have wished him to say, about a proper children's playground with swings and roundabouts to keep them from their normal destructive activities in the street, Miss Porteous rose from the second row and received a respectful hearing when she stated that in a rural district, such as their own was still fortunate in being, surely Mother Nature could provide all the playground their children required.

It was finally decided to let the question of the War Memorial stand over till the next meeting in three months' time, but before the real excitement of the evening, the perennial dispute over the street-lighting, could be started, Martha decided that she had had enough and nudging Ralph to follow her, got up and stumbled out, whispering hurriedly to Wendy, her next-door neighbour, some confused excuses about not leaving Nanny alone too long. Back in their own armchairs, highball in hand, they agreed that the Parish Council was clearly not the right medium through which to influence the village.

Margaret, leaving work the next Friday to go to the cinema, was astonished to find Roy waiting for her outside the hospital gate. 'Why, Roy –' she began in pleased surprise, but he caught her arm and pulled her away from the departing crowds further down the suburban by-road. 'Look, I'm ever so sorry,' he began, 'but I'm afraid the pictures tonight is off. I'd clean forgotten it was Mum's birthday, and it was only this morning Edie told me she'd fixed it that we'd all go to the pictures together this evening to celebrate. She's a great organiser, is Edie, and there wasn't any way I could get out of it, not without a lot of questions. I was afraid I wouldn't be able to find you before you'd got to the Plaza, which would have been a bit awkward.' He grinned at her uncomfortably, and she said, 'Of course that's all right, Roy. I'm glad you managed to find me.' She couldn't help her voice showing a bit how disappointed she was.

She could hear that Roy was disappointed too. He said disconsolately, 'It's a long time to next Friday,' and then she had to tell him that it was getting a bit difficult, that her mother was saying she didn't like her making regular appointments that kept her away from home '– though, of course, she doesn't know I'm with you,' she finished in hurried confusion.

Roy burst out, 'But we've *got* to see each other,' and Margaret waited in silent acquiescence. 'There's no way we can ever get in touch with each other,' he said, and they walked a few more steps in worried cogitation.

Then Roy said quickly, 'Look here, I've got an idea. You get an hour for your dinner, don't you, same as me? I could get a quick bite at the canteen and be along here, say, by one, and then we could go for a bit of a walk for half an hour. It'ud be better than nothing, wouldn't it? I mean, that's to say, if you'd like to.'

147

'I *would* like it,' Margaret agreed shyly. 'It's always nice to get a bit of fresh air in the middle of the day. But I don't always get –' she was going to say 'lunch' but in instinctive deference to Roy she changed it, '– I don't always get dinner at the same time every day, and I wouldn't have any way of letting you know. I mean, I don't want you to come right from the other end of town just for nothing.'

'Oh, I don't mind about that,' Roy said, elaborately off-hand. 'It's a nice walk after all,' and that was how they left it, Monday if possible, and if not Tuesday, and anyway it would be a nice walk, a nice breath of air.

But as it turned out it was Monday and Tuesday and Wednesday, in fact every day that week except Thursday when the Country Clinic threw everything out. Each day at one Roy would be waiting outside the gates, and each day they'd been together down the street to the right, away from the High Street and the shops and the crowds, down among the little quiet streets of ugly Victorian villas, the untidy laburnums drooping over their straggling fences, the stucco peeling from the walls, the rust flaking from the dilapidated balconies. 'I wouldn't like to live in one of those old houses,' Margaret said one day and Roy agreed with her, but for the most part they didn't notice their surroundings, just ambled through the streets at random, arm in arm. They talked to each other quite easily now, or rather, for the most part Roy talked and Margaret listened. He'd talk to her about life at home, about the row Maureen had had with Gran last evening, and how Jim had heard tell of a half-house going at

Bentworth and if it came off, he and Edie could get married in the autumn. He'd tell her the village gossip, not the sly malicious gossip that flew among the older people, but the little factual gossip about the children throwing stones at the siren and Mr Timms saying he'd spank young Jenny Wilkins who was worse than the boys, just like they used to say about Maureen. And Mr Birch's arthritis had got so bad he didn't know how long he'd be able to carry on for Miss Evadne, pity, wasn't it, an old boy like that and working at the Hall these last twenty years, even if it was only about once a week now it would still break his heart not to be able to carry on. Or sometimes he'd tell her funny things that had happened in the Army and about the comic ways they had abroad, like women doing the hard work in the fields in Egypt, or in France serving the vegetables separate from the meat course. He found himself collecting all the funny things that happened at work so that he could tell Margaret, who received them with pleased smiles as if they were ripe fruit he'd gathered especially for her, not like at home where – well, maybe, he admitted, they might have liked him to talk like that at home, they were always saying he sat there mum without anything to say for himself, but it was different, somehow, telling things to Margaret. You could always tell by their lagging footsteps how sorry they were when the dinner-hour was over and it was time for Roy to leave Margaret at the hospital and hurry back to Thatcher's.

It was Sheila who first noticed that Miss Moodie had got a little dog. Officially Wood View still took no count of Fernlea's

149

doings, and the fact that Miss Porteous was now going about saying that Miss Moodie was really an extremely nice woman had been received by Priory Hill with a certain exasperation. No one, they said, doubted that Miss Moodie was a nice woman, but that was hardly the point, was it, and the point was simply whether one had certain standards or not. It was all very well for Miss Porteous, who often liked to take up an unpopular point of view with self-righteous humility, but after all, she lived right down at the bottom of the hill and didn't have Miss Moodie for a neighbour. In fact, for a week or two Trixie Beltram had enjoyed an unprecedented popularity as she made her little excuses to call at this house and that, dropping her jealous poison in every ear.

But as usual an overdose of Miss Beltram produced the inevitable effect, and however right she was, you couldn't help taking the other point of view, even though you knew it was nothing but sheer pig-headedness. 'After all,' Mrs Paynter-Smith said one day to Wendy when she'd come to exchange some raspberries for bottling for half-a-dozen eggs, 'people have got to start somewhere, haven't they? Goodness knows I'm no snob, but Trixie Beltram's father was only a wholesale butcher, when all's said and done,' and it became tacitly agreed that, though no overt steps of recognition need be taken, an opportunity for acceptance arising naturally would not be rejected.

So when Sheila saw the little dachshund puppy tumbling up the road on its brand-new lead she somehow knew that it wouldn't do any harm to stop and say, 'Oh, what a darling little thing!' and smile half at Miss Moodie and half at the dog. Though Sheila's present ambition was to be Senior Mathematics Mistress at whatever then happened to be the best girls' school in England, it wasn't so long since she'd wanted to run a stables and some breeding-kennels, both together, and so it was easy and natural for her to follow up her initial enthusiasms with questions that elicited that the puppy was a little gentleman just eight weeks old and his name was Paddy, and that Miss Moodie was afraid he'd soon have to have his first distemper injection, but one didn't like to think of it, did one, hurting a little thing like that, even though it was for his own good. Sheila was able to reassure Miss Moodie that there was absolutely no need to do anything about it until he was six months old and really there was nothing to worry about, and Miss Moodie seemed to accept her assurances as from someone who knew, even though Sheila had never been able to have a dog herself, naturally not, with all the chickens, and had to make do with Peterkins, the fat old black cat who'd been around so long that he was hardly noticed any more except for the difficulty of feeding him.

And after this it became common form for the Priory Hill ladies to smile graciously at Miss Moodie when they passed her in the road, trundling their wheeled shopping-baskets behind them, and even to stop and say, 'What a little darling!' with an extra-gracious smile. 'It's really a dear little creature, that dog of Miss Moodie's,' they admitted to each other, 'not like that horrid fat mongrel of Mrs Brotherton's,' and indeed it wasn't anything like Mrs Brotherton's mongrel, any more than a nice quiet tweed suit is anything like a stockinette frock with a cardigan over it.

CHAPTER TEN

The Wetheralls had by now almost completely dropped
out of the more intimate social life of Priory Hill. Everyone
went to the Church Fête, of course; you couldn't let personal
feelings make a difference. If somebody gathered up their
resources and gave a more or less formal party, as Mr and
Mrs Paynter-Smith had in May and the Bruces in June,
then the Wetheralls were automatically asked and came, and
they, in their turn, gave two or three small parties at which
all the Priory Hill set turned up. They were chatted to in
the streets and a general atmosphere of friendliness was
taken for granted, but it was equally taken for granted that
the Wetheralls' real social life soared beyond Priory Dean,
took place in the Bentworth Country Club and the big neo-
Georgian homes of the rich businessmen on the Bentworth
outskirts, took place in the Thatcher mansion and even in
restaurants twenty miles away in London. They had expanded
beyond Priory Dean before they could ever be asked fully to
penetrate the cosy intimacies of the sewing-parties in the
afternoons, the coffee-parties in the evening, the men's glass
of beer after church on Sunday mornings in the saloon bar of
the Master-At-Arms. Even Margaret Trevor, who probably

liked Martha Wetherall more than anyone else in the village did, seemed to have stopped dropping in, and Wendy, quiescently accepting order once more established, had almost forgotten the high hopes she had formerly placed on the new arrivals at Green Lawns. It came as a great surprise to her, then, when one day in July she answered the telephone and heard Martha at the other end.

'Hallo,' said Martha, with that upward intonation so subtly different from the English greeting. She worked dutifully through all the social preliminaries – 'Well, now how are you getting along?' – 'Yes, we'll have to water the grass if this dry weather keeps on, whatever the government may tell us,' – and then said, 'I was wondering if you'd let us take Margaret out to dinner next Thursday evening. My step-brother Toby is coming over for a spot of leave, and we thought we might go over to the Country Club so's they could dance – you know, just a young people's party.'

Wendy wondered for a moment whether she should say that they didn't let Margaret go to clubs, just, so to speak, to re-establish the picture of Margaret the sheltered debutante, just to show that they didn't need to accept any favours and knew what was what. But through her social caution flooded the revival of her hopes. 'I'd be delighted for her to go,' she said enthusiastically, wondering if perhaps it wasn't all going to come true after all, the new people at Green Lawns, the opening of opportunities, and at last the arrival of the eligible young man.

'We're not dressing,' said Martha. 'Tell Margaret just something light and pretty,' and rang off.

Margaret received the news of the invitation with mixed feelings among which relief, perhaps, predominated. For three weeks, now, she'd been going for walks with Roy in the lunch-hour, and however hard you didn't really think about it, it was impossible not to admit now and again that one had settled down to a clandestine relationship, infinitely contenting, infinitely disturbing, and with no possible future. You couldn't help seeing what Wendy meant when she spoke of Ralph Wetherall's young step-brother being the excuse for this dinner-party, and if it all turned out as it just conceivably might, there would be an end to this queer disturbing half-life, and a future unassailable and secure.

The right frock for the party was, as always, a problem. 'Something pretty and light' clearly meant, ideally, something like those fluttery voiles in which young girls stood by refrigerators in American magazines. But when you stopped to think how unlikely it was that you'd be able to buy a ready-made dress with that much material in it when cotton dresses were seven coupons and the material two coupons a yard, it was obvious that no one was going to have one just hanging in their wardrobe, and certainly nothing of the sort had ever turned up in any of the parcels from New Zealand.

The arrangement about Margaret's wages, firmly imposed by Wendy, had been that she paid her mother a pound every week for her board and lodging – 'Goodness knows I'd rather not take a penny, but it's the principle of the thing, and anyway it doesn't go near covering what she costs' – retained ten shillings for her fares and lunches and banked the rest in the Post Office for an emergency. Now this invitation, Wendy decided, was as suitable an emergency as could be devised for drawing five pounds out of the Post Office and buying a frock which she couldn't honestly say would be practical but which might well come in handy for similar occasions in the future.

'You slip out in your lunch-hour tomorrow and see what you can get,' Wendy ordered. 'Or had I better come with you?' She considered the problem while Margaret held her breath, terrified of the chance encounter with Roy outside the hospital gates, but Wendy finally decided no, Margaret was old enough to choose for herself and it would be good experience for her.

This was Wednesday, a day on which so far it had always been possible to meet and walk with Roy. Of course it would have been perfectly easy to meet him as usual and explain that just today, because of this party, she'd have to go off shopping – but then she found that she didn't in the least want to. The occasion for which the frock was to be bought seemed, if you looked at it one way, a kind of treachery to Roy; and if you looked at it another way, it seemed oddly to diminish Roy, to make the meetings, the whole relationship, something low and degrading of which now, for the first time, she felt ashamed.

So she asked Sister if she could, as a special favour, take her lunch-time late that day, and slipped out of the hospital at a time when she was sure Roy would have given her up and gone back to work. She didn't feel happy about it, and it was a relief to remember that she wouldn't have to face him next day because of the Thursday Clinic, in fact not until Friday when the party would be over and something – though she didn't know what – settled one way or another. But even with everything so conveniently arranged, even with a powder-blue linen frock with white embroidery round the neck that Wendy graciously commended as 'a really nice dress, thoroughly ladylike and yet pretty at the same time', Margaret couldn't rid herself of a sense of guilt, a consciousness of behaving badly to Roy.

She was asked to Green Lawns at seven o'clock so that there'd be time for a drink before setting off. In the drive in front of the house she was excited to see a car that by its very appearance called up all sorts of ideas of sophisticated glamour, a long low black car absolutely roofless, with big silver tubes coming out of the bonnet. No car could have been better devised to fit in with her half-formed anticipation of the evening ahead. She rang the bell and almost before the melodious chimes had begun their tinkle Ralph was opening the door to her and ushering her in.

'Is that Margaret?' Martha's voice called. 'Come on in, darling,' and Margaret went into the drawing-room, and Martha was getting up from her chair, coming forward to welcome her.

But beyond Martha, on the big peach velvet sofa, two people were sitting. One was a young man who was everything a dreamed-of young man ought to be, long-limbed and well-dressed, good-looking, incredibly – what was the word – smooth, no, self-confident in a worldly kind of way. And beside him was sitting an unbelievably beautiful girl with smooth fair hair and an exquisitely made-up face, a girl just as sophisticated as the young man himself, and wearing a dress simultaneously far more elaborate and yet simpler than anything Margaret had ever seen in the American magazines.

Martha's hand was on her arm, guiding her forward. 'Come and meet everyone,' she said gaily. 'Margaret, this is Sandra Thatcher – I don't know if you two girls know each other?'

Sandra shook her head with a smile of polite regret, and Martha explained, 'Sandra's the niece of our friend Alan Thatcher at Bentworth Park. And this, as you've probably guessed, is my young brother-in-law, Toby. Oh –' and she turned round to someone in the wing armchair who had been invisible to Margaret until now, '– of course you know Roger Gregory, don't you?'

Margaret, bewildered by the unexpectedness of this gathering, was shepherded to a chair and handed a sherry, while the talk went on. Toby Wetherall was making a long involved story of his drive up from London with Sandra, of losing his way here and there, misunderstanding Martha's directions – 'Mind you, it would have been all right if I hadn't got this wench with me,' he said, nodding to Sandra, 'but sooner than that she cast doubts on my competence as a driver, I thought I'd better get my story in first. And anyway, it was having her there that distressed me and shook my self-confidence.'

'Would you have condemned the poor girl to our unspeakable railway line just to keep your self-confidence intact?' laughed Ralph, and Martha broke in with mock self-reproach, 'And I thought it was such a lovely idea you bringing Sandra and killing so many birds with one stone. And if I'd only thought of it,' she added, turning to Roger, 'he could have picked you up at the hospital and brought you along too.'

'Gregory looks like a man who'd have kept me on the straight and narrow,' said Toby laughing, and Margaret, unable to contribute to this kind of conversation, looked at Roger sitting in the big armchair and thought how different he looked from these two Wetherall men in their smooth well-cut grey suits, poor Roger in his navy blue obviously hot and uncomfortable with his hair in a thick untidy thatch on his head and a boil starting on his neck. Forgetting her usual dislike of him, she smiled at him with tentative kindness but was shocked that, looking straight at her, he ignored the smile and dropped his eyes quickly to his glass, draining it in an untidy gulp.

'Well, we'd better get going,' said Ralph heartily. 'You'll take your car, won't you, Toby? How shall we arrange everyone?'

Toby half turned to Sandra but before anything could be said Martha suggested smoothly, 'Toby, you take Margaret in your death-trap and the rest of us can squeeze into the Humber. Then coming back we can change over.'

Margaret, watching her, saw her give a quick nod of complicity at Toby and half realised that it was the coming back that mattered and that Toby would be coming back with Sandra. Disturbed, not quite comprehending, she obediently climbed into the low black open car.

Toby said kindly, 'You'd better tie something over your head or you'll be blown to pieces. I think Sandra left a scarf in that pigeonhole,' and Margaret searched and found a heavy-silk scarf printed with fantastic convolutions of roses and smelling of a perfume both evocative and exciting. 'That's right,' said Toby. 'Tie it on now, there's a good girl,' and Margaret knotted the thick silk under her chin and then instinctively clutched the side of the door as the black car accelerated and shot down the drive.

Conversationally the Trevors took the ownership of cars for granted, but the fact remained that Margaret had, as far back as she remembered, very seldom been in one. Of the Priory Road people only Miss Evadne and the Paynter-Smiths had cars, and the latter's had been laid up on blocks in the garage ever since 1940. Miss Evadne had a small allowance of petrol because she was on the Hospital Driving rota, but there had never been any occasion for Margaret to go in Miss Evadne's car. The village taxi was used mainly to transport schoolchildren to special classes in Bentworth and anyway, with what Porter charged, there was never any need to use it when there was a perfectly good bus. Just to go in a car was unusual enough, but to go in a car like this one was so breath-taking and thrilling an experience that Margaret never noticed that Toby didn't bother to speak to her on the swift three-mile journey, but just sat there as relaxed as if he were still in the drawing-room, whistling a tuneless little song.

He drew up before the striped awning of the club's front door and said to Margaret, 'You hop out and I'll go and park her.' So Margaret untied the scarf and climbed out, then, not knowing what to do, waited uneasily on the steps until the Humber drew up on the well-swept sandy gravel.

'What have you done with Toby?' Martha asked.

'He's just parking the car, I think,' said Margaret, and Martha said, 'Well, let's go in and find a table,' and led them through the door into the thickly-carpeted hall.

The next day, when Wendy kept asking impatiently what the club was *like*, Margaret found it very hard to explain. There were little tables, she said, and a dance-floor and a band wearing white dinner-jackets like you saw in the American films – but she couldn't explain any more clearly, and to Wendy's further demand to be told who was there, she had nothing to offer. She passed most of the evening in a state of bemusement, trying all the time to get the pattern of a routine of talking, eating, dancing, behaving that she had never met before and that clearly, at least to Martha and Ralph, Sandra and Toby, was one they took completely for granted. 'That would be lovely,' she said, when someone suggested what she might like to eat, and, 'Yes, I'd like to,' when someone suggested she should get up and dance. She didn't even try to join in the conversation, only smiled politely when people, trying to include her, smiled at her.

But gradually it began to be apparent to her that Roger wasn't much more at ease there than she was herself. Because he had been talking loudly where she had been silent, she had originally included him with the others to whom these surroundings, this way of behaving, was easy and familiar. But later, as the dinner was cleared away and they sat over their coffee, she couldn't help noticing that Roger's talk had a loud desperation of effort very different from the casualness of the others. He was talking about cars with Sandra and Toby, making over-confident statements full of names Margaret had never heard of, while the other two sat and smiled at him lazily, as if, Margaret thought, they knew he was all wrong but wasn't worth contradicting. It seemed to her so improbable that they would want to include her in their conversation that she would never have noticed she had been left out of it had not Martha said with a little laugh, 'Roger, if you're going to neglect your dinner-partner, you'd better move across and let me sit next to her; Margaret and I haven't managed to have a word all evening.'

So Roger was her dinner-partner, not Toby. Toby was Sandra's dinner-partner and he'd been talking to her all evening, but Roger, who was Margaret's, hadn't yet addressed a spontaneous word to her. Mind you, I don't like him either, Margaret admitted fairly to herself, but it wouldn't hurt him to be friendly. She wondered what ever had given Martha the idea of asking Roger – and then Martha was sitting beside her, hoping so much she was enjoying herself, and of course Margaret had to say that it was lovely, it was sweet of them to ask her, she was having a marvellous time.

But long before it was time to go, it seemed to Margaret as if the evening had dragged on for ever. She got more and more tired and sleepy, yes, and bored, sitting at the table among the ever-replenished drinks she herself consistently refused, a part of the group and yet not integrated into it, wondering how the others could possibly keep up their light friendly banter, how it was possible they could be enjoying themselves as much as they seemed to be. Even when the three men fell to talking together, and Margaret and Sandra and Martha were left to chat as a feminine group, there was no point at which Margaret's experiences could make contact with their conversation. A five-pound dress from a shop in Walbridge gave you nothing to say about expensive clothes in London, a drop of Wendy's hoarded Coty scent behind the ears as recommended by *Woman and Beauty* had no relevance to a discussion about perfume smuggled from Paris. But I can talk all right to Martha when she's alone, she thought despairingly, talk about cooking and children and the village, but this was Martha's real life too and only a tiny part of it had ever been given to Margaret. It was people like Sandra who could share Martha's life, people like Sandra whom Martha naturally looked on as the counterpart of Ralph's step-brother Toby. Margaret was suddenly overwhelmed with the realisation that she and Wendy had been deceiving themselves from the start. Martha never had, never could have thought of Margaret Trevor as someone for Toby. Sandra for Toby – and then Martha had looked around and picked on Roger, the only young man in the village suitable for Margaret. Roger would do for Margaret, Martha thought that Roger would do for Margaret, and nothing else had ever entered Martha's head.

'Well, I don't know about you people, but I'm just about ready for bed,' Martha said at last, and they were packed into the two cars, but this time Sandra and Toby whirled off together into the night and Margaret and Roger were settled in the back of the big Humber.

As they came up Archery Lane and swept round the village green, Martha leant over to the back and said, 'Roger, I know you'll not mind seeing Margaret up the hill, and, Margaret, you'll forgive us not running you there, but Toby and Sandra will have arrived long ago and I'm sure they'll forget all about not waking up the children.'

Ralph quickly opened his mouth to say something, but bit it off abruptly as his wife gave him a sharp meaningful dig in the ribs.

So again Margaret was walking up the hill in the dark with a young man. She had not perceived Martha's manoeuvre in the car, but Roger had, and he was furious. He too had understood the pairing-off that had gone on in Martha's mind, Sandra for Toby and Margaret for himself, and he was outraged that Martha should think him unworthy of Sandra, the sort of girl he had always longed for and never been able to make, outraged with a frenzy of frustration that Martha should think a dull plain girl like Margaret Trevor a fitting partner for him. Never before had he been in such close contact with a girl like Sandra, glamorous, sophisticated, exactly the sort of girl on whom his most lurid dreams were based, and now he desired her fervently and there was only Margaret walking silently by his side. Suddenly he stopped and caught hold of her, pulled her against him and kissed her brutally and clumsily, determined to vent on her his passionate dissatisfaction. He felt Margaret tremble, he felt her twisting away her lips and knew that she hated this as much as he did, but still he went on kissing her angrily until at last he didn't care any more and let her go.

'I'm sorry,' he muttered, and he saw her twisted face in the moonlight and thought she was going to cry, and he quickly turned and walked away.

Margaret waited a minute and then walked slowly to the end of the road, hardly knowing what she was doing. She stood and looked over the field where she and Roy had waited, listening to the crunch of Mr Rowe's cows tearing the grass a few feet away from her, waited unthinking, with the cool soft air against her bruised cheeks.

Then she heard herself say aloud, 'It's no good.' Startled, she wondered why she had spoken, why the words had forced themselves out of her mouth. It's no good, she repeated silently – she began to know that what was no good was the half-formed hope she had had of change and release. There was no good to come from the Wetheralls, nothing they could offer that she knew how to accept or even to want. There was no good from Toby who had never been real for her, no good from Roger who was all there could ever be. There was no escape: there was only – perhaps – safety.

CHAPTER ELEVEN

'Well, I should say that was a very successful evening,' remarked Ralph Wetherall, pushing away his coffee-cup, lighting his first after-breakfast cigarette. 'Toby and Sandra still in bed?'

'I think I heard Sandra in the bathroom,' said Martha. 'I told them not to hurry up. After all, Toby is on leave, and Sandra's not the girl to be up with the lark.'

'Think something's going to come of it?' he asked casually.

'You can't be sure,' said Martha. 'I know they've been running around together for some time. It wouldn't be such a bad idea. She's certainly a lovely girl.'

'And there's plenty of money there,' Ralph agreed. He started to fold the *Daily Telegraph* tidily so that it could be passed on to Martha the way she liked it, an apparently pristine newspaper. 'And what about Margaret and young what's-his-name? I thought she looked prettier last night than I've ever seen her.'

'I'm not so sure it mightn't come off,' Martha said, 'if it gets given a nice helpful push from time to time. Of course they're both very shy. I don't suppose they're either of them used to going about very much, but they seemed to be getting on all right last night, and he certainly wasn't averse to the chance of seeing her home. The trouble with the Trevors is I don't think it ever occurs to them that if you want something, you've got to go right out and get it.'

'Lucky they've got you to think for them then,' he said laughing. 'I must say I'd like to see Margaret happily married. She's so quiet, she's the sort that just gets left behind unless there's someone to give her a helping hand. Though mind you,' he added, 'there's not much the Trevors *can* give her, when it's clear they've hardly got two pennies to rub together.'

'How much do you think they really *have* got?' Martha asked curiously.

'About five or six pounds a week, I should say,' Ralph answered, and Martha broke in with a horrified, 'But, Ralph, that's unbelievable! Why, only yesterday Edie was telling me that there's never less than twenty-five pounds a week coming into their home and often it's nearer thirty. And they're only working-people.'

'Class doesn't go by money, though, does it?' said Ralph. 'Why, it doesn't even in America. Plenty of your old Boston families are nearly as poor as the Trevors, but they still look down their noses at everyone else.'

'But they're a very small group,' Martha protested, 'and anyway, they're mostly an older generation that's dying out. I'll agree there are people like university professors who don't earn what they deserve, but generally speaking a man's earnings are a pretty fair guide to what he's worth.'

'Fair enough,' said Ralph, 'and in our new society there's no doubt the Wilsons will be worth more than the Trevors. But neither the Wilsons nor the Trevors think so, and that's the important thing.'

'Five to six pounds a week,' Martha repeated. 'But darling, on that they can barely get enough to eat.'

'You've got to remember that English incomes are very much lower than American ones,' said Ralph. 'You must double it at least if you're going to think in American terms, but even so I agree they probably go pretty empty on it. Still, from all I hear there's just a chance a bit of good fortune may be coming Trevor's way. I don't know if you've heard, but in the new town-planning maps Priory Dean has been scheduled as an industrial area.'

'But we don't want to live in an industrial area!' Martha exclaimed in dismay. 'Why, one of the reasons we came here was that it was so rural.'

'It won't mean more than one or two small factories,' said Ralph soothingly. 'And that wouldn't be such a bad thing, bring money into the neighbourhood and stir it up a bit. But what I'm thinking is that the only place they could put them is at the Priory Hill end. Well, if I'm right, it means land values there will go up very considerably and Trevor ought to be able to part with that field of his for a very nice little sum. In fact, I'm not sure I won't make him an offer for it myself. We'll just wait a bit and see if the plans look like coming to anything.'

'And do you think,' Daisy asked mysteriously, 'that anything *will* come of it?'

Wendy, taking her elevenses in Daisy's kitchen, understood perfectly. 'Mind you, it's like squeezing blood from a stone ever to get a word out of Margaret,' she said, 'but reading between the lines, I think one could see she'd enjoyed herself. And the way she was so unwilling to say a word about this Toby made me think that perhaps things hadn't gone too badly.'

'He drove her there in his car, you said?' hinted Daisy encouragingly.

'So I eventually gathered,' said Wendy, 'and it finally came out that he'd danced with her several times. Of course, one wants to be careful, but – though I didn't tell her so, of course – I must admit she was really looking quite pretty last night.'

'And how would you feel,' asked Daisy, 'if – well, if something did come of it?'

'Well, of course, the Wetheralls aren't exactly out of the top drawer,' said Wendy judiciously, 'but in these times I suppose one oughtn't to be too particular about such things. They've got money, of course, and nowadays that seems to be the only thing that counts.'

'Is he going to see her again soon do you know?' Daisy asked.

'I'd rather gathered he'd only got a very short leave,' Wendy answered, 'but after all, he'll be over here again, no doubt – these things are often best left to simmer for a bit.'

Both women were unconsciously assuming that for Toby to meet a girl was as rare an event as for Margaret to meet a man, and just as Margaret's life would presumably pursue its isolated tenor between possible meetings, so they assumed that Toby's would too.

'I hear they asked Roger Gregory too,' Daisy remarked. 'I didn't know that the Wetheralls and the Gregorys were all that thick.'

'Oh, Margaret said there was some niece of the Thatchers there too,' Wendy casually dismissed the subject. 'I suppose they got Roger along for her.'

To atone for her contemplated betrayal of Roy, Margaret, strolling through the quiet streets with him, eagerly and volubly betrayed her evening with the Wetheralls. Usually she was content to let Roy do most of the talking but today he could hardly get a word in edgeways as she insisted on telling about the previous evening. She told him about the car and the band and the supper and the drinks and the people at the tables around, all the things she hadn't been able to remember for Wendy came pouring out in tumultuous confession. 'And I was so bored,' she kept saying, 'so bored, I couldn't see how anyone could call that enjoying themselves. And that girl, Roy, you've never seen anything like her, almost like a film star, but so stuck-up, not really human at all.'

'And what was the chap like?' Roy asked once or twice, but each time Margaret quickly brushed Toby aside with, 'Oh, just ordinary, nothing to write home about.' She didn't mention Roger at all.

Her continued febrile chatter about the evening obscurely troubled Roy. 'Course, she kept saying she hadn't enjoyed it, but still he felt it as a threat. It had been offered as pleasure, and pleasure of a kind he would never have thought or known how to provide. It was subconsciously with the idea of

169

competing in the provision of enjoyment that he suddenly remembered something and turned eagerly to Margaret, cutting her off in the middle of a sentence. 'What do you say we make that trip to Little Poulteney we were talking about?'

She looked at him uncomprehendingly, and he nervously urged, 'You know – that time you said you'd never seen a real forge working. Come on – we'll go on Sunday – what do you say?'

It was a jerk forward, a foreboding of sudden change. Margaret said in bewilderment, 'I'd like to, I really would. But how ever could we manage it?'

Now Roy could confidently plan and sweep Margaret along with him. 'We'll go this very Sunday as ever is,' he decided. 'You've got a bike, haven't you? You tell your Mum you're going off for the day with a pal and we'll meet on Bentworth Common by the pub. I'll get Maureen to make some sandwiches and we'll have a picnic.'

'You won't tell her who it's for?' Margaret begged, and therewith gave her assent to the whole scheme.

Now it was no longer possible to pretend there was no deceit. No innovation could easily be introduced at Wood View, and a sudden whim to go off for a day's bicycling would need documenting at every point. As she sat at her typewriter that afternoon, making out the little slips for the patients, Margaret's brain continuously wrestled with the problem of inventing a total screen of uniform opacity. Jill suggested, she began – no, not Jill, she had let Jill be assumed too often lately – Evelyn, the girl I work with at the hospital, she tried

– but that wouldn't do either, because it wasn't utterly impossible that Wendy might one day meet Evelyn, perhaps coming out of the hospital or perhaps Wendy or someone else from Priory Dean coming in for an X-ray and then saying something to Evelyn about a picnic and then it all coming out. A nurse whom I sometimes talk to at lunch, she started – yes, that would do, a nurse could easily leave the hospital, never be available as a hostile witness. A nurse whom I sometimes talk to at lunch, then, she said to herself, asked me if I'd go for a long bicycle ride with her on Sunday. She invented little objections from Wendy. 'Why doesn't she come to the house to pick you up?' Because, she thought, because – because she's spending the weekend with friends the other side of Bentworth – I'm not quite sure where, she interpolated hurriedly – and it's easier to meet her there so that we can go further, and that's the reason why she can't come back for a bite, just a scratch meal as it's Sunday. 'And what is your friend's name?' she imagined Wendy asking, and making up a name was the hardest of all, but Margaret finally decided that her friend was called Mary Brown, which wasn't quite so obvious as Smith.

She tried it when she was washing up the supper things and Wendy was getting the table ready for breakfast. She had told it to herself so often that it was disconcerting when Wendy put in the unrehearsed suggestion. 'Why don't you take Sheila along too? I'm sure it would do her good.' Margaret didn't know what to say, but fortunately Sheila broke in protesting that she'd got oceans of homework and anyway it was much too hot to go pedalling all over the country. 'It *is* rather hot,'

Wendy said doubtfully. 'Are you sure, Margaret, that it won't be too much for you?' but luckily at that moment the back-door bell rang and Wendy said, 'Whoever can it be this time of night?' – went to open it and it was old Mrs Wilkins, the daily woman.

She said, 'I'm ever so sorry to disturb you, mum, but me and Wilkins was wondering if you'd be so kind as to help us. It's one of those government forms, mum, and me and Wilkins can't make head nor tail of it, and in the end Wilkins said to me, why not ask Mrs Trevor, he said, she'd know all about that kind of thing, he said.' She stood waiting on the doorstep, not humbly, but confident of her right to bring to the gentry those problems with which the gentry were best fitted to deal.

Instinctively Wendy admitted this claim. 'I don't know if I'll be able to cope with it,' she said for form's sake, 'but come on in, Mrs Wilkins, and we'll see what we can make of it. What's it all about?'

'It's about Wilkins' pension, see,' said Mrs Wilkins, stepping into the kitchen and producing from her big shabby handbag a piece of buff paper, folded and refolded at every corner, obviously passed around from one non-comprehending gaze to another for many days. Wendy unfolded it and said with a laugh, 'It looks pretty complicated, doesn't it?' and Margaret in the corner silently went on with the washing-up, thankfully relieved for the timely inter-ruption.

Wendy scanned the form hurriedly and then said, 'You know, Mrs Wilkins, this really ought to be filled in by your husband. I'll do it for you, if you like, but I don't know if you'll be able to answer all the questions for him.'

'I'll do me best, mum,' said Mrs Wilkins, and Wendy successfully elicited the easy name and address and then came on to the question of George Wilkins' date of birth.

'Well, I can't rightly say as to that,' said Mrs Wilkins, 'but seventy-two is what Wilkins says he is and I reckon that's about right.'

Wendy hurriedly did a subtraction sum, hoping that approximate accuracy would satisfy the Ministry of Pensions. It was easy to fill in Mr Wilkins' occupation, which was that of agricultural labourer in the employ of Rowe, the dairyman who rented the fields at the end of Priory Hill. Then Wendy looked through the next section and said to Mrs Wilkins, 'This seems to be about the insurances you already carry. I think it might be better if you took this back to your husband and got him to fill it in for himself.'

But Mrs Wilkins made no move to take the proffered paper. 'Me and Wilkins have never cared much for reading,' she said with a trace of uneasiness. 'If you would be so kind as just to fill it in as you think best, mum, I'm sure that would do very nicely.'

Wendy looked up sharply, seemed about to protest – then said, 'Oh, very well. Suppose you tell me about the insurances then.' Slowly she elicited from Mrs Wilkins that there was the burial club they'd been paying into ever since Louie was born which was twenty-nine years ago come next November, a penny a week that was, and five pounds benefit if it should so chance that anything was to happen. And then there was the burial club they paid into for themselves and had done ever since they were married, threepence a week that one was, and twelve pounds for the funeral whichever of them was the first to go.

'But, Mummy –' said Margaret, startled at the sink, but Wendy quickly shushed her and went on taking down the slowly, laboriously extracted details.

'There you are,' she said at last, 'now all Wilkins has got to do is to sign his name just there, and then you hand it in at the post-office.'

'Would it do if I was to write it for him?' asked Mrs Wilkins. Wendy looked doubtful and in a surge of confidence Mrs Wilkins said, 'It's not that he can't do it, mum, not if I guide his hand, like, but he doesn't fancy it, if you take my meaning. I've never minded the writing myself, not my own name, that is, but to Wilkins, mum, it's a regular burden and that's all there is to it.'

'I see,' Wendy said gravely, 'but I think you'd better guide his hand for this one, as it's for the government.'

'Well, I'll do my best, mum,' Mrs Wilkins said doubtfully, 'and thank you, mum, for taking the trouble. I do hope as how I didn't disturb you, coming along like that, but Wilkins, see, he said to me –' and slowly Wendy edged her to the door and at last managed to guide the flow of talk into a final parting.

She came back in the kitchen and said with a laugh, 'Poor old thing. I thought I'd never get rid of her. One thing people of that sort never learn is how to take their leave gracefully.'

'But, Mummy,' said Margaret, who had been bottling it up. 'Did you hear what she said about the insurance? I mean, I'm rotten at arithmetic, but surely they've paid dozens of times over for what they'll get in the end?'

'Of course it's a wicked fraud,' agreed Wendy, 'but what can you expect with people like that who are simply asking to be taken advantage of? They can't either read or write, so you can hardly expect them to be able to do arithmetic.'

'Do you mean they really can't read?' asked Margaret in stupefaction. 'I thought Mrs Wilkins just said they didn't like to?'

'That's merely a polite way of putting it,' said Wendy, smiling. 'You'd be surprised how often you find it among working-class people. Honestly, it makes me see red sometimes to think that people like that have got the vote. Still, I suppose it's them and their sort that gave us the government we've got now.'

'Do you think people oughtn't to be allowed to vote if they can't read or write?' Margaret asked.

Wendy gave a short laugh. 'I know it's unfashionable to say so just now,' she admitted, 'but to my way of thinking, the country was a good deal better off when it was governed by people of our sort and you didn't have every uneducated Tom, Dick and Harry asked to give his opinion on matters he couldn't know anything about. Why, you've only got to look for yourself. Take Mrs Wilson: in many ways she's a very sensible woman, but are you honestly going to tell me that you want to be governed by someone like that? I talked to her about politics one day and she as good as told me she was going to vote Socialist, obviously without knowing the first thing about it.'

'But I don't know anything about politics,' Margaret objected, 'and I suppose I'll have a vote when I'm twenty-one.'

'That's different,' said Wendy. 'You've had an education, you can read the newspapers and find out what's going on. But Mrs Wilkins, now, she can't even read, and you can see that when she wants something done, it's people like us she naturally turns to. And as for people like the Wilsons, I don't suppose they ever look at the papers except to do the football pools.'

She had finished laying the table and went to sit down in the sitting-room where Gerald had already got the wireless on so as to be sure to be in good time for Arthur Askey. But Margaret lingered in the kitchen, slowly drying the plates and putting them away in the cupboard, appalled at the gulf of contempt that Wendy had opened, and discovering that she was feeling for Wendy an entirely new kind of suspicion and mistrust.

CHAPTER TWELVE

It was ten miles from Bentworth Common to Little Poulteney and the road climbed all the way. The direct way to go was to follow the main road for at least nine of the ten miles and this was the route Roy and Margaret naturally took after they had met, at eleven o'clock, opposite the pub on the Common. But it was a hot August weekend and despite the petrol rationing the road was crowded. The private cars dodged in and out of the big coaches and Green Line buses, the cyclists dodged in and out of both, and Roy and Margaret, trying to pedal along sedately on their now old-fashioned bicycles, were constantly separated and forced to swerve away from each other by the groups from the cycling-clubs, girls and boys alike in shorts, all bent over low-twisted rubber-covered handle-bars, one horizontal line over the machine from buttock to neck and the head jerked up to scan the road ahead.

But neither Margaret nor Roy wore shorts – he in grey flannel trousers and a white cotton shirt with rolled-up sleeves, open at the neck, she in the new blue linen dress; 'grossly unsuitable,' Wendy had said crossly, but Margaret had hurriedly explained, the words slipping easily from her lips, that her friend had said they might have tea with a great-aunt in

Little Poulteney, an old lady, very old-fashioned. And neither Roy nor Margaret had come out for the pleasure of being a-wheel, and so when they were about halfway there and up on the flank of the downs, Roy cycled in close to her and suggested, 'What do you say we strike off to the left and take to the lanes? I've a pretty good bump of direction, and with all this traffic, it'll probably be quicker in the end.'

'I think it would be nicer,' Margaret agreed, and in the next village they turned off the main road between a shabby petrol-station and a triangle of waste-ground covered with rusting metal-scrap.

Soon this smaller road emerged from the square brick bungalows and the corrugated iron hutments and meandered up and up over the Downs. 'I think we go this way – or this way,' said Roy each time it forked, but both he and Margaret knew that he was choosing at random as they rode slowly side by side along smaller and smaller lanes.

And at last they had turned on to a lane so narrow that it might only just take a car, a lane that curved between hedges so high and untended that nothing could be seen over them but the pure calm sky. 'Shall we stop off soon and eat our lunch?' asked Roy and at the next field-gate they dismounted and leant their bicycles against it, unpacked the parcels from the carriers, and climbed over into the field beyond.

Now the countryside was open before them. The hay had long been cut and beyond the new bright grass stretched field after field, golden and green and yellow and at last dark blue, lying against the paler sky. The air was heavy with the smell of grass and clover and honeysuckle, and vibrating with the buzzing and whirring of bees and grasshoppers. 'Over there,' said Margaret, pointing to a chestnut tree a little way from the hedge, and they picked their way slowly through the cool ankle-deep grass, and sat down under the big tree, under the leaves lit and shadowed by the thrusting sunlight.

Then they smiled at each other contentedly. 'I'll unpack the lunch,' said Margaret lazily. 'I made a cake,' and she unpacked it proudly, unwrapped the knife she had been careful to remember, and then Maureen's sandwiches and the hard-boiled eggs and the bottles of ginger-beer.

'I didn't know if you liked beer or not,' Roy said and Margaret said no, not yet, not much, she liked ginger-beer much better. They ate their lunch, Roy praising Margaret's sponge-cake which was, she knew, one of the lightest she'd ever made, and when they'd finished Margaret carefully packed up all the bottles and the greasy paper to put back in the bicycle-baskets and dispose of properly when she got home. Then she clasped her hands and looked ahead at the tranquil sunlit countryside, feeling the breeze stir gently on her neck and face, thinking of nothing at all, knowing nothing but happiness.

Roy leant back against the tree and put his arms behind his head. 'I suppose we ought to be pushing on,' he said, 'if we're going to get to Little Poulteney.' He sighed contentedly and said, 'It's so nice here.'

'We don't *have* to go to Little Poulteney,' said Margaret, still looking ahead at the view.

'Then let's not,' said Roy, 'I like being here. Let's just do nothing but sit and talk.'

Now Margaret loosened her hands from her knees and lay in the grass beside Roy, her head against the tree, her fingers playing idly with the grasses beside her. Roy's hand came from behind his head and rested on hers, slowly tightening on hers. Neither looked at these contented hands, only up at the sky, dark blue through the heavy drooping leaves.

'I wish it were summer for ever,' said Roy.

Margaret said, 'I do too.'

They were silent for a time. Then Margaret asked, 'Would you like to live in the country?'

'Not really, I don't think,' Roy answered. 'Not to work in, that's to say. I reckon it's people like you and me who can come to the country for pleasure that get the best of it, not those that have to get their living out of it, whatever the weather.'

'Yes, it must be horribly bleak and cold here in winter,' said Margaret, but winter wasn't really imaginable in this golden sunlight, this soft warm air.

'Mind you, I wouldn't like to live right in a town,' said Roy, 'not even in Walbridge, let alone somewhere like London or Birmingham. What I like is something betwixt and between, somewhere where you've got a few amenities, like, and still got room for a house to yourself and a bit of a garden. In fact, somewhere like Priory Dean would do me fine, though I wouldn't say no to a cinema.'

'It would save the bus-ride,' agreed Margaret, 'but it would be horrid to have to live right in a town and perhaps even in a flat.'

'No flats for me,' said Roy decisively. 'I want my own front door and my garden to myself, say a few flower-beds in the front, just enough to stop people looking in at the windows, and at the back a bit of lawn and enough room to grow some vegetables and perhaps keep chickens.'

'I hate chickens,' said Margaret, with a little shudder. 'I've had enough of them for a lifetime. Ducks, if you like.'

'We'll make it ducks,' said Roy. His fingers began to caress hers, to creep up and down her hand, to play with the hollows between her fingers. 'How many rooms would we want?'

'Well, a kitchen,' said Margaret. 'I like one big enough to eat in, don't you? And then a sitting-room, not too big, just cosy, with an open fire.'

'And not kept for best,' said Roy; 'the sort of room that really gets used. And we wouldn't have any of those hideous wallpapers. I'd paint the walls a nice warm colour.'

'Primrose yellow,' said Margaret dreamily.

'Primrose yellow,' Roy agreed, 'and two comfortable armchairs, and that sort of carved oak furniture, Tudor, they call it. But I'll tell you a funny idea I've always had. I've always thought I'd like to have one of those old-fashioned dressers with some pewter beer-mugs on it and some willow-pattern plates.'

'And a warming-pan on the wall,' said Margaret, 'and I'd cover the armchairs in blue and have linen curtains with flowers on them.'

'And we'd sit there in the evenings,' said Roy, 'one of us on each side of the fire and the curtains drawn so's no one could see in and the radio on –' His voice trailed away, and in a voice that died as his had died Margaret whispered, 'It would be lovely.'

He jerked himself up and leant over her. He said, 'We must. We must. Why shouldn't we?'

'Oh, Roy,' said Margaret, in an anguish of longing, and he demanded fiercely, 'Margaret, you must marry me. Say you'll marry me.'

'Oh, Roy,' she repeated, and then he bent his head to hers and they kissed in bliss.

At last he lifted his head and looked into her eyes. 'I love you,' he said despairingly, and Margaret sighed, 'Oh, Roy, I love you too. I love you,' and he kissed her again, but this time they clung together for fear of loss and kissed in desperation.

When this kiss ended, their lips were trembling and their faces troubled. 'Oh, Margaret, I need you so much,' whispered Roy. 'You're what I've always wanted, we could be so happy –' He buried his face in her neck, the touch of his lips bringing to both a warm excited content.

Tentatively Margaret's hands began to touch his neck, to stroke his hair. 'Let's go on pretending,' she said softly, 'do let's go on pretending. Tell me about the rest of the house.'

He dragged himself upright and leant back against the tree, pulling her against him so that she leant on his shoulder, his arm around her and his other hand playing with her hands. 'There'd be a hall with a barometer,' he said, 'and I'd tap it to see if I was going to dig in the garden or go off to the pub.'

'I'd come to the pub with you,' said Margaret tenderly.

'We'll make it a rainy day then,' he said. 'We'd go to the pub and have a couple of pints, and then we'd go along home in the dark, arm in arm – then –'

'How many bedrooms should we have?' asked Margaret, instinctively postponing the end of his sentence.

'One for us,' said Roy. Shyness held his fingers still for a moment. 'And one for – well, we'd have kiddies, wouldn't we?'

'Two,' said Margaret, looking down at the grass.

In a different, unnatural voice, Roy said to the air, 'I often think about it and work out how it would be.'

Margaret said, 'So do I.'

'We always did play make-up games,' said Roy, with a half-laugh, a half-sob. It wasn't possible to pretend any more. His hold on her tightened – in a voice empty of everything but urgency he demanded, 'Margaret, why shouldn't we marry? We love each other, we want the same things exactly. We're both people.'

'I *will* marry you,' said Margaret with a rush. 'I want to – there's no real reason – I mean, it's just silly.'

'We're both people,' repeated Roy desperately. 'That's true, isn't it? There isn't any reason why we shouldn't marry, just a lot of old-fashioned ideas. I'm in a good job, I could make you happy, I know I could.'

Margaret said, 'It's the other people.'

'I know,' cried Roy, 'but what do they matter? It's no business of theirs. It's you and me.'

'I'm not twenty-one,' said Margaret. 'I'd have to get their permission. I mean – Roy, when were you thinking of?'

'We'd have to find somewhere to live,' said Roy thoughtfully. 'But that's all. I don't see there's anything else need make us wait. That's all we need wait for, just to find somewhere to live.'

'That might be ages,' said Margaret, with a sigh.

'I'll tell you what I'll do,' said Roy. 'I'll put us down at the Town Hall right away. Not that it'll do much good, with the waiting-list what it is, but it's something done, isn't it?'

'Can you, if you're not married?' asked Margaret.

'You can if you're engaged,' answered Roy. 'Margaret, we are engaged, aren't we?'

'I'm engaged to you,' said Margaret, turning to him. 'Are you engaged to me?'

Roy said gravely, 'I'm engaged to you all right.'

'But we needn't tell anyone,' urged Margaret, suddenly panic-stricken. 'I mean, we can't do anything till we've got somewhere to live, can we, and if we've got somewhere, then they can't really stop us, can they, not if we've made up our minds? But if we told them now, they'd only say beastly things –' She stopped abruptly. It was inescapable that 'they' were Margaret's family and friends and that the beastly things would all be said about Roy.

She wept in his arms and cried, 'Roy, why has it got to be like this? What you said is true, we're both people. Why shouldn't we get married like anyone else?' But as she wept, she knew that weeping was different when she was held by Roy and sure of his comforting.

He held her to him and assured her firmly that it would be all right, there was nothing could stop them once they'd

184

made up their own minds, they'd just keep quiet about it while they were on the look-out for somewhere to live. And Margaret gladly let herself be comforted and soon they fell to kissing again and playing with each other's ears, each other's hands, each delicate tentative caress an ecstasy of giving and receiving.

'I love you,' they murmured, lip to lip, and at one with their kisses was the smell of each other's flesh as they clung together, the smell of the grass, the songs of the birds and the dazzling sky seen through transparent fingers, a mesh of eyelashes, a rainbow of hair.

At last, dazed and drowsy, they sat up and gradually the grass and the leaves and the distant horizon recovered their normal focus again. 'We must go,' said Margaret, 'or they'll be wondering –' and they rode home side by side, silent in the golden evening light.

They parted on the Common at Bentworth where they had met. 'I'll give you half an hour,' said Roy, 'that ought to give you enough time to get right in. See you tomorrow outside the hospital.'

She nodded, and he held her bicycle for her to remount. 'Don't forget you're engaged,' he whispered, his lips against her ear, brushing her hair, and she smiled contentedly and rode away.

CHAPTER THIRTEEN

Try as she would, Margaret couldn't help feeling a bit different, even after she'd put the bicycle away in the shed and come into the kitchen where Wendy was just putting the cold supper out on the table. It was as though there was new blood in her veins that flowed faster and more strongly than the old so that she wanted to smile and laugh and talk, to let her eyes sparkle with gaiety and the words tumble out of her mouth. It was impossible exactly to re-adjust the old mask of polite acquiescence, and Wendy, looking up, said, 'Well, you *have* got sunburnt. Did you have a good time?'

'Lovely,' said Margaret, letting her emphasis on the word drain away some of the overflowing excitement. Something seemed unusual to Wendy and she said sharply, 'I hope you didn't go to tea with your friend's aunt with your dress all crumpled like that.'

'Oh, we never got as far as that,' said Margaret laughing. 'We stopped in a field and ate our lunch, and then we just stayed there and talked.' Her lips curved with pleasure as the words brought recollection, and Wendy said with uncomprehended suspicion, 'Well, you seem very gay and cheerful,' and wondered if this friend was really a nice girl or perhaps another of those awful vulgar creatures Margaret seemed to pick up. 'Jill Morton won't like being neglected for your new friend,' she said, though goodness knows she couldn't care less about what Jill Morton liked or didn't like, and Margaret, still laughing, answered, 'Oh, that's all right. Jill won't mind, I'll be seeing her soon, anyway,' flushing with fresh excitement at the thought of seeing Jill and telling Jill and hearing all that Jill would say.

But Wendy forgot her momentary uneasiness in the days that followed, and noticed only that Margaret seemed somehow healthier and more contented than she had been lately. 'I really think she's growing up at last,' she said with pleasure to Daisy, 'and I shouldn't wonder if that evening at the Wetheralls didn't have something to do with it,' and Daisy agreed and hinted and enticed Wendy further into complacency.

There were still only the lunch-hour meetings for Roy and Margaret, but now these were quite different. Languidly they would saunter arm in arm through the almost deserted back-streets, hardly bothering to walk, only moving because it was less noticeable than standing still, and talking, for ever talking, of their married life together. Mostly they found it easiest to express this in the concrete terms of the pink rather than the red rambler roses, the radio extension in the kitchen so that Margaret could hear it while she worked, and never an artichoke in the house, not if Roy knew anything about it. And, in these public streets, love was easiest spoken of when they talked of the children, the boy first and then the girl in their cots in the room that Roy would stencil with pictures of animals, the children whom they'd never allow to run in the street like hooligans, and they wouldn't want to, not if Roy made them a sandpit in the garden, because children only played in the streets when there was nothing for them to do at home. Roy had put his name down on the housing-list at the Town Hall the very next day after they went to the country, and though neither of them expected anything from this (not having any pull, which was what everyone said you needed if you were to get anything out of the Council) it was still a responsible, far-sighted thing to have done, and gave official standing to the engagement that might otherwise have seemed no more than an idea in their two minds.

'I'm not taking my holiday this summer,' Roy said one day. 'I'm due for it now, but what I thought was, supposing something turns up, then I've got it in hand, so to speak.'

'I'm not due for one yet,' said Margaret. 'I've only been there six months. But if they do offer it, I suppose I'd better do the same.'

'Don't you give yours up,' said Roy. 'You're not going back to work after we're married.'

Margaret said timidly, 'Well, I don't want to. But I didn't know – I thought maybe the money –'

'Well, if you're going to want fur coats and diamond necklaces maybe you'd better,' said Roy, 'but it's not my idea. Don't you worry, Mrs Wilson, you'll have plenty to do keeping my home nice for me when once the honeymoon's over.'

Margaret pressed closer to him and asked, 'Where shall we go for our honeymoon?'

'Somewhere nice and quiet where we can be right on our own,' said Roy decidedly, and then, 'Do you – do you look forward to it?'

Margaret nodded. It wasn't the sort of thing you could put into words. Roy swallowed, and then managed to say, 'I have been meaning to tell you – I mean, I don't want there to be anything come between us, sort of. You know I'd never look at another girl now I've got you, but this was before I knew you, when I was in Germany. It was one night, there was a whole lot of us and I got drunk – it was only once – I thought I ought to tell you.'

Margaret could see he hated telling her, could see how he'd rather it hadn't even been just once, only him and her. 'Well, it's all behind us,' she said awkwardly. 'I mean, it's not really anything to do with me,' and then she remembered something that made her cold with shame and she whispered, her eyes on the pavement, 'I did something worse because it was after I met you. I went out with someone – I didn't want to, I had to – and he kissed me. I couldn't help it, I didn't want him to – but I wish he hadn't.'

Now, both released by confession from remorse, they felt their love deepened and made secure. 'I wish we could go on walking for ever,' he said, his mouth close to her hair, and then he laughed and added, 'No, not for ever, just until we get a house.'

They were turning into the road that led to the hospital now, and they dropped each other's arms and walked sedately side by side. 'Has anything turned up for Jim and Edie?' she asked and he said, 'Yes, it seems almost certain they'll get that half-house I told you of in Bentworth. They're just waiting to hear definitely. Wouldn't it be nice,' he said, 'if we could get hold of one of the pre-fabs for ourselves and then we could have a double wedding?' and Margaret agreed it would be lovely to have a pre-fab, it would be just the thing to begin with, but there was no reality in the suggestion, for both of them knew there was no chance of the pre-fabs going to the people of Priory Dean.

There was a lot of feeling growing in the village about the new housing. You'd have thought, people said, what with the Archery Lane estate on their very doorstep, so to speak, and the pre-fabs right in the village, there'd have been something to spare for Priory Dean people, and it wasn't liked at all when it became clear that the Walbridge Urban had put up the Archery Lane houses just for some of their own over-flow population and that all the pre-fabs were meant for the builders and their families – and mostly Irish too, people said disgustedly – who were coming to put up the new paper-mills in Bentworth and other new building projects that were as yet only hinted at. But what made it all particularly galling was that practically everyone in the village had taken the chance to go over a pre-fab while they were being built, stumbling over the drainpipe ditches in the thick red clay, and all agreed that gimcrack though they looked, they were really lovely inside with everything fitted in and more modern conveni-ences than anyone in Priory Dean, except Mrs Wetherall, had ever dreamed of. 'Why, I'd hardly mind living in one myself,' exclaimed Wendy with a little laugh to show it was just a joke, and all the ladies of Priory Hill echoed the words and the laugh, but to the rest of Priory Dean the idea of living in a pre-fab was very far from being a joke when there was scarcely a family that wasn't on the look-out for a home for one or other of its members.

Afterwards no one could say exactly when village indignation had started to concentrate around Broomfields. A big early-Victorian house standing well back from the Walbridge road on the outskirts of the village, Broomfields had been empty and neglected since 1941 when old Mrs Peachbody, who'd lived there ever since anyone could remember, had died. It was known that the house had since then been in the hands of solicitors who were willing to sell it if they could get a good enough price, but it had never been modernised and not even the Army had been willing to go to the bother of putting in electric light and telephones when so many more suitable houses were readily available. For years now the village children had played in its overgrown gardens, torn bricks out of its surrounding walls to make little hovels with, and now and then broken a ground-floor window either to go exploring in its dank recesses or else just for sheer fun. It had been known for some time that some friends of the Wetheralls were thinking of it, and occasionally a gleaming Bentley was seen drawn up outside the crumbling portico, and a lady in a mink coat would get out and fit a key into the keyhole and go in. It was said they'd been bargaining for it in a leisurely way, not being in any hurry and knowing there was no one else after it; and perhaps it was the knowledge of that leisurely approach that began to rile people who, as soon as they heard the faintest rumour of a house, must rush in and clinch it without having time to stop and think about it or a chance in the world of knocking down the price asked. 'It's all right for them that have got money,' people started saying to each other. 'It isn't right, not in these times, it isn't.' But even so, the discontent would never have boiled into action had it not been for the example of the London squatters.

But the London squatters had moved into their flats and their hotels, and triumphantly held the police and all the authorities at bay, encouraged by a public opinion almost wholly sympathetic to them. And one day Margaret came home from work to be greeted excitedly by Sheila with, 'Margaret, what do you think? The squatters have moved into Broomfields!'

'I thought those friends of the Wetheralls had just decided,' said Margaret in amazement. 'Surely people can't move in if a house has just been sold? And who are the squatters, anyway? Surely London people wouldn't come all the way up here?'

'It's mostly Station Road people,' said Sheila, almost overcome with excitement. 'Mummy says Mrs Wilkins says her daughter Louie is one of them. Don't you think it's exciting? It's almost like the Peasants' Revolt.'

For a shocked second Margaret wondered if Roy could be among the trespassers, but she quickly chided herself for stupidity. Roy wasn't the sort to go and do something showy like that; everything done decently and in order was the way he always said he liked things, and because a thing was the sort of thing ordinary Station Road people would do, there was no need to worry about Roy doing it. He was different.

'Mummy's gone to the WI' said Sheila, 'and Daddy's gone into Bentworth to see about some pullets. I thought I'd walk along to Broomfields and see what's going on. Want to come?'

Margaret shook her head. Even though she was quite certain it wasn't the sort of episode Roy would have taken part in, she still instinctively recoiled from going to see something the Station Road people had done as if it and they were a kind of show. 'It'll give me a chance to have a chat with Jill,' she offered as an excuse, for she and Sheila didn't hide from each other their annoyance in being unable to indulge in long private telephone calls from home, and when Sheila had gone, she realised that this was, indeed, a good chance to speak to Jill and went and rang her up.

'Well, you're a poor sort of a friend,' came Jill's loud cheerful voice over the phone. 'A month it is since I've heard anything of you, and me not daring to ring you up in case I disturb one of your little plans.'

'I'm really sorry,' pleaded Margaret contritely. 'It's just that everything's been so complicated, but I'm longing to see you and tell you all about it. Could you possibly do this Friday?'

'I daren't go out,' said Jill. 'I was out last Friday and the parents are strong on the old we-never-see-anything-of-you line. But look here, why don't you come and have dinner with us? I know Mummy'd love to see you – she always thought you were a good influence on me.'

'I'd love to,' said Margaret gratefully, for she must tell someone her secret soon and telling Jill didn't really count as telling, no more than digging a hole in the ground and whispering your secret into its earthy depths.

Usually Sheila took no interest at all in what went on in Priory Dean; everything that she felt really concerned her was outside it, her friends, her lessons, and all her future life. But what she had heard of the squatters seemed to her, as it did to many other people, exciting in a strange romantic kind of way. Sheila was too young to remember Mr Chamberlain flying off to see Hitler, but something of the same element was present in both episodes, the element of the ordinary man, the little man, taking matters into his own hands and doing the sort of thing he always said ought to be done as he pontificated at his own fireside or in the bar-parlour. 'If I had anything to do with it,' he would say, 'I'd pretty soon cut through all the red tape and –' and now the squatters had cut through all the red tape, and you couldn't help, people said to each other, but admire them, though mind you, if people didn't have a respect for private property, there was no telling where it would stop. But Sheila was too young to have reservations about the sacredness of private property, and so she was hurrying down the hill to see what was going on, with what was, for her, an entirely new and admiring interest in the village people and their affairs.

There were quite a few sightseers clustered round the gates of Broomfields and little knots of people all along the drive. Sheila walked along it, looking eagerly about her, but there was nothing unusual to be seen until just before the drive widened out before the house, and there was an old gate fixed across it, held up with boards and packing-cases and on one side of it stood Mr Timms the policeman and on the other a rough common-looking man without his coat on, and with a waistcoat over a shirt with rolled-up sleeves, whom Sheila recognised as Calder who was forever coming round with a barrow, ready to buy any kind of trash people could be persuaded to part with. He and Mr Timms seemed to be chatting amiably together. Sheila looked avidly over the barrier and beyond, but there was nothing unusual to be seen except a line of washing strung from one of the upstairs windows to the next. Then Sheila glanced around, and a few yards away from her she saw Maureen Wilson eyeing her consideringly.

Both girls had secretly been curious about each other for a long time. They were the same age, they were both clever and they were both lonely for want of intelligent companionship. Both had wondered – not thinking of it seriously, of course, just wondering – whether it mightn't, perhaps, be nice to know each other if such a thing was possible. Of course Sheila knew that Maureen was quick-tempered and wild and had got a lot of Socialistic ideas, and Maureen knew that Sheila was one of that stuck-up Priory Hill lot who treated the rest of the world as if it was so much dirt. It was only that it might have been nice – it might be nice – and gradually, casually, on the pretext of seeing a bit better what was going on over the barrier, they edged closer until they were both standing together on the same side of the drive under the tall untrimmed rhododendrons.

Oh, come on, said Maureen to herself, somebody's got to start, and nervously, aggressively she said with a mock-refined accent in a voice that was meant to be jocular, 'Quaint, isn't it, to see how the lower-classes carry on?'

The moment was gone for ever. Angrier, more outraged because of her momentary impulse of friendship, Sheila stood silent in rigid fury. She'd come to have a look like everyone else, she had a perfect right to come and have a look, and all that happened if you for a moment demeaned yourself to think of nasty common people was that they took advantage and sneered at you. She forced herself to look at Maureen, to look her up and down with deliberate superciliousness, and then she turned and walked quickly down the drive again. In that moment of what she and Maureen both saw as deliberate insult, from one to the other, both their political attitudes had been irrevocably set for ever.

By the end of the week rumours began to float around that the occupation of Broomfields had been undertaken with the Council's covert acquiescence or, some even said, with its approval. It was reported that the situation was to be regularised by requisitioning, and to most of the village people this seemed the proper action to take in a situation that some of them might conventionally deplore but few could morally condemn.

Martha and Ralph Wetherall were probably the people most outraged by the situation. Ralph, during his energetic rise to prosperity, had in most cases developed a tolerance for actions forced upon people less capable than himself, but this one seemed to strike at the roots of his hard-won security. Usually he took great pleasure in correcting Martha's misapprehensions about English habits and ways, but this time he could only agree when she stormed that it was an outrageous violation of human rights, and that if you once started disregarding the rights of property, there was no knowing where it would end.

'You English must be blind,' she said angrily, 'to let the Communists get away with a thing like that.' Ralph, in a last despairing blow for impartiality, did try to put in that whoever organised the squatters in London, Calder, of Station Road, who seemed to be the ringleader here, was said to be only a Socialist, though he couldn't help but agree when Martha snorted that she'd bet any money he was really a Crypto, and that people would only see the truth of what she said when it was too late. 'And besides,' she wailed, 'it really is too bad for poor Freddie and Moira. They'd fallen in love with Priory Dean and Moira says she's quite broken-hearted. She's asked me to look out for something else for her, but I don't see anywhere else at all possible. It really seems wicked when you come to think of it, the Rector and his wife just living in a corner of that lovely house, which would be just the right size for them. Or there's the Hall which is exactly the sort of thing Moira would go for in a big way. I know it's all Miss Evadne can do to keep it up, and it's much too big for her anyway. I wonder if I just hinted –?' but here Ralph put his foot down and said firmly that nothing was to be hinted to Miss Evadne, and that Freddie and Moira would just have to look elsewhere.

But on the issue of the squatters, Martha felt it her positive duty to open the eyes of her neighbours to the secret danger so insidiously threatening them, and the fact that they seemed so unwilling to be convinced only made her the more certain of the reality of the danger. After church, for instance, she'd had a word with George Bruce who should, goodness knows, have been a responsible person, a Conservative, a householder and a lawyer, but he had only answered deprecatingly, 'You don't want to make too much of it, you know. Nobody here takes the Communists seriously – they're just a joke. No, you'll find the English people are much too level-headed to be taken in by that kind of thing,' and his words were more or less echoed by everyone Martha spoke to along Priory Road except for Trixie Beltram, and to be agreed with by Trixie Beltram was almost enough, Martha felt, to turn her into a Commie herself.

But at last Martha found agreement and solace. She was standing at the bus-stop one day after lunch, waiting to go into Walbridge to try to buy some baby chicks in the market for her children, when Mrs Green came along and waited with her, and almost despairingly, after the initial conventionalities about the weather had been exchanged, Martha started with her opening gambit. 'I really am amazed at the casual way everyone seems to have taken this disgraceful business at Broomfields,' she said, and waited, without hope, for Mrs Green to explain that there was no need to worry about it, it wasn't so bad as all that.

But Mrs Green only edged a little closer to her and said with what was unmistakably relief, 'Well, I can't tell you, Mrs Wetherall, how glad I am to hear you speaking right out like that. Only yesterday my husband was saying to me, I'm sure

Mr and Mrs Wetherall, he said, are people who will see it in the proper light. Mind you, in our position Mr Green and me have to be very careful what we say to people. In fact, to listen to some of the customers, you'd think we didn't ought to hold any opinions of our own because, whatever you say, you're sure to offend someone. But I know that what I say to you, Mrs Wetherall, won't go any further, and I can't deny that I think it's a shocking affair. People that haven't any respect for property aren't likely to stop there, and to my way of thinking it's not at all a nice business.'

The bus came along then and they climbed into it and the conversation ended. But just as the affair at Broomfields had irrevocably severed any hope of a relationship between Sheila and Maureen, so it had established a community of interests between Martha and Mrs Green. Martha began to feel that the village tradespeople could be relied on, and without perceiving any connection between the two events cancelled her weekly order from Harrods and registered for her rations in the village shops. And Mrs Green retailed the conversation with suitable embellishments to all her friends, and soon the tradespeople had come to look up to the Wetheralls as the proper figureheads of village opinion.

CHAPTER FOURTEEN

On their Friday midday walk, Margaret arranged with Roy that he should fetch her from Jill's that evening. 'I won't stay late,' she said. 'I'll get away at half-past nine, and that'll give us a bit of time together before the last bus.'

'I'd better not come up to the house for you, had I?' asked Roy, and Margaret agreed that it was better not, they'd been so careful this far, it was better not to take any chances.

'Wait outside the gate and I'll come out,' she said, and 'Roy, would you mind most frightfully if I brought Jill? She's my best friend and I know she'd simply love to meet you when she hears about it.'

Roy was rather relieved than otherwise that at last Margaret was going to tell someone. He saw, as well as she, the complete undesirability of letting it out in Priory Dean, but he didn't like all this hole-and-corner business over what, to be proper and respectable, should be public knowledge. There wasn't any friend *he* could tell without being sure it would be right round the village in no time flat, and so he welcomed the prospect of this friend of Margaret's being able to look on them as an engaged couple. 'Do you think she'll be pleased?' he asked for form's sake, and when Margaret said enthusiastically that she knew Jill would be absolutely thrilled, he agreed to wait outside the gate at half-past nine without any more ado.

There wasn't any chance to talk to Jill before dinner because all her family was there, and the girls had to content themselves with meaning glances until the meal was over. 'No, I won't have any coffee, thanks,' said Margaret, and Jill said, 'I won't either,' and then they were free to rush up to Jill's bedroom and sprawl comfortably on the carpet.

'And now, Meggie,' said Jill, 'come clean.'

Margaret clasped her hands round her knees and turned to Jill a face gleaming with happiness. 'Oh Jill,' she sighed, 'it's just so wonderful I can't believe it's really true. I can't tell you how happy I am – I didn't know it was possible to be so happy.'

'You're in love all right,' said Jill dryly, 'but you're not being very communicative, you know. Who is he?'

'His name's Roy,' said Margaret, 'and he's an absolute darling. He wants all the same kinds of things that I do, and we think just the same about practically everything. We're going to have a little home with a garden and we've decided exactly how we're going to furnish it. Oh, and Jill, you *will* be my bridesmaid, won't you?'

'I'd love to,' said Jill, 'but I wish you'd come out of love's young dream and tell me a bit more about him. Who is he? Has he got any money?'

'He's a printer,' said Margaret, 'and he earns more than enough for both of us.'

'What do you mean, he's a printer?' asked Jill, who liked to know exactly where she was. 'Has he got a printing-works, or what?'

'No, he's a printer,' explained Margaret, 'a compositor, whatever that is. He works at Thatcher's, you know, that big printing place over on our side of Walbridge.'

'You don't mean he's a real printer,' said Jill, 'not a work-man?'

'Yes, I suppose he is,' answered Margaret uneasily.

Jill was cast into a turmoil of confusion. Probably, she thought quickly, Margaret didn't mean what she gave the impression of meaning, after all lots of people went through factories and things to learn everything from the bottom up. That must be what Margaret meant but it would be as well to get the point cleared up and she asked, 'What's his full name? Where did you meet him?'

'His surname's Wilson,' said Margaret, 'and I've known him for ages. We used to play together as children.'

'Oh, the doctor's son,' exclaimed Jill with relief; so it was all just Margaret's funny way of putting things. 'But I thought you didn't like him.'

'Not Roger,' contradicted Margaret with contempt. 'You're getting muddled up. Roger's Dr Gregory's son and he's quite horrid. No, I must have talked to you about Roy. His mother used to work for us.'

'Do you mean to say,' asked Jill in cold stupefaction, 'that he's the son of the woman who used to be your mother's char?'

The happiness was blotted out from Margaret's face. She'd never thought of Jill being – well, funny about it. She stammered miserably. 'She wasn't really a char – I like her awfully –' and then, with a spurt of defiance, 'anyway, what's that got to do with it?'

'Well, after all –' said Jill. 'I mean –' and then angrily, 'Well, if you can't see what that's got to do with it, I don't suppose anyone can explain it to you. Whatever did your parents have to say?'

'I haven't told them yet,' said Margaret, drowned in unhappiness. 'I've only told you. I thought you'd be nice about it –' she broke off and looked imploringly at Jill.

Jill was not insensible to the pathos of Margaret's appeal. It was only, she thought quickly, that it had been sprung on her so suddenly without any preparation. Of course it made a difference, it would be silly to pretend it didn't, but even if they couldn't be the same sort of friends as before, she wasn't going to let Margaret down just because she was marrying beneath her. Of course there could be no question of her being a bridesmaid now, but it would be easy enough to find an excuse for that when the time came. Meanwhile she rather liked the idea of being the one broadminded person who stood by her unconventional friend – and then suddenly it occurred to her that perhaps she hadn't got the whole story, perhaps Margaret wasn't being so unconventional after all, and she asked, 'Is he a Communist?'

'No, I'm sure he isn't,' Margaret answered bewildered. 'As a matter of fact, I think he voted Socialist, but I'm sure he wouldn't be a Communist. Why do you want to know?'

'I just wondered,' said Jill evasively. So *that* was out; one of the girls at her boarding-house had a friend who was a Communist and she'd married a workman who was a Communist too, and Jill, who was very quick at picking up social nuances, had gathered that for Communists to do that kind of thing wasn't at all *déclassé*. But Margaret was still gazing imploringly at her and Jill tried to pull herself together and said with a little laugh, 'You know, Meggie, you took me quite by surprise. You're such a secretive little thing, I'd no idea you'd got anything like this up your sleeve.' To herself her voice sounded entirely false, but Margaret desperately wanted to believe in her.

She said wistfully, 'I did think you'd understand, Jill, though I know it sounds a bit funny at first. But we really do love each other, and I know we'll be frightfully happy.'

'I'm sure you will,' said Jill heartily; I'm talking just like I would to a maid, she realised suddenly, and was momentarily sickened, but sincerity was impossible and she could only patronise.

Margaret had hoped that she'd be able to tell Jill about the plans for the house, but she knew now that it would be no good. She sighed and tried to make her voice sound interested as she noted, 'And what about you? What about that foursome you talked about?' She knew as soon as she'd said it that it was the wrong thing, but it had just slipped out.

Jill laughed again, the same bright artificial laugh, and said kindly, 'Oh, my affairs aren't anything like so interesting as yours.' Her Humphrey, an intellectual, a witty ironical copy-writer in the advertising agency that did most of the stuff in *Vogue*, would be sullied by mention in the same breath as Margaret's working-class printer who wasn't even a Communist. Then suddenly she had an idea, a good idea, a brilliant idea, the sort of idea that could only be put to Margaret by a true friend, and she leant forward and said eagerly, 'Look here, Meggie, why marry him? Why not just have an affair and then when it's over, it's over?'

Margaret was so stupefied that for a moment she couldn't quite take it in. Then she scrambled to her feet and reached for her jacket with shaking hands. 'You're disgusting,' she whispered, 'you're disgusting. Roy and I aren't like that, we don't want each other like that – I tell you, we love each other –' She couldn't even look at Jill again, she just picked up her bag and went out of the room, down the stairs, out of the house.

Outside the gate she stopped and tried to control herself. She knew, in a kind of way, that Jill hadn't meant to be unkind – but the contempt contained in the suggestion was unforgivable. She looked at her watch; it was twenty-past nine, ten minutes before Roy would come and fetch her, ten minutes in which to get over this outrage and make up an excuse to Roy for Jill not coming out to meet him. It didn't occur to her to tell Roy what had happened; as long as she could, in every way she could, she must deny the barrier that stood between them. That wasn't the sort of thing you could talk about, and instinctively neither she nor Roy ever talked of it. They knew that one day it would have to be faced and surmounted – but if you could do it without talking about it, they both felt, so much the better. Of course Margaret would never see Jill again, but no one must ever know why; and by the time Roy came round the corner she had the story ready for him about the bad headache that had sent Jill early to bed.

'Well, I'm glad in a way,' said Roy, who looked worried, 'though I'd like to have met her. But when I got home for supper I found Gran was real bad. She'd had a bad chill all week, but today she seemed so poorly Mum sent for the Doctor, and he says it's turned to pneumonia, and he doesn't seem to think that at her age there's much hope. I just slipped out to meet you, but I really think I'd better be getting back right away in case there's anything I can do.'

'Of course,' said Margaret. She slipped her arm into his and they started to walk back towards the bus. 'I wish I could do something,' she said, and she meant it; it was awful to think of Roy's family in trouble and not be able to do anything to help. It made her feel kind of shut out, but Roy pressed her arm and said, 'Now, you're not to worry. Dr Gregory said he'd send Nurse in later, and Mum's not a one to lose her head. It's only that I feel I ought to be there, just in case anything happens.'

'You'll let me know how she goes on?' begged Margaret and Roy said, 'Of course I will,' and then, in dismay, 'Well, I can't very well till Monday, can I? There's no way I can get in touch with you over the weekend.'

Less than half a mile separated their two houses and Margaret's was on the telephone, but there was no way they could be in touch with each other in Priory Dean. Margaret had no right to help Roy's family or be there to comfort him just when he'd most like to have her by him, and it was with desperation that he said, just before they carefully parted round the corner from the bus-station, 'We can't go on like this much longer. We'll have to do something about it soon.'

But before she met Roy on Monday, Margaret had heard that Gran was dead. The news had come from Daisy who had heard it from Mrs Wilkins who'd heard it from Mrs Birch who lived next door to the Wilsons, and Wendy had said, 'Well, I don't suppose the Wilsons will be all that sorry. I'd rather gathered from Edith that the old lady was a bit of a tyrant round the house. Do you think I should send a wreath?' she asked Gerald who said no, he didn't think it was necessary, it wasn't as if she'd known the old lady after all. 'No, I don't think there's really any need,' agreed Wendy with relief, because wreaths cost the earth, and with those sort of people if you were going to do a thing, you had to do it handsomely. 'I'll just say a word to Edith next time I see her in the village. After all, it isn't as if she was still working here,' and Gran's death dropped from the conversation.

Margaret passed a miserable weekend. She couldn't easily get over losing Jill, and in such a horrid way too, and now there was all this trouble at Roy's home and she couldn't do anything to help. She could hardly bear to wait to see Roy on Monday and offer her sympathy, but when she came out of the gate and saw him standing there, she found, to her huge surprise, that though there was a black band round the sleeve of his jacket, there was an enormous grin on his face.

He took a quick step towards her, and, regardless of their normal restraint when other people were around, he eagerly clutched her arm. 'Come quickly,' he urged, 'let's get some-where we can talk.'

'Roy, what is it?' she begged, but he only shook his head and urged her on. 'We'll go into the Park,' he said. 'We've got to be able to sit down and talk.' He had evidently got it all planned in advance, and Margaret, trying to keep up with his quick footsteps as he almost dragged her along, said with breathless anxiety, 'Roy, there's nothing wrong, is there?'

He paused then, and looked down at her, grinning. 'Wrong?' he repeated. 'I should say not,' but he wouldn't tell her any more until, as he had planned, they were sitting on one of the benches in the trim municipal park.

Then, 'We've got a house,' he said.

It wasn't believable, it couldn't be true. 'Oh Roy,' cried Margaret, and then, forgetting all about the spectators, she was lying in his arms and he was hugging her tight and laughing and trying to talk at the same time.

At last she was sitting on the bench pressed closely against him, his arm tightly round her, and she could say, 'Darling, I just can't believe it's true. Now tell me all about it, and where it is and how it happened.'

'Well, it's Auntie's house,' said Roy, and Margaret said, 'You mean Mrs Taylor down Archery Lane?' Roy nodded and Margaret exclaimed, 'Why it's a lovely little house! It's got everything we wanted and it's got that lovely thick hedge in front of it. And you did say it had two bedrooms, didn't you? But how did it happen? Why is Mrs Taylor giving it up?'

'It's like this,' said Roy, his arm tightly round her. 'On Sunday night, see, we were all sitting there talking, and Auntie said to Mum, what was she going to do about Gran's room, was Edie and Jim going to take it over? And Mum explained how Edie and Jim had got this place in Bentworth for certain now and she hadn't thought what to do with Gran's room, Maureen having her room to herself when Edie goes off. And Auntie said, "Edith," she said, "I wonder how you'd feel about it if I was to move in with you, because my arthritis is getting so bad," she said, "there's mornings I can't hardly move my fingers to light the gas and I don't like to be on my own any more, particularly now Miss Fairlie's got this new job in London, and I don't fancy taking another lodger." And the whole thing came to me in a flash and I said as quick as lightning, "Auntie," I said, "what are you going to do about your house?" And she said she'd not made up her mind whether to sell it or let it, so I nipped in and said I knew someone wanting one something desperate and would she give me first chance of it and she said she would.'

'But did your mother say she'd take her?' Margaret asked, somewhat bewildered.

'Oh, there was never any doubt about that,' said Roy. 'Mum and Auntie have always got on like a house on fire, and once Edie goes Mum'll be glad of the company. Mind you, I didn't say who I wanted it for, but that Maureen, she's as sharp as a needle and she said at once, sly-like, "You wouldn't be the fellow that's in desperate want of a house?" she said, and there was I blushing like a fool, and all of them going on at me, to know who it was.'

'You didn't tell them, did you?' asked Margaret anxiously.

209

'No, I didn't let on,' said Roy, 'but this makes a bit of difference, doesn't it? I mean there's no reason now why we shouldn't get married as soon as we like.' He paused, and then went on with conscious dignity, 'And what I was thinking, Margaret, seeing how things are, that it's only right and proper I should come up tonight and have a bit of a talk with your father.'

Margaret's bliss was shot through with apprehension. 'Oh Roy,' she gasped, not daring to say any more, and Roy clutched her hand tight and muttered, 'Well, it'd got to happen sooner or later, hadn't it? It couldn't be put off for ever. Don't you worry, Margaret, it'll be all right, you see if it isn't. After all,' he said desperately, 'I've got a house and I've got a good job and that's more than most chaps have got to offer nowadays.'

Margaret begged, 'Whatever he says, you won't let it make any difference.'

'Not me,' he said gruffly. 'When I make up my mind to a thing there's nothing can stop me. I've got nothing to be ashamed of. I'm as good as the next man, aren't I?'

Margaret said with a rush of tenderness, 'You're the best man in the world for me, anyway,' and he took her hand and held it and said gently, 'It's all a bit silly, isn't it, us getting the wind up like this? I mean, it isn't as if I was a black man or something,' and they were both glad of the chance to laugh before they had to get up and leave and part.

While they had been sitting on the bench they had been too much absorbed in each other to notice Trixie Beltram

stroll down the path towards them, start, stare, then quickly
turn and hurry away, the collar of her coat held up to hide
her face.

CHAPTER FIFTEEN

So it was only just in time that Roy rang the front door bell that evening. The Trevors were sitting in the drawing-room, listening to the radio, Margaret in an agony of apprehension that she tried to still by knitting furiously at a pullover for Gerald's birthday.

'See who that is, Sheila,' said Wendy, and Sheila came back from the door to say, 'It's Roy Wilson. He wants to see Daddy.'

'But why the front door, may I ask?' commented Wendy coldly, registering again in her mind the feeling she'd had at the dance, that there was a young man who was getting too big for his boots. 'I wonder what he wants?' she said.

'It may be about that boys' club they were talking about,' said Gerald. 'I'll take him into the dining-room,' and he went to fetch Roy from the doorstep where Sheila had naturally left him, sure in his own mind that Roy had come to ask him to accept the Presidency of the new boys' club, and what could be more suitable than an ex-officer like himself, accustomed to command, and to receive the deferential respect of his men. 'Come in, come in,' he said jovially and led Roy into the dining-room. 'So you're out of the Army now, are you? Gone back to your old job?' It was only right to try to put the lad at his ease in these unaccustomed surroundings as he stood there awkwardly in his blue serge suit and his clumsy black shoes.

'Yes, I've gone back to Thatcher's,' said Roy.

'Quite right too,' said Gerald. 'And how's your mother? We were sorry to hear about your grandmother's death.'

'Mum's quite well,' said Roy. That sort of lad never knew how to get on with it, thought Gerald, and he asked helpfully, 'Well, what can I do for you?'

Roy said, 'I want to marry Margaret.'

The clock on the mantelpiece ticked loudly in the silence. Then Gerald repeated, 'You want to marry Miss Margaret?'

'That's right,' said Roy.

Gerald said, 'You must be mad.' Again the silence surged around them. Suddenly Gerald demanded, 'Does Margaret know about this?'

'Of course she does,' said Roy.

Gerald turned sharply round and rushed to the door, fumbling with the handle, unable to make it turn in his frantic haste. At last he got it open and 'Wendy,' he shouted. 'Wendy, come here quickly.'

Wendy was in the passage beside him. 'What's the matter?' she said. 'What's wrong?'

'Come here,' he gasped and took her by the arm and half dragged her into the dining-room where Roy still stood stiffly by the mantelpiece. 'Now,' he ordered, 'you repeat to Mrs Trevor what you said to me.'

Roy repeated doggedly, 'I want to marry Margaret,' and then, to their glazed staring eyes he added, 'and she wants to marry me.'

Unlike Gerald, Wendy did not experience even an initial incredulity. Instantaneously she perceived that what Roy said was true, that something had been happening that nullified all her complacency and all her hopes. Pulling out a chair with nervous awkward hands she sat down on it heavily, telling herself that all her wits, every ounce of her energy must be called up to combat this situation.

Gerald looked at her and looked at Roy, and then realised that Wendy had accepted the truth of words that he could not believe to have been more than mad outrageous impertinence. 'He wants –' he began, 'he wants –' but he couldn't find any more words, and Wendy said with heavy calm, 'I think we'd better have Margaret in here, too,' and Gerald went to fetch her, leaving Roy and Wendy staring silently at each other.

Margaret came in with Gerald behind her and Wendy saw Roy's eyes move towards her, saw them flicker some signal she knew to be reassurance. So it's true, she thought, but she hadn't really doubted it from the moment she had heard Roy speak.

Roy cleared his throat and said, not looking at one or the other, 'Margaret and me have come to an understanding and we want to get married. I'm in a good position and I can keep her comfortably. We've got somewhere to live and –' His eyes searched Wendy's face, searched Gerald's, but there was nothing to be seen but distaste on the one and – could it be? – fear on the other. He ended in a different pleading tone – 'and we love each other.'

Wendy stirred on her chair and, looking at her fingers clenched on the table, said, 'Well, that all sounds very nice.

What are the Major and I supposed to do? Stand up and cheer?'

Roy said, 'Margaret's not twenty-one yet. We want to get married soon and so we're asking for your permission.'

Wendy said softly, 'Do you have to get married soon?'

Margaret looked up in bewilderment, not understanding. Roy flushed an angry red and said, 'Me and Margaret respect each other, Mrs Trevor. It's not right of you to suggest a thing like that.'

Wendy laughed an icy tinkling little laugh and said, 'I see I must beg your pardon for hurting your feelings. But so much deceit seems to have been practised, you can hardly blame people for wondering just how far it went.'

Now Margaret came forward and said quickly, 'We didn't mean to deceive you, Mummy, honestly we didn't. Lots of people fall in love secretly and we've only just got engaged.'

'Oh,' said Wendy, with cold politeness, 'so you're engaged, are you? And we, I suppose, are the last people to be told?'

'That's not so, Mrs Trevor,' said Roy. 'There's nobody else knows about it. We thought it only right and proper that you and the Major should be the first.'

Gerald screamed suddenly, 'How dare you? How dare you? Wendy, throw him out. How can you listen to what he says?'

'That's not the way to deal with it,' said Wendy softly. As Gerald shouted and trembled, she had decided on her line of approach. In a different voice she said, 'This has all been rather a shock to us. You'll have to give us a little time to take it in. Suppose you sit down and we all talk it over quietly, without losing our tempers?'

Roy took a quick step forward as if he were going to speak, then changed his mind and sat down stiffly on one of the leather-covered dining-room chairs next to Margaret. 'Sit down,' said Wendy to Gerald, and at last he slowly moved to a chair and sat down beside her.

Roy spoke to Wendy. 'I can see this has been a bit of a shock to you,' he said, 'but it just happened, sort of, and we couldn't either of us help it. I'm not pretending people aren't likely to do a bit of talking about it, but it doesn't take much to set Priory Dean tongues wagging, and if you don't mind me saying so, Mrs Trevor, it's that me and Margaret are going to be happy that matters.'

'I'm going to talk to you frankly,' said Wendy. 'If I was sure of my child's happiness, believe me, I wouldn't let anything stand in her way. But that you and Margaret would be happy together I very much doubt. I'm not denying that you think you're in love with each other now,' she said, as Margaret leant forward, her mouth opened to protest, 'but Margaret hasn't seen a great deal of the world yet and her horizon is still very limited. I'm not suggesting for a moment that you took advantage of her, but I do suggest that there's a great deal more to marriage than just being in love.'

'I do know that, Mummy,' said Margaret fervently.

Wendy brushed her aside. 'I'm speaking to Roy,' she said, 'and I think he understands what I'm trying to say. We may not all of us approve of the way society is organised today, but we've got to live in the world as it is. I'm perfectly prepared to admit that to be, if I may use the word, gentlefolk doesn't mean very much any more, but there are many people still to whom that fact has a certain importance. I don't think, Roy,' she said, with exquisite kindness, 'that when you break the news to your mother, you'll find she takes quite the same casual view of it that you do.'

'I'm not denying,' said Roy, an angry red, and obviously trying hard to keep control of himself, 'that we're only plain working-people, but if Margaret doesn't let that make any difference, Mrs Trevor, I don't see why you should.'

'Believe me, Roy,' said Wendy earnestly, 'I'm not saying a word against working-class people, since you've chosen to use the term. There are few people I respect as much as I do your mother, and working-class or not working-class has got nothing to do with it. What happens to be true, whether we like it or not, is that people from different backgrounds have been brought up quite differently, have got different ways of looking at things, different habits, different ways of thought. I'm sure that neither Margaret nor you thinks any of these things matter just now, but believe me, after a very little while, you'd come to find that they matter very much indeed.'

'But, Mummy, what ways am I different from Roy?' cried Margaret.

'You won't like the answer,' said Wendy with sadness, 'but remember it was you who asked the question, not me, and I'm going to answer you frankly. For one thing, you speak quite differently from Roy. Now mind you, I'm not saying that one kind of voice is better than another kind, although,' and she laughed again, 'the BBC seems to have very definite views on the subject.' She hurried on before they could speak. 'I don't want to go into details that are only going to hurt people's feelings, I'm just trying to answer Margaret's question. In my own mind there is no doubt whatsoever that for a successful marriage it is essential that people have a common background in every sense of the word. After all, marriage doesn't take place in a vacuum. One's got to think of one's friends, for instance. Can Roy honestly tell me that he'd be perfectly happy and at his ease mixing with people like – oh, say, Miss Evadne or Miss Porteous or the Wetheralls.'

'But they're not my friends, Mummy,' said Margaret, almost crying. 'They're your friends. They're much older than me and –'

Gerald thrust his head forward and demanded, 'And how do you think we're going to feel with a son-in-law we're ashamed to introduce to *our* friends?'

'Be quiet,' hissed Wendy fiercely. Roy suddenly laughed, sharply and contemptuously. Then he composed his face and leant over the table and said calmly to Wendy, 'Seems to me, Mrs Trevor, we're not getting anywhere. I've come to ask you to let me marry Margaret. I'm earning pretty well fifteen quid a week with overtime –' He hesitated a moment, as Gerald gave a sharp involuntary gasp, '– and I've got two hundred and thirty pounds saved in the Post Office against a rainy day and there's my gratuity to buy furniture with, and I've got the offer of a house. I've listened to everything you've got to say, and all I want to know now is, what's your answer, yes or no?'

'No, damn you,' shouted Gerald. Wendy stood up and pushed back her chair, and Roy rose too. 'I must ask you to excuse the Major,' she said. 'As you probably know, he's not at all strong and this has been a very great shock to him, as it has to me. I don't deny that my own inclination is to say, more or less politely, what my husband has just said, but in view of the way you both feel, I can't convince myself that it would be a very useful answer. So I'm going to make you a proposal. If you and Margaret will agree not to see each other or tell anyone about this for three months, I'll give the matter my most earnest consideration. After all, you can hardly expect me to say yes at a minute's notice, and I think this is a very fair offer.'

'No,' said Roy, 'it isn't. Margaret and me are engaged. You can't hardly expect us not to see each other for three months while you decide to say no at the end of it.'

'You don't seem very sure of the lasting quality of your affections,' commented Wendy lightly.

Roy said, 'It's not fair, what you're asking, Mrs Trevor, and you know it. We'll keep it more or less quiet for a while, if you like, but I've had my fill of acting on the sly and so has Margaret. We've got nothing to be ashamed of, without you behaving as if we have.'

Wendy seized on the hint of a compromise. 'All I'm asking,' she said, 'is that you don't get yourselves talked about round the village until the Major and I have a chance to make up our minds. I don't know how or where you've been meeting, but so long as you continue to be discreet, I'll make a concession on that point. I won't ask any questions, in fact, I'm pretty certain I'd rather not know.'

'I must tell Mum and Dad,' muttered Roy, and Wendy said, 'By all means tell your parents. I should be delighted for you to do so, because I'm pretty sure they'll feel exactly the same about the whole business as we do.'

'Well, we'll leave it like that for a bit then,' said Roy, 'but it's only fair to warn you, Mrs Trevor, if you're hoping we're going to change our minds, you're in for a big disappointment.'

'We'll let Margaret speak for herself later on, shall we?' said Wendy smoothly, and Roy, on the point of going, stopped and said to Wendy, 'There's just one more thing, Mrs Trevor. I'd like to be sure you're not going to take it out of Margaret, like, after I've gone.'

'My dear Roy,' said Wendy, in mock surprise, 'the very fact that you could make such a remark shows that you haven't, as I said before, the faintest conception of how people like ourselves behave. I shouldn't dream of taking it out of Margaret, as you so charmingly put it. I very much trust there won't be any need and that she'll come to her senses without any word of mine.'

'She was never out of them,' said Roy firmly. 'Margaret, you coming to see me down the road?'

'May I, Mummy?' asked Margaret timidly.

Wendy glanced out of the window. 'Oh, all right, as it's nearly dark,' she conceded. 'But remember, I'm relying on you to observe a certain discretion. Judging by the successful way you've betrayed our trust so far, that shouldn't be difficult.'

'Good night then,' said Roy, and walked out of the room with Margaret.

Outside the gate he drew a deep breath. 'Well,' he said explosively, 'that's over. It wasn't so bad, was it?'

'They were beastly,' wailed Margaret, openly crying now and clinging to his arm.

'Well, I can't say I enjoyed it,' he said frankly. 'Your Mum's got a wicked tongue when she lets herself go. But I never expected it would be a piece of cake, so to speak.'

'But I hated them hurting your feelings like that,' said Margaret.

'Don't you worry about me,' said Roy. 'I've had a good few dressings-down in my time, and it just rolls off like water off a duck's back. No, what worries me is in case you're going to go and let yourself be upset by it.'

'I can't help being a bit,' said Margaret, 'but so long as I know you really love me, I don't mind anything.'

Roy said, 'Let's go up to the field. I've got something to show you.'

Arm in arm they walked up the hill to the end of the road where over the fence the cows cropped the grass in the moonlight. Then Roy put his hand into his pocket and brought it out with a little square box in it.

'I got you a ring,' he said. 'I thought it might all be a bit of a – well, that you'd be all upset after it and I thought it'd cheer you up.' He opened the little box and there was a diamond ring, shining coldly on its cream velvet bed.

'Oh, Roy,' breathed Margaret, and he took the ring out of its box and very gently eased it on to the fourth finger of her left hand, and then he lifted her hand to his lips and kissed it. 'Now we're properly engaged,' he said.

'Oh, Roy, it's lovely,' said Margaret, looking at her hand as if she'd never seen it before. 'This does make us properly engaged, doesn't it? Only you won't mind if I wear it round my neck for a bit until it's all all right?'

'I won't mind anything,' said Roy, 'so long as I'm sure you'll go on loving me.'

'Oh, I will, you know I will,' cried Margaret. Then she added nervously, 'Roy, why do you love me?'

Roy said jokingly, 'I just do.'

Margaret pleaded. 'No, but really. I do want to know. I mean, I'm not pretty or glamorous or anything. I just can't see why it happened.'

'Well, I do know, in a kind of way,' said Roy slowly, 'and it's something to do with what your Mum was saying, though not how she meant it. The first time I saw you after you were grown up, at the dance, I thought how nice and quiet and ladylike you looked. I don't mean ladylike like your Mum would mean it, talking in a lahdidah way and thinking yourself too good to set to and turn out a room. What I mean is – well, it's hard to explain, but being quiet and not showy and – well, refined.' He grinned awkwardly, and said, 'It's much more of a surprise to me, you falling for me.'

'But you're so good,' said Margaret fervently. 'I feel so safe with you.'

He held her closely against him and whispered, 'You go on feeling safe with me, my girl, that's all I want. And don't let anything any of them say make any difference, see? Promise you won't?'

'I promise,' said Margaret, and they stood wrapped in a silent contented embrace.

As the front door closed behind them, Wendy said quickly, 'I'm going to bed, and you'd better come too. I don't want to face any more of this tonight.'

Gerald was staring fixedly at the chair on which Roy had been sitting. 'Did you hear what he said?' he asked, almost to himself. 'Fifteen pounds a week he's earning, a boy like that. It's outrageous.' He swung round and faced Wendy. 'It's outrageous,' he repeated. 'Don't you think it's outrageous?'

'Well, I don't think it's surprising the country's in the mess it's in,' said Wendy lightly. 'Come along to bed, now. There's nothing more we can do about it tonight.'

'Why are you so polite to him?' Gerald demanded. 'My God, the one thing I wanted to do was to take a horsewhip to him.'

Wendy leant across the table and spoke warningly. 'It's no use losing your temper over this,' she said. 'It needs very careful handling, and you'd better leave it to me.'

'But you're not going to agree?' Gerald cried. 'You can't! We'd never be able to hold up our heads again.'

'Of course I'm not going to agree,' said Wendy. 'Do you think I've got no pride, that I enjoyed humbling myself to a boy like that? But you can see the girl's infatuated with him, and that gives him the whip-hand over us. Give her a bit of time, and she'll see him for what he is and come to her senses. It'll be all right so long as no one finds out about it in the meantime. The one thing we've got to be careful about is that no one finds out.'

But of course, within twenty-four hours of Miss Beltram seeing them on the park bench, the news was all round the village.

CHAPTER SIXTEEN

Trixie had been doing a bit of shopping, had had lunch at Fuller's in the High Street, and was walking across the park to spend the rest of the day with an old family friend, the matron of a private nursing-home in South Walbridge. But after she'd seen what she'd seen, she didn't feel like going on and having a nice cosy chatty afternoon. It was always upsetting and disgusting to see people embracing in public, but when such people turned out to be a lady and a working-class man, the whole thing was too entirely repellent just to pass on and go out to tea with somebody who didn't know either of the parties concerned. Goodness only knew how far it had gone already, but if Margaret Trevor thought that public opinion would stand for that kind of thing, she'd find herself very much mistaken. And in these times too, she muttered, as she hurried across the park to the telephone-box to ring up her friend and explain that she couldn't come after all. She needn't think she's going to get away with it, she said, joining the bus-queue, jolting back to Priory Dean. I know my duty, she declared in righteous indignation, and let herself into Kelmscott and walked into the drawing-room, and there was Miss Porteous, who'd said she was going to lie down on her bed with her new library-book, giving tea to Miss Moodie.

'Well!' she exclaimed explosively, and Miss Porteous looked quickly up, and what was on her smooth, well-bred face was unmistakably guilt. 'I thought you were going to have tea with Miss Cartwright,' she exclaimed, and Trixie snorted and said, 'In these times you can't be sure what's going to happen from one minute to the next.'

'You know Miss Moodie, don't you?' said Miss Porteous. 'She's come to see my knitted counterpane.'

'Yes, I know Miss Moodie, all right,' said Trixie grimly: it was nothing but a vast conspiracy, they were like spiders, like earwigs, crawling in everywhere.

Miss Porteous grew impatient. 'Well, take off your things and come and have some tea, now you're here,' she said testily, but Trixie tossed her head and said, 'No, thank you. I know when I'm not wanted,' and walked out of the room, leaving the door ajar so that she couldn't help hearing Miss Porteous apologising, 'I'm afraid poor Trixie is rather difficult at times – I suppose it's only natural, at her age.'

So it has come to that, she thought, shaking with fury in the hall. Never did I think I'd live to hear my friends making excuses for me to a woman like that. I'll show them, she thought, I'll show them, and before she knew what she was doing she was out of Kelmscott again and had closed its door behind her.

Then she wondered whom she should go to first. She walked uncertainly down the path, into the street, and then stood there, wondering what to do next.

'Why, Miss Beltram!' said a voice beside her. 'Are you all right? You don't look yourself at all,' and there was Mrs Green standing beside her, a solicitous smile on her broad ruddy face.

Trixie suddenly knew instinctively that here was someone who would be as shocked at her news as she was herself. 'I won't deny I'm upset,' she said sharply; '– so would you be, Mrs Green, if you'd seen what I've just seen, which was Miss Margaret Trevor and that Roy Wilson hugging and kissing each other on a public bench in Walbridge Park.'

She couldn't have wished for a better reception. 'Roy Wilson!' repeated Mrs Green, 'and Miss Trevor! No, Miss Beltram, I can't hardly believe it!'

'It's not the sort of thing I'm likely to make up,' said Trixie tartly, 'though I'll admit I was so shocked I could hardly believe my eyes.'

'And no wonder,' agreed Mrs Green with outraged delight. 'I can't hardly take it in. Roy Wilson and Miss Trevor! Well, you don't say! And I shouldn't wonder,' she added, 'if poor Mrs Trevor didn't know anything about it.'

'I'm quite sure she doesn't,' said Trixie. 'It's a terrible thing, isn't it? I wonder if I ought to go and give her a word of warning.'

'No, I shouldn't do that,' said Mrs Green hurriedly. She was a kind-hearted woman, and to be told that sort of thing about your daughter by Miss Beltram was something you wouldn't wish on your worst enemy. 'If I were you, Miss Beltram, I'd go and have a nice lie-down,' she urged. 'I can see it's upset you, and no wonder.' For herself, she could hardly wait to get along to Edna Pickering and drop in her ear the dreadful delicious news.

But Trixie was feeling strengthened by the meeting, and avid for more and still more. 'I was just on my way to have tea with Mrs Paynter-Smith,' she said, and they parted, one up the hill and one down, each pregnant with calamity.

The eddies widened in the pool. From Miss Beltram to Mrs Paynter-Smith, from Mrs Paynter-Smith to Daisy Bruce, from Daisy and George talking over the breakfast-table overheard by Mrs Wilkins, and from Mrs Wilkins to Station Road. From Mrs Green to Mrs Pickering, to Mr Pickering and then to the Rector, from Mrs Pickering to Rosemary and Ted, and so out around the bar of the Month-Of-May. 'Isn't it terrible, Doctor?' said one. 'I couldn't hardly believe my ears,' said another, and so whispering, chattering, titupping, the eddies widened and spread.

Bill Cotterell, the Wetherall gardener, heard the news when he knocked off work that evening. It couldn't help reminding him that he wasn't sure whether he'd remembered to lock up the shed and if he hadn't, Master David might get in and cut himself on one of the sharp tools, and so back he went and blessed if he hadn't locked up after all, but being back it didn't seem unreasonable to beckon Nanny out into the garden and tell her the news. 'Well-I-never-did,' said Nanny, and when Mrs Wetherall came in to say good night to the children it seemed only right to tell her what was being said, knowing how highly she thought of Miss Trevor.

Martha was stupefied. She cut short her goodnights to the children and went quickly downstairs to see if Ralph was back, but it was one of his late evenings and he got in only when the dinner was on the table. Martha was just going to blurt out the news when she suddenly remembered that Edie, deftly handing the dishes, was Roy's sister, and so she bottled it up inside her until Edie had cleared the coffee-tray and said, 'Good night, Madam,' and gone; true, she could have started while they were actually drinking the coffee, but she instinctively felt that such news as this would be better broken when the comments on it could proceed steadily and unchecked.

So, 'Ralph,' she said, the minute Edie closed the door behind her, 'Nanny tells me there's a rumour going round the village that there's something going on between Margaret and Edie's brother Roy.'

'Something going on?' said Ralph. 'What do they mean, something going on? Is she supposed to be going to bed with him, or what?'

'That was the impression I got,' said Martha, and Ralph snorted and said, 'Well, I just don't believe it. Margaret's the last girl to do anything like that. It's just typical village gossip.'

'I think there might be something in it,' Martha objected uneasily. 'She's been rather funny lately and she's not been to see me for weeks. I'd rather thought something was brewing between her and Roger, to tell you the truth, and I didn't like to poke my nose in. But it may have been this other business, after all.'

'Well, I hope not,' said Ralph, looking alarmed. 'I wouldn't like to be in her shoes if there's any truth in it.'

'I agree with you. I don't think for a minute she's sleeping around,' said Martha, 'but you know what gossip is, always getting hold of the wrong end of the stick. I'll admit I was rather preening myself on having brought the Roger business off, but this other mightn't be such a bad idea. Edie often speaks of her brother, and from all she says he's a bright young man who may well go far.'

'If you're suggesting they might get married – that is, assuming there's anything in it, which I very much doubt,' said Ralph, 'you'd better put the idea out of your head right now.'

'But it's quite a good idea,' protested Martha. 'You remember, when we were talking about the Wilsons a few months ago, you said that boy would be earning more than the whole Trevor income put together.'

'And I remember telling you at the same time,' said Ralph grimly, 'that class was what counted in England and not money. People marry inside their own class in this country.'

'But that's not true,' said Martha vigorously. 'Look at all the novels you read about the rich manufacturer marrying the impoverished daughter of the aristocracy.'

'That's different,' said Ralph, 'the impoverished daughter of the aristocracy is in an unassailable position, whoever she marries, and anyway she lifts her husband up to her own level. But the Trevors' position is far from unassailable, in fact, it's damned precarious. Their standard of living is lower than the poorest paid workers' and nothing keeps them in the middle-class except their own absolute refusal to be recognised as anything else. Let them once mix with the working-classes

– who are on the up and up, mind you – and their own identity would be submerged in no time.'

'And you call yourselves a democracy,' said Martha contemptuously. 'Personally, I've no patience with all this snob-talk. In America we value people for what they make of themselves, not for what their parents are. Roy Wilson may start in a low-income group, but if he can make a success, well, he's worth more than people who can't and he's got a perfect right to marry whom he pleases. We look on every bell-hop as a future President and treat him accordingly, but from what you say, people like Roy Wilson are condemned to be second-class citizens all their lives. Thank God we've got nothing like that in the United States. We value people for what they show themselves to be worth, not for where they happen to be born.'

'After which Declaration of Independence,' said Ralph, 'I think I'll elaborate to you an idea which has often occurred to me, which is that the position of the working-classes in this country is very like that of negroes in the United States.'

'Why, Ralph,' exclaimed Martha in outraged protest, but Ralph held up his hand and said calmly, 'Now don't get me wrong. I'm not talking of the negroes in the Southern States but in the enlightened North. They've got equal rights to relief and schooling and welfare and they're equal before the law. They've got the vote. There's no discrimination against them in restaurants – but I've never seen a negro in Larue's any more than I've seen a working-man in the Ritz. There's no official discrimination against them in jobs, but I've very seldom been to see a top executive in the States and found him a negro, any more than I've found working-men in the same positions here. No negro family would employ a white servant any more than those gentlewomen who advertise for positions in *The Times* would dream of going to people they thought were common. A negro doctor can hang out his shingle but he wouldn't get any white patients, just as the upper-classes here wouldn't dream of going to a doctor who wasn't a gentleman. Progressives in Greenwich Village get a kick out of having negro friends, but then Bloomsbury intellectuals get a kick out of having working-class friends here. Why, you even get the same guff about the ladder of advancement being open to all, and when a Bunche or a Bevin makes the grade, everyone pats each other on the back and says that's democracy. Many's the time I've sat in your mother's apartment in New York and heard you all talking in a broadminded way about treating the negro properly, but I've never come in and found a black man dropped in casually for cocktails, and I wouldn't expect it, any more than I'd expect to find the Trevors accepting Roy Wilson as a son-in-law.' He got up and stood in front of the electric log-fire, and looked down at her.

'But, Ralph, you're exaggerating –' stammered Martha.

He interrupted her. 'Am I?' he demanded. 'Just you think about it a bit, and see if I'm not right. Mind you, I'm all in favour of a certain amount of discrimination myself, but that doesn't mean to say I don't recognise it when I see it, whether it's against a Jew or a negro or a working-man. Honestly, now, you wouldn't have married a negro, would you? You'd do your damnedest to stop your sister from marrying a negro. Well, you take my word for it, the Trevors will feel just the same way about Margaret marrying Roy Wilson, if there's any question of it, which I very much doubt.'

Daisy said to little Mrs Winterton, 'And the trouble is, I just don't know where my duty lies. I mean, Wendy ought to hear about it, the way everyone's talking, but I don't fancy being the one to tell her.'

'It's very difficult,' sighed Mrs Winterton. 'One wants to do the right thing, and yet it's often hard to see what the right thing is.'

'What's worrying me,' said Daisy, 'is Margaret herself. I'm perfectly prepared to believe it's all perfectly innocent – trust Trixie Beltram to see the worst in everything – but I do feel someone ought to warn Margaret that she's playing with fire. I'm sure she hasn't got a wrong thought in her head, but you can't expect someone like Roy Wilson not to take advantage of her. I mean, people like that just aren't used to controlling themselves, and it's hardly likely he's going after her for any other reason.'

'It sounds wicked to say so when people are in such bad trouble,' said Edna Pickering to her husband, 'but you can't help seeing the funny side, can you? There's the Trevors that think they're too grand to have any dealings with us unless it's over the counter, and then there's their girl goes and falls, not for a nice boy like it might be our Ted, but for one of the Station Road people. Well, you can't help laughing, can you?'

Miss Evadne was the least easy person in the village to approach with gossip and probably the last to hear it. It was Doctor Gregory who told her when he came to keep an eye on her heart, which had been troublesome lately. 'Bad business, this, about Margaret Trevor and that Wilson boy,' he said gruffly, as he drained the glass of sherry she always offered him at the end of his visits, 'but what can you expect with this government we've got in power and every jumped-up Jack thinking he's as good as his master,' and then he saw from her face that she knew nothing about it and was sorry he'd mentioned it, though there was nothing for it then but to repeat the rumours that had greeted him on all his visits that morning.

'Oh, the poor things,' said Miss Evadne. 'It *would* be Miss Beltram who saw them together, wouldn't it?'

Doctor Gregory and Miss Evadne were the last of the village gentry, the last whose fathers had been born in the village and their fathers before them, and they alone looked on the story, the one with almost Olympian detachment, the other with a rising sense of personal responsibility. 'I'm afraid the Trevors will take it hard,' said Doctor Gregory, shaking his head. 'They've got precious little but their dignity left, and they're bound to feel it as a sad disgrace.'

'Does anyone know how far it's actually gone?' asked Miss Evadne, and Doctor Gregory answered, 'I should very much doubt if it's gone anywhere, if you ask me. The Wilsons are a thoroughly respectable family, and young Roy's the last sort to play fast and loose on his own doorstep, let alone with a girl like Margaret Trevor. Mind you, I wouldn't dream of saying so outside these four walls, but to marry a boy like Roy Wilson would probably be the making of her. She'd make a good working-class wife and mother and that's about all she's cut out for – she's got no more brains than would cover a sixpence. And with the money these people earn nowadays, young Wilson could keep her in luxury such as she's never known. Personally, I've no patience with the sort of attitude that thinks more of gentility than letting a girl perform her natural functions with a good husband, even if he does eat his peas with a knife.'

'I entirely agree with you,' said Miss Evadne vigorously. Then she added slyly, 'but you wouldn't like Roger to marry a milkmaid, would you?'

'That's different,' said the doctor straight away. 'Certain things are expected of a professional man, but there's certainly no one expects anything of the Trevors.'

'Except themselves,' said Miss Evadne compassionately. She added questioningly, 'I suppose a marriage *is* out of the question?'

'We don't even know that they themselves want it,' said the doctor, rising. 'I don't suppose they've got enough sense to think of it.'

'No, I suppose not,' said Miss Evadne, rising too. 'How is your wife?' she asked, accompanying him into the hall, the only person in the village who ever dared to make the inquiry. But the doctor liked to hear it from Miss Evadne who remembered Mrs Gregory when she was a pretty light-hearted young woman before the birth of Roger had brought on her trouble. 'About the same,' he said, as he always said, and he struggled into his overcoat and went away.

When he had gone Miss Evadne wandered out into the garden where old Birch was putting in the broad beans. She knew enough of the workings of village gossip to realise that he must know all about it, and he, straightening himself on his dibber, looked at her and saw that she now knew too.

'It's a sad thing, isn't it?' he said, and she didn't pretend not to understand. She sighed and said, 'Times are changing, Birch. Everyone's standards are different from what they used to be.'

'And no better for that,' he said. 'Over forty years I've been gardening in Priory Dean, man and boy. Started at twelve, I did, up at the Grange, garden-boy and then to second gardener till I come here to the Squire twenty years ago, before there was any of those houses up Priory Hill. You hear a lot of talk nowadays about the bad old times, but to my way of thinking they wasn't anything like so bad as the times we've got now.'

'They're better for some people,' said Miss Evadne; this was an argument they both knew inside out, and it followed its recognised course. 'There was some shameful poverty in the village when I was a girl.'

'And would be still, if people had their just deserts,' said Birch obstinately, 'instead of being cosseted by a government that's got nothing to do but put its hands into the pockets of people that can't afford it. There's never any good comes of interference with nature. Nature must take her course, which is what all those people who drop atom bombs and upset the weather are always forgetting.'

'But it's natural for young people to fall in love with each other,' said Miss Evadne, half-pleadingly.

'Not outside of their own class, it isn't,' said Birch firmly. 'Kind mates with kind, that's the rule all the world over. You don't find cats mating with dogs or cattle with horses.'

Miss Evadne said, 'But people are – well, they're all people –'

Birch wagged his head obstinately. 'It's nature's way there should be differences between people,' he maintained, 'you're not the same sort as me, Miss Evadne, and we don't neither of us ever forget it; you know your place and I know mine. I'm not saying,' he added with fine contempt, 'that there's the same degree of difference between the two people we're talking about as there is between you and me, but there's more than enough to make it a sad and shocking thing.'

'By the way, do you want me to order any more weed-killer?' asked Miss Evadne.

Birch graciously ceded his argument; it was Miss Evadne's privilege to change the conversation when she thought proper. 'I'm not saying we couldn't do with a gallon or two,' he said, and they talked about weed-killer for a few minutes and then Miss Evadne moved away, saying as she went, 'Come up to the house, Birch, before you go off. I've a note I want you to take to the Rector.'

By that evening a new rumour had gone the rounds. To someone who had just hinted, ever so delicately, to Edith Wilson that things were being said, Edith was reported to have stated firmly that if her Roy was thinking of getting married, she couldn't see what business it was of anyone else.

CHAPTER SEVENTEEN

It was with trembling nervousness that Margaret had come downstairs to get the breakfast that morning. She didn't quite know what attitude she expected her parents to adopt, but Wendy's cold 'Good morning,' and Gerald immediately picking up the paper and hiding behind it seemed to fit all her apprehensiveness. Sheila couldn't help being conscious of the uneasy atmosphere, but scenes were to be avoided whenever possible and so she just ignored the obvious tension and ate her breakfast in silence, a textbook on her knee.

Suddenly Wendy said to Margaret, 'What's this house we heard so much about last night?'

'It's Roy's auntie's,' said Margaret over-eagerly, clutching at the question as a concession of interest. 'She's going to live with the Wilsons and she said Roy could have it.'

'By "auntie" I suppose you mean what we in this family are accustomed to call "aunt",' Wendy commented, 'but I suppose the deterioration of your vocabulary is one of the things we shall have to get used to.'

Sheila looked up from her book. 'What are you all talking about?' she asked. 'What's Roy Wilson's aunt-or-auntie's house to do with Margaret?'

Wendy said, 'I suppose you had better know. Your father and I have just been informed that Margaret and Roy Wilson propose to get married.'

Sheila's book fell from her knees on to the floor. She exclaimed vehemently, 'How disgusting!' and then, turning to Wendy, 'Mummy, it's not true, you won't let her do it. Think what people would say.'

'I'm afraid your sister is far too concerned with her own affairs to spare a thought for *our* feelings in the matter,' said Wendy with mock-lightness.

Sheila pushed back her chair and stood up. She said to Margaret, 'I think you're absolutely disgusting. If you marry Roy Wilson, I'll never have anything to do with you again.'

She rushed out of the room, and Wendy sighed and said to the air, 'Poor Sheila. I was afraid she'd take it hard. I only hope for her sake it doesn't get out at school.'

Margaret stood up, and with shaking hands began to put the breakfast things together.

'Leave them,' said Wendy, 'you'll be late. I don't doubt that two pounds-ten a week seems very little compared with the riches you're offered, but there's many a slip, you know, and I wouldn't be too eager to get the sack if I were you.'

'I'm not,' said Margaret, half-crying, but it was no use trying to say anything and she could only try to put up with it as Roy had said and try to believe it would be all right.

When she'd gone out of the room, Gerald threw down his paper and said, 'Isn't there anyone who'd talk her out of it?'

'I just don't know,' said Wendy. 'I've got a kind of hope that Edith may go off the deep end about it. She's always been a very sensible woman, and I've no doubt that she'll see it in the same light that we do. In fact, I wouldn't be a bit surprised if she didn't come along and see me about it in the very near future.'

'Well, I hope you're right,' said Gerald, 'but isn't there anyone else? What about the Rector? It's really his job, after all.'

'This one?' said Wendy contemptuously. 'He wouldn't begin to know what we were talking about. Why, he isn't even a gentleman! What a pity that old Mr Hall isn't still alive; he'd have been the very person to help us.'

By the time Roy met Margaret that afternoon he already knew that it was too late for discretion. 'Flying a bit high, aren't you?' Reg Summers had said on the bus, with a nudge in the ribs, and when Roy had demanded, as naturally as he could, 'Here, what are you talking about?' Reg had answered with a guffaw, 'Don't you get up on your high horse, young feller-me-lad. It's all round the village.'

How it had got out Roy couldn't imagine, but he wasn't surprised. Knowing what the village was, he'd marvelled they'd managed to keep it dark so long, and he only thanked his stars he'd been along to the Trevors before they'd heard from anyone else.

So when he met Margaret he said boldly, 'Let's go along the High Street today and have a look at some furniture,' and when Margaret said shrinkingly, 'Oh, but Roy, we promised –' he explained, 'It's too late for that now. I don't know how it's got out, but it's all round the village. The best thing we can do is to put a good face on it, and not act like we'd got anything to be ashamed of.'

'Mummy and Daddy will be so angry,' said Margaret. 'They'll think we've told,' and Roy answered, 'Well, it wasn't us, and we know it wasn't, and if you ask me it's not such a bad thing. I never liked the idea of creeping around as if we'd got something to hide, and to my way of thinking it's likely to force their hands. So come along now, hold your head up and look as if you're proud of me.'

Margaret couldn't help laughing at that, and she didn't raise any more objections. As they walked along, Margaret asked nervously, 'Roy, what did your parents say?'

'It was a bit of a shock for them, of course,' said Roy, frowning. It was difficult to tell Margaret about it without making unfavourable comparisons between his parents and her own. 'Dad didn't like it at first, I'll tell you straight, but in the end he said, "Well, it's your own business," he said, "and if Miss Trevor's prepared to take us as she finds us," he said, "I'll be glad to give her a welcome."'

'That was nice of him,' said Margaret gratefully, 'and what about your mother?'

'Mum was real upset,' said Roy, 'but don't get me wrong,' he added hurriedly, 'it wasn't you she was upset about, but your mother. She's really fond of your mother, is Mum, and it was how *she* was going to take it that kept on worrying her. "If things were different, Roy," she kept on saying, "there's no one I'd sooner see you marry than someone like Miss Margaret," and Maureen went on telling her not to be silly, that things were different now. Now there's someone who's real pleased, and that's Maureen. I tell you, I had the surprise of my life when she up and said how much she liked you, because usually she hasn't got a good word to say for anyone who isn't what she calls one of the workers. Anyway, in the end Mum came round, and she said I was to tell you that if you liked to call around any time she'd be glad to see you.'

'You'd come with me, wouldn't you, Roy?' whispered Margaret.

'Now, you're not shy of Mum, are you?' Roy exclaimed. ''Smatter of fact, I did tell her I didn't think you could come while we'd promised your parents to keep it dark, so to speak. That's what worries her, of course, knowing that Mrs Trevor and the Major don't fancy it. As Dad said, it wasn't to be expected that they would, but she doesn't like the idea of setting herself up against your mother. Still, now people have got to know about it, it may make a bit of difference all round.'

Much as Miss Evadne disliked calling on him for anything, there was no doubt that the Rector was the proper person to speak to about the matter. 'You must forgive my calling you out like this,' she said, when in obedience to her note he came round to the Hall next morning. 'My excuse is that whatever goes on in the village used to be my family's business, and I'm afraid I can't get out of the old-fashioned way of regarding it as such.'

This, the Rector felt, was right and proper. This was just what he'd pictured when he first heard he'd been appointed to a country living – being invited to discuss village affairs with the lady of the manor. True, Miss Evadne, with her untidy ginger hair and cheap shapeless tweeds, didn't really fit in with the gracious, dignified lady he'd envisaged, but it was the first time she'd called him in like this, and surely it meant that at last he was beginning to make his mark.

'It's about this business of Margaret Trevor and Roy Wilson,' said Miss Evadne. 'I suppose you've heard about it?' and the Rector, chiming in with what he was sure must be her attitude, said gravely, 'Yes, I'm afraid I have.'

Miss Evadne looked at him sharply. 'Do you know if there's any question of a marriage?' she asked, and the Rector answered, 'Well, according to what I heard this morning, it seems there is. They say Mrs Wilson's going round boasting to everyone that her son's going to marry Miss Trevor.'

'From what I know of Mrs Wilson, that's most unlikely,' said Miss Evadne. 'She's never been one for spreading her affairs all over the village. Still, if marriage *has* been talked about, that makes it easier. I'd go to the Trevors myself, but I'm afraid they'd think I was trying to patronise them, and that would only put their backs up. You're the only person who could do it.'

'Do what?' asked the Rector, uneasily.

'Go and see the Trevors and persuade them to put a good face on it,' said Miss Evadne impatiently. 'Mind you, they may be doing so already for all I know, but I should think it's most unlikely. And anyway, if they had, we'd have heard of an engagement by now instead of all these nasty rumours that aren't doing anyone any good.'

'But, Miss Graham,' stammered the Rector, 'you're not in favour of it, are you? You – in your position?'

'Why not?' said Miss Evadne curtly. 'Here's a poor girl without any chances in life, and a respectable young man willing to give her a good home. What's against it?'

The Rector found it practically impossible to put his opinions into words. 'Well – they do come from very different walks of life, don't they?' he tried.

Miss Evadne said, 'I shouldn't have thought that would have worried you. Don't you teach that everyone's equal in the sight of God?'

With relief the Rector moved on to his own ground. 'In the sight of God, yes – but that refers to the spiritual life, not the worldly life on this earth. I don't need to remind you, Miss Graham, of the Christian duty expressed in the Catechism, that we should do our duty in the station of life to which it may please God to call us.'

'But may it not be,' suggested Miss Evadne, 'that He has called Margaret Trevor to the same station of life as Roy Wilson?'

The Rector wanted to say testily that this was mere quibbling, but he was unaccustomed to parishioners who questioned his theological dicta, and was wary of proceeding. Instead, he shifted his ground. 'We are also reminded of the duty we owe to our parents,' he said. 'If Major and Mrs Trevor are in favour of this match, no words of mine are needed. But if, as I don't doubt is the case, they're against it, then it's not for me to encourage their daughter in what can only be regarded as wilful disobedience.'

'But what harm can there be,' asked Miss Evadne, 'in trying to reconcile the parents to it?'

'I'm sorry,' said the Rector stiffly. 'I'm afraid I don't see it as my duty to interfere. I'll tell you frankly that personally I'm against the match.'

Miss Evadne asked, 'Why?'

The Rector tried to answer, to produce a respectable, conventional, orthodox answer, but he found he could not. He raised troubled eyes to Miss Evadne, and looking at him, she saw the distance he had come, the impossibility of his doing anything that should make that distance seem less great or less important. 'Don't worry,' she said gently. 'I quite understand how you feel about it.' 'I wish –' he began, but Miss Evadne stopped him. 'Don't worry,' she said again, 'I'll see to it myself.' One always, she thought, had to see to things oneself in the end.

But that evening Miss Evadne had another of the heart attacks that had been troubling her intermittently for the last few years, and this time she had to take to her bed. It worried her that she could do nothing when she most wanted to help, but the doctor was adamant, and she had to console herself with his half-promise that if she behaved herself he'd let her see visitors at the end of the week.

Martha Wetherall, however, from entirely different motives, felt an equally strong need to do something about the situation, and a few days later she tackled Ralph about it again. 'From all I hear,' she said, 'there's no doubt that those two want to get married and the Trevors won't hear of it. Now I've had an idea. Suppose the young man got a white-collar job, do you think that would make any difference to the situation?

I mean, of course, a real good leg up the ladder so that they could see he was all set to go ahead.'

'It might,' said Ralph cautiously. 'What put the idea in your head?'

'I was pumping Edie,' said Martha. 'She's thrilled with the whole situation, and she told me that in printing you can go over from the sort of job Roy's got to the management side.'

'By the way, when do we lose Edie?' asked Ralph.

'The end of the week,' said Martha. 'She's getting married the Wednesday after, and she said that would give her time enough. Of course,' she said doggedly, disregarding Ralph's red herring, 'she didn't know why I was pumping her. But what I was thinking was, you could go to Alan Thatcher and persuade him to give Roy a leg up.'

'I could,' said Ralph, 'but there's one very important factor you're forgetting.'

'And what's that?' Martha demanded.

'The young man himself,' said Ralph. 'It's my experience, and I've no doubt it's Alan's too, that there's nothing harder than to persuade that sort of young man to go over to management. After all, why should they? They've served a long apprenticeship for a highly-skilled job, and they're earning enough to do all they want to do. Besides, there's always a feeling of treachery in making the change-over, a kind of feeling that they've gone over to the enemy, so to speak.'

'But there's more money, surely?' said Martha, 'and you can't get to the top unless you go over to the management side?'

Ralph looked at her quizzically and said, 'Believe it or not, darling, the average British workman doesn't want to get to the top. If he's in the sort of job Roy Wilson's in, he's usually perfectly happy as he is.' He watched with amusement the incredulous consternation that momentarily held her silent.

Then she said, 'Well, I'm sure Roy isn't like that. After all, Margaret would hardly want to marry him if he was. Promise me, darling, you'll at least ask Alan to give him the chance.'

'If Alan thinks he's good enough,' said Ralph. 'I'm not going to ask Alan to upset his works just so that your *protégée* can marry into the upper classes.'

Towards the end of the week Gerald said irritably, 'Well, what's happening? Aren't you going to do anything about it?'

'What can I do?' said Wendy. 'The only thing is to do nothing and hope it dies away naturally. All I hope and pray is that no one finds out anything about it.'

'What will you do if it comes out?' asked Gerald anxiously.

'God alone knows,' said Wendy, sighing heavily. 'There's nothing we could do, I suppose, but put a good face on it, insist on a long engagement, and then do what we're doing now, just leave it to time. But if it does come out, I'm afraid it may make a very considerable difference to Margaret's chances elsewhere.'

'If only he wasn't what he is,' groaned Gerald. 'I mean, when you come to think of it, fifteen quid a week isn't bad, is it? And you heard what he said about all that he's got put away. I only hope that when the right man comes along, he'll have as much to offer.'

Wendy said reflectively, 'You know, I'm very much surprised that Edith Wilson hasn't been up to see me yet.'

'Talbot,' said Miss Evadne to her maid, 'I want you to go along to the bus-stop at about six this evening, and try to catch Miss Trevor as she comes off the bus. Ask her if she'd be so very kind as to come in and see me over the weekend, any time that suits her.'

'It's fair getting on my nerves,' said Roy to Margaret as they stood looking in at the window of the furnishing-shop. 'There we are, all set to go, and yet we just can't get a move on. Have they said anything more to you about us?'

Margaret shook her head. She didn't want Roy to know anything about how it was at home, Wendy's cold, cutting little comments, Gerald embarrassedly avoiding her, and Sheila, frankly outraged, refusing to have anything to do with her. It was she who was pleading now. 'Roy, you will go on loving me, won't you? You won't let all this waiting make any difference?'

'Of course I'll go on loving you,' muttered Roy irritably, 'but I must say I'm getting a bit fed up with being treated as if I was dirt. Why can't it be with us like it is with Edie and Jim, everyone as pleased as punch and showing it? I'm not a criminal, and I'm sick of being treated as if I was.'

'I'll have to be getting back now,' said Margaret miserably. There was nothing she could do to disperse the miasma of misery and discouragement that seemed to be settling on them. At the hospital gate Roy suddenly clutched her hand and said, 'It'll be all right, just so long as we can get a move on soon. Don't you worry too much.' But not even Roy's confident optimism could now tell her not to worry at all.

'Well, I've spoken to Alan,' said Ralph, 'but I'm afraid you're going to be disappointed.'

'Damn,' said Martha sharply. 'Well, come on, tell me exactly what happened.'

'I had a word with him a couple of nights ago at the Country Club,' said Ralph, 'when you were chattering about schools with Sylvia. Of course he didn't know anything about young Wilson offhand, but he said he'd look into it. Well, I had lunch with him today, and he told me what had transpired. He'd called for a report on this boy, first of all, and it was good enough, he said, as far as it went – a good workman, keen at his job, nothing known against him, but – well, not exactly the sort one would recommend for a change-over to management, if you know what I mean.'

'I take it you mean not of the right class,' said Martha coldly.

'No,' said Ralph, 'I don't mean that at all. Men like Alan and me haven't got time to worry what a man's class is, so long as he can do the job. But it happens to be a fact that working-class people have very seldom got the – well, I don't know what you'd call it – I suppose I mean the capacity for leadership of better-educated people.'

'They would have, if you had universal state education like we do in the States,' put in Martha.

'You're probably right,' agreed Ralph politely, 'though I seem to remember your telling me that you yourself went to an extremely expensive and very exclusive private school. But that's beside the point. As I say, there wasn't anything against the boy, and though in the ordinary way he's not one of those he'd have picked out for that kind of promotion, as a favour to me Alan agreed to give him the chance. So he put it up to him – not personally, of course, but through the proper channels – and I gather young Wilson's reply was a polite but firm negative.'

Martha frowned. 'It was made quite clear to him that there'd be real social and financial advantages, that it would provide a solid chance of getting his feet on the ladder?' she asked.

'Everyone perfectly understands the meaning of all the available jobs in their own line of country,' Ralph said patiently. 'I don't know whether it was explained in detail or not, but I can assure you it had no need to be. You've got to remember, as Alan put it to me, that printers regard themselves as the aristocracy of the working-classes. As I told you the other evening, it's a very hard trade to get into, with a very long apprenticeship, the wages are fantastically high, and, Alan says, the numbers are deliberately kept down so that there's never any danger of unemployment. Anyway, young Wilson was quoted as saying that he liked his job and he didn't see any reason to make a change.'

'Then,' said Martha, 'I wash my hands of the whole business. I'd be ashamed to take any more trouble over someone who hasn't a spark of ambition or initiative. I can only say that I'm very, very sorry for poor Margaret.'

Ralph drained his glass. 'I did get one useful piece of

information out of Alan,' he remarked. 'It seems that scheme up at the top of the hill is coming off after all, so I suppose I'd better take some steps about it.'

Margaret came timidly into Miss Evadne's bedroom where she lay on her high brass bed in a flowered flannel nightgown with a Shetland shawl over her shoulders. 'It was very nice of you to come along and see me,' Miss Evadne said. 'Sit down, now, and make yourself comfortable.' Margaret seated herself on a little chintz-covered Victorian chair, and Miss Evadne said, 'I'm afraid you're going to think me a very interfering person, but can you tell me if it's true that you're going to marry Roy Wilson?'

A week earlier Margaret would have replied Yes, it was true, she and Roy were going to get married as soon as they could. Now she twisted her fingers in and out of each other, and answered hesitantly, 'Well, I want to.'

'Your parents are very much against it, I suppose?' asked Miss Evadne.

'Yes,' said Margaret dully. Then she perceived that Miss Evadne was not antagonistic, had not sent for her to berate her, and she burst out, 'They were horrid, Miss Evadne. They said such beastly things to Roy. He pretended he didn't mind, but I know he did. Nothing's been the same since he came to see them. If it goes on like this much longer, I know it'll spoil everything.' She stopped abruptly; what spoiling everything might mean she didn't dare to examine.

'You're quite sure you love him?' questioned Miss Evadne. Margaret nodded. 'And that you'd really be happy with him?

You know your parents may have put things tactlessly if they are upset or angry, but you mustn't blind your eyes to the fact that you'd have some very real differences to overcome.'

Margaret said hesitantly, 'Miss Evadne, Roy's sister Maureen once said to me as a joke that I hadn't got any sense of class, and I'm afraid that's true. If other people didn't bring it up all the time and make me think of it, I'd never think of Roy as being any different from me. I mean, he isn't really. We like just the same things and we see everything the same way, and if people didn't talk about there being a difference, I'd never think of it, really I wouldn't.'

'And does Roy feel the same about it?' asked Miss Evadne.

'He does, really,' said Margaret, frowning, 'but though it sounds horrid to say so, Miss Evadne, it isn't so easy for him as for me. I mean, though it's a beastly way of looking at it, I'm the one who's on top, aren't I, and it's harder for him.'

Miss Evadne smiled kindly and sadly. She knew perfectly well in what sense Margaret felt she was on top, and in her heart she approved the moral validity of this claim. But practical validity nowadays was another matter; in every practical sense the advantages were all on Roy's side.

She said: 'Margaret, I want to tell you what happened to me when I was the same age as you are now.' It didn't occur to her to ask Margaret to respect her confidence: had she not been sure it would be respected, she would not have spoken. 'As you know, I've lived here at the Hall all my life. My mother died when I was ten, and as soon as I grew up I started keeping house for my father. Life in the village was very restricted in those days, and in any case my father preferred to live quietly, so I met very few people. But even so, I did manage to fall in love.'

She paused and sighed. 'He was a dentist in Walbridge,' she said. 'I used to go to him to have my teeth seen to, and I remember old Talbot, who was with us even then, always used to come with me and wait for me in the waiting-room. A dentist doesn't sound very romantic, I know, but he was a very nice and honourable young man, and though we could only meet on my professional visits, we managed to fall very deeply in love, and in the end he came to my father and asked for my hand.

'My father wouldn't hear of it,' said Miss Evadne. 'I'm ashamed to say I listened outside the library door, and I heard him call Matthew an impertinent young puppy and a fortune-hunter – though goodness knows I hadn't any fortune to speak of. Then he called me in and tried to make me promise I wouldn't see Matthew again, but I wouldn't promise, and Matthew and I both swore that we'd wait until I was twenty-one and then we would get married whatever he said.'

'And what happened?' breathed Margaret.

'It just died away,' said Miss Evadne. 'Three years is too long for young love to last without anything to feed on. At first we wrote to each other regularly, but soon it all began to seem unreal. And then my father would continually tell me that Matthew was beneath me, that he'd never be successful, that I'd have plenty more chances with people of my own class, and, to tell you the truth, when, in the end, I got a letter from Matthew – a very manly letter – saying that he felt we'd both made a mistake and that he had no right to bind me, I was relieved and felt that my father had saved me from a *mésalliance*. I sat and waited smugly for the other chances to come along, and then they never came.'

Margaret asked, 'And what happened to Matthew?'

'He married,' said Miss Evadne, 'he married two or three years later, and eventually, so I heard, he took a practice up north somewhere. I never saw him again, but naturally I kept my ears open to hear anything I could of him. I gather my father was right in that he never made a substantial success in his profession.'

'Do you mean your father was right to stop you marrying him then?' asked Margaret.

'No, indeed, my dear,' said Miss Evadne. 'That was the last impression I wanted to give you. What I do believe is that Matthew and I could have been very happy together and that worldly success was the last thing that should have entered into anyone's consideration.'

'It's only Mummy and Daddy that think about it,' said Margaret. 'I don't. And anyway, in his own job, Roy *is* successful, and that's what matters.'

'The last thing I want to do,' said Miss Evadne, for this formal protest was conventionally necessary, 'is to persuade you to go against your parents' wishes.' Can they possibly make a success of it here, she wondered. Wouldn't they be wiser to go away, right away? But she realised instinctively that the lightest order would weigh heavily with Margaret's uncertainty, and she went on firmly. 'But, as you see, I know only too well how a love that could have blossomed into lasting happiness can be blighted by other people's opposition. I should like to feel that you have the strength I lacked, and that you and your young man will be able to conquer these present difficulties and make a happy life together.'

Margaret said desperately, 'Miss Evadne, what can I do?'

'What is Mr and Mrs Wilson's attitude?' Miss Evadne asked.

'Roy said they didn't mind, except for Mrs Wilson worrying about Mummy,' said Margaret. 'I like Mrs Wilson awfully, Miss Evadne, and I like Maureen too. Roy said Mrs Wilson would like me to go and see them, but I didn't like to while things were like this.'

'Then my advice to you,' said Miss Evadne firmly, 'is to go and see Mrs Wilson straight away. If they like you, and you've got them on your side, that's half the struggle. It means that you and the young man have got it respectably accepted by half the families, and it will help him to feel better about it. Now I want you to promise me, as soon as you leave here, that you'll go right away and call on Mrs Wilson.'

'Oh, I will!' promised Margaret. 'I did want to, and I'm awfully glad you think it's a good idea. And do you think Mummy and Daddy will come round?'

'That entirely depends on you,' Miss Evadne said. 'If they see that you are firm and resolute, and that nothing they say can change you, I'm sure they will in the end. And if you feel like wavering, you think of me and my lonely life, and remember it was just because I hadn't the courage to stand out for what I wanted.'

Margaret timidly got up and put her hand on Miss Evadne's. 'I don't know how to thank you,' she said. 'I'll really do my best, but the trouble is I'm not awfully brave or anything, and I'm sure I'm much more frightened of people than you are.'

Miss Evadne held her hand tightly and said, 'Nonsense!' She felt herself swept by a strong feeling of tenderness towards Margaret, and the thought flashed through her mind that she'd like to leave Margaret the books in the rosewood bookcase. She realised immediately what a silly idea this was, Margaret not being at all the sort of girl to like them, but she still wanted to give her something, and she directed, 'Will you fetch me that Indian box from the chest-of-drawers?'

While Margaret was carrying it to her, she hurriedly pondered its contents. Nothing valuable, of course, it wouldn't be suitable, and in any case valuable jewels – not that hers were anything to write home about – should stay in the family. Slowly she opened the box, wondering what – and there was the very thing, a mother-of-pearl locket shaped like a rose on a thin silver chain.

'This belonged to my mother,' she said, 'she had it as a little girl from the daughter of a very famous preacher, and when I was a child I used to wear it with my white dresses on Sunday. I want you to take it as a wedding present – I hope it's the first you've received – and give it to *your* little girl to wear with her pretty frocks.' She lifted up the charming trinket, dropped it into Margaret's hands and held them tightly closed over it with her own. 'Be strong and happy,' she said, and there were tears in her eyes as there were in Margaret's, who leant over her and kissed her cheek.

So, quickly, before there was any temptation to dilly and dally and perhaps put it off, Margaret came out of Miss Evadne's gate, skirted the Green, and turned down Station Road. Perhaps Roy might be there, she thought, it was a Saturday afternoon and he'd said they were all busy with the preparations for Edie's wedding; it would be nice if Roy was there and surely he'd be pleased she'd come. Walking quickly down the road she found she had caught up with Maureen who was sauntering along more slowly. 'Hallo,' she said shyly, and Maureen said, 'Hallo-allo-allo!' There was a moment's awkward silence. Maureen had made one mistake with Sheila and it had badly shaken her self-confidence. It was Margaret who broke it by saying, 'I was coming along to see your mother. Do you think she'd mind?'

Now Maureen knew where she was, and she clapped Margaret on the back, saying heartily, 'There's nothing Mum'd like more. Come right along,' and the two girls walked down the road together.

Maureen pushed the door open. 'Mum!' she shouted, 'here's young Margaret come along to pay us a formal call,' and out of the kitchen came Mrs Wilson, as flustered, as blushing, as embarrassed as Margaret herself.

Margaret – she never knew afterwards what had made her do it – took an impulsive step forward and suddenly, clumsily, gave Mrs Wilson a kiss. Then Mrs Wilson's arms were round her and she was saying, half-laughing, half-crying, 'There now, and me in my apron, never thinking of you coming along! I was just getting on with the cake for Edie's wedding. Maureen!' she called, 'you just take Miss Margaret into the parlour and I'll be along in two jiffs.'

'Oh, can't I come in the kitchen?' begged Margaret. 'I'd love to watch you making the cake.'

Mrs Wilson looked at her. 'Well, I don't know why not, come to think of it,' she said slowly, then her face crinkled into a complete smile. 'After all, if you're going to be one of the family, you'll have to start taking us as you find us. Come along then, Miss Margaret – or I suppose I ought to be saying Margaret, seeing how things are.'

'Please,' said Margaret, as she followed Mrs Wilson into the kitchen, where the big yellow bowls were set out on the kitchen table. 'Is there anything I can do to help?' she asked, and Mrs Wilson looked round her doubtfully, and then suggested, 'Would you like to get on with peeling the almonds? You remember the way I used to show you, pour boiling water on them and then just pop them out?'

'Yes, I remember,' said Margaret. She lifted the steaming kettle off the stove, poured the water over the almonds, and began sliding them out of their slippery wrinkled skins. Maureen had tactfully disappeared. It was easier to work together than talk, and for a time they kept on with their jobs in sympathetic silence.

At last the almonds were finished, and Margaret pushed the bowl away and emptied the skins into the scrap-bucket she saw under the sink. 'You always was a tidy worker,' said Edith Wilson, watching her. 'Many's the time I've said to your mother, you'd make someone a good wife one of these days, but never did I think it would be my Roy.'

'You don't mind?' said Margaret apprehensively.

'Well, I'll tell you frankly I was a bit taken aback at first,' said Edith, 'but as Dad said, it's the boy's life, he said, and I hope he's got too much sense to let any nonsense stand in his way. Mind you, I don't see the way clear ahead, and there's no use pretending I do. It's going to cause a lot of awkwardness all round, and it's not a bit of good shutting our eyes to the fact.'

'I'm sorry about Mummy and Daddy,' said Margaret, and at the sight of her woebegone face Edith said reassuringly, 'Well, we can't have everything the way we want it, or the world wouldn't be what it is. To tell you the truth, I was in two minds whether to go and have a word with your mother, but then I said to myself, it's best to let things work themselves out, I said. Times are very different from what they used to be, and I'm sure that once they see that you and our Roy are really fond of each other, they'll want to do what makes you happy.'

It was so nice and comfortable sitting there in the warm kitchen with Mrs Wilson that Margaret began to feel happier. She told Mrs Wilson about Miss Evadne's advice – not, of course, about Miss Evadne's private story – and showed her the pretty locket, and Mrs Wilson was thoroughly pleased and gratified. 'There now,' she said, 'it's to be wished everyone had as much sense as she's got –' but she didn't finish the sentence, and at last Margaret dared to ask, 'Where's Roy?'

'He went out – let me see, it can't have been more than ten minutes before you came along,' Mrs Wilson said. 'He's gone into Walbridge with Alice Evans to see about the photographer for the wedding.'

'Is that Alice Evans from the Cake Shoppe?' Margaret asked.

'That's right,' said Mrs Wilson. 'Edie's best friend at school she was, and she and Maureen are going to be the bridesmaids. She's been ever so good about helping with all the odd jobs.'

Margaret had never known jealousy and she didn't recognise it. She only knew that she'd stopped feeling happy and safe, and that some new unformed apprehension was beginning to clutch at her. 'I'd better be getting back now,' she said, standing up, and Mrs Wilson urged, 'Won't you stay for a cup of tea? I know it's a bit late for it, but Roy and Alice shouldn't be that long, and I wouldn't like him to come back and find you'd been and gone.'

But Margaret shook her head. 'I really mustn't,' she said, 'they'll be waiting for me at home,' and now she was in a hurry to get away, terrified lest she should meet Roy with Alice Evans on the hill, perhaps laughing and joking and not missing her at all.

CHAPTER EIGHTEEN

Gerald had received a letter that morning and he and Wendy had been pondering over it all day. It was from one of the Walbridge estate agents, and it purported to be on behalf of an unnamed client who wanted to buy the field at the back of Wood View. It was a polite and a deferential letter, and the price offered was startlingly tempting, at least five times what Gerald had paid twenty years back for a piece of ground that for some time now had been little more than a reminder of failure. In the ordinary way both Gerald and Wendy would have worried about it and argued about it for days and even weeks, but at the end of the letter was a paragraph which said that a speedy decision would be appreciated as their client had other properties in view, and they both felt that if they *did* decide in favour it would be a pity to lose the chance by dithering.

'I wish we knew who it was,' said Wendy for the hundredth time, and for the hundredth time Gerald surmised that he was sure it was Rowe, the dairyman, who already owned the adjacent fields at the top end of Priory Hill. 'I don't see who else it could be,' he said again and again, and Wendy agreed that it was true, one couldn't think who else it could be, who else could possibly want an odd field. They wondered whether to ask Rowe – after all, it was easy to ring him up and just ask, but then if he'd wanted his name brought into it, he'd have come out into the open, probably he'd felt a bit awkward about asking and had thought it better to make a formal offer. 'It couldn't possibly be for *building*,' Wendy occasionally threw into the discussion, but, as Gerald pointed out, it wasn't much use to anyone for building since it could be reached only through the fields already belonging to Rowe, or through the garden of Wood View. 'It *must* be Rowe,' they decided at last, and after they'd settled that it wouldn't really detract from the value of the house, supposing they ever wanted to sell, it was such a good price and a bird in the hand after all – after they'd weighed up every possible consideration they could envisage, Gerald tapped out a formal letter on the old typewriter, accepting the offer.

'I'd post it right away,' Wendy said, 'so that they're sure to get it first thing on Monday,' and then they discovered they'd finished the last stamp-book and that he'd just have time to go down to the village and slip it in the letter-box before tea.

It was on his way to the post-office that he passed Roy's father in the street, a big fat hulk of a man padding along with smiling preoccupied dignity. They caught sight of each other simultaneously, checked their steps, looked hard at each other. A flicker of comprehension, almost of sympathy, passed between them, a glance that agreed that there it was, a rare old mess and none of their doing but that talking about it was the women's business, not theirs. And then they looked away and were passed and gone, Mr Wilson back home for tea and Gerald on to the post-office.

He bought his stamp and slipped his letter in the box and started back home. And it was then that he noticed, on the rotting fence that filled the gap that had never been built over between the Post Office and the Drapery, the roughly chalked letters that said 'Roy loves Margaret' and underneath them a crudely drawn heart with an arrow through it, and scratched in the middle of it the initials RW and MT.

It struck Gerald like the blast from a bomb. All through this unhappy week the one thing that he and Wendy had comforted themselves with was that no one else except the Wilsons knew about it. And now, facing him within glaring affront, was the evidence that the shameful news was the property of everyone in the village, down to the little urchins who scribbled with a bit of chalk to insult and mock.

The people on the pavement, the children sucking sherbet-powder, the housewives with their prams, the young people hurrying out with their sweet-coupons on the last day of the month, saw Gerald standing there staring at the fence and nudged each other with significant glances. And suddenly he became conscious of them, of the nightmare of this knowledge that was in all the watching eyes, and he turned and pushed through them blindly, and hurried, hurried up the hill.

'So that's that,' said Wendy drearily. 'I suppose we were fools to think we could keep it dark.'

'Everyone must have been laughing at us,' gulped Gerald, 'laughing at us all the time.'

'I must think,' said Wendy fiercely, and then she said, 'If everyone knows all about it, there's no reason why I shouldn't have some advice. I'm going over to talk to Daisy.'

Daisy was at the door before Wendy reached it. 'I saw you through the window,' she whispered. 'I've got Trixie Beltram here, unfortunately. Come into the kitchen for a minute; I said I was just going to make the tea.'

Wendy followed Daisy into the kitchen and shut the door. 'Daisy,' she said calmly, 'did you know about Margaret?'

Daisy looked up quickly and the water from the tap sprang to the top of the kettle and overflowed. 'What did you say?' she asked, so flustered she hardly knew what she was saying, and Wendy watched her and nodded. 'So you *did* know,' she said.

Daisy said humbly, 'Wendy, I just didn't know whether I should say anything to you or not. I mean, if you didn't know, I hardly wanted to be the first to tell you.'

Wendy had to say with affronted dignity, 'I've known for some time. Naturally Margaret told me about it right away.'

'You've agreed to it, then?' Daisy asked warily.

Wendy abandoned her pretence of dignity and spoke frankly. 'No, we're not agreed yet,' she said, 'but what else can we do? I gather it's all round the village now, and I can't see anything for it but to put a good face on it.'

'But you'd like to stop it?' questioned Daisy.

'What do you think?' asked Wendy. 'I'd give a million pounds – if I'd got it, which I haven't – to see an end to it. But Margaret's so infatuated no one can say a word to her, and I just don't see any way out.'

Daisy said, 'I'm not sure that there isn't a way out in this very house right now.'

Wendy demanded loudly, 'What do you mean?'

'Hush,' said Daisy. 'I told you that so-and-so Trixie Beltram was here – it was she who told me about it in the first place, as a matter of fact.' Wendy made a gesture of distaste and Daisy went on, 'Well, she's come with another of her horrid little stories, but this one may be the very thing you want to put an end to the whole business.'

Wendy got home only a few minutes before Margaret, just in time to tell Gerald her news. 'Do you think it'll do the trick?' he asked eagerly, and Wendy said she didn't see how it could help but do it, not if Margaret still retained any sense of dignity at all.

So they were waiting for her when with lagging steps she came into the house. 'Come into the dining-room,' said Wendy. 'Daddy and I have something we want to say to you,' and Margaret paled and followed them silently in.

'I'm afraid I've got rather a nasty story for you,' said Wendy gravely, 'and I'm not going to deny that it comes from an unpleasant source, though one that is, I'm sorry to say, usually accurate. I mean Miss Beltram, who was, I now learn, the person who so kindly informed the whole village of our private affairs, though how she learnt about them I don't know. Perhaps you can enlighten me.'

Margaret dumbly shook her head, her sad, worried eyes fixed on Wendy's face.

'Well, however that may be,' said Wendy, 'it appears that

she's for some time known another piece of village gossip which is that your predecessor in Roy Wilson's affections was Alice Evans, that fair girl at the Cake Shoppe.' Margaret gave a sharp wince, and Wendy noticed it with satisfaction. She's heard something already, she said to herself, and she went on with more confidence, 'It seems they were generally known to be walking out together – which I believe is the right expression – until he was sent off to the East, and then people rather forgot about it. Anyway, it seems that Miss Beltram happened to be in Walbridge this afternoon and who should she see but Roy Wilson and this girl walking along arm in arm and looking, Miss Beltram said, as if they hadn't got eyes for anything but each other.'

Margaret was silent, her eyes, expressionless now, still on Wendy's face. She was silent so long that Wendy felt forced to fill the silence, to begin with rising impatience, 'Of course, if you're prepared to share him . . .'

Then Margaret spoke with a taut shivering intensity. 'I'm not prepared to share him,' she said, 'and I'm not prepared to give him up either. Even if I didn't love him like I do, I wouldn't be prepared to give him up. You talk a lot about people like us and not letting down standards, and what do we get out of it? If I don't marry Roy, what is there ahead of me but working at a job I loathe that will never be any different or lead to anything better? I slave at my beastly job all day and then I come home and I slave at home, and you none of you even thank me, you just take it for granted that I'm the stupid one and I'm not worth anything better. You never do anything for me, buy me pretty clothes or take me out where I could meet people, or even behave as if you love me.' She stopped, aghast at herself. She didn't know what had come over her. When she'd opened her mouth she hadn't known it was for more than a hopeless capitulation.

'Margaret, we *do* love you!' cried Wendy.

Margaret shook herself impatiently and then heard herself speaking again, speaking to her parents with an angry ecstasy that she had not even known she felt towards them. 'You don't love me,' she said, 'if you did, you wouldn't try to take away my only chance of being happy. It's Roy who loves me and who wants to look after me. Roy's got money, he's rich compared to you. If I marry Roy, I'll never have to hear people going on about money again. I'll be safe.' She broke off and looked at them thoughtfully. 'Yes,' she repeated, 'I'll be safe.'

Wendy found herself pleading with this new, stern Margaret who stood there judging them. 'It's your happiness we want,' she said, 'you must believe that. Daddy and I know that Roy can give you more in the way of material things than we can. If he was only our class, I give you my word we wouldn't hesitate for a moment.'

'Class,' said Margaret with a new contempt. 'What's class? What's class ever done for you or me or any of us? Roy and I are people, I tell you, and a thing called class isn't going to stand between us. If class is something that says that one kind of people can fall in love and another kind can't, then it's a wicked thing. Roy is good and kind and he loves me and he'll take care of me, and class hasn't got anything to do with it. We're people, I tell you. That's all that matters, that we're people who love each other. You're going to give me

266

permission to get married, or if you don't, I'll get married anyhow, and I don't mind if they do put me in prison. Anyway, you'd have more scandal then, if that's what you're frightened of, than you would by just saying yes.'

She stopped and looked at them and she saw that she had won. She had won with an exhibition of power such as she had never imagined herself possessing and never would possess again. 'I'll go and get Roy and you can tell him,' she said, and she went from the room, leaving them staring, defeated, at the door through which she had gone.

It crossed her mind for a second as she went down the hill, that perhaps Alice Evans would be there, perhaps there would be another battle to be fought and won. But whatever faced her, she would be confident of victory until this rhythmic exultation that upheld her had ebbed and died away, and it was without apprehension that she rang the bell at the Wilsons' front door, and it was no more than she expected when it opened and Roy stood before her.

'Roy, it's all right,' she said, speaking with such confident calm that he looked at her with wonder. 'They've agreed. I said I'd come and fetch you so that they could tell you themselves.'

She watched Roy's expression slowly change from disbelief to utter triumph. 'It's all right,' he cried, and his arms were round her, hugging her tightly, he was laughing and kissing her and trying to talk, all at the same time. It was all right. The danger, the miseries, the misapprehensions were over. It was all right.

'Here,' came Mr Wilson's voice from the kitchen door, 'what's going on here?'

Roy whirled round, his arm round Margaret. 'It's all right!' he shouted. 'They've agreed! Margaret's parents have agreed!' and then they were all crowding round them, slapping them on the backs, kissing them, delight and happiness on every face.

Suddenly Roy turned round to Margaret and demanded, 'Here, you haven't told us what happened. However did they come to agree after all that to-do?'

'I just told them to,' said Margaret firmly, and the faces round her changed slowly from incredulity to respect. 'By God,' said Roy softly, 'I believe that's just what you did do. Here,' he said, feeling instinctively that his authority must be asserted now if it was to last for ever, 'now's the moment to put on your ring and flaunt it before the world,' and then Margaret relaxed and giggled and happily slipped her ring from the ribbon round her neck on to the fourth finger of her left hand.

When they got back to Wood View, the Trevors were still sitting as Margaret had left them, silently staring in front of them. The only difference was that Wendy's hand lay in Gerald's for comfort.

As they came in, Wendy nodded to her husband and he staggered to his feet, holding on to the table for support as if he were drunk. He lifted his head and looked at Roy, and at last he assumed the dignity he always tried to believe he possessed.

He said, 'I withdraw my objections to your marriage. I'm

not going to say we didn't think they were well-founded, but Margaret has shown us that circumstances alter cases. We do sincerely hope you'll both be very happy.'

'Thank you, sir,' said Roy. Wendy spoke, her voice heavy and dragging as if she was overcome by a fatigue that almost overwhelmed her.

'I'm going to ask a favour of you, Roy,' she said, 'it's a big favour and I'm not going to pretend that it isn't. I want to ask you if you'll consider living anywhere else but Priory Dean. I know you think we're wicked to think of these things,' she said wearily, 'but for what it's worth, our social life is almost all we've got left. I want you to think sympathetically, if you can, of what it'll be like for all of us if you go on living here. I'm not arguing now whether it's right or wrong, I'm just trying to look facts in the face, and the fact remains that in a village like ours people move in very definite circles that don't mix with each other. If you both stay here, there's going to be constant difficulties and awkwardnesses and embarrassment and – maybe I'm a coward – I just feel I can't face them.'

Roy and Margaret looked at each other. Both thought swiftly of the little house down Archery Lane and then regretfully let it slip into the past behind them. Roy imagined having, say, Reg Summers and Jim and Edie for the evening and then the Major and Mrs Trevor dropping in, casual-like. Margaret thought of taking Roy to dinner at the Wetheralls and Edie – no, not Edie but probably a friend of Edie's, someone they both knew as a friend – handing round the plates, an unsmiling automaton who couldn't join in the conversation. Roy said slowly, 'I want to be fair, Mrs Trevor. I don't like what you say, but I can't deny there's a lot of truth in it.' He looked again at Margaret and saw agreement in her eyes.

'I don't want to do you any harm,' Wendy pleaded, 'I was wondering if you couldn't get as good a job elsewhere – I mean, there are big printers all over the country, aren't there?'

'There's never any difficulty about a good job for a trained compositor,' Roy stated with natural pride. Then he added frowning, thinking it out as he spoke, 'But I don't know as how I fancy just moving to somewhere else, like that, as if we'd got something to be ashamed of. I don't know as I wouldn't rather make a clean break, go off somewhere like New Zealand, say, where this sort of thing doesn't matter so much anyhow.'

'Not New Zealand,' said Wendy quickly before she had time to think. 'There's Aunt Doris in New Zealand.'

Roy let out a curt explosive laugh. 'Seems as if it does matter in New Zealand after all,' he commented. 'Well, if I'm not to be here, it's all one to me. We'll make it Australia. You haven't,' he asked Wendy ironically, 'got any relatives in Australia?'

Wendy said helplessly, 'I'm sorry, Roy. I didn't mean to hurt your feelings, but you see what I mean. I suppose one day we'll all take this sort of thing for granted, but we've got to face up to life as it is, and something like that would be happening all the time.'

Margaret spoke with her old timidity. 'I'd like it,' she said, 'I'd like to get right away – start afresh without anyone to say anything or think anything. It's not as if I'd ever been very happy here.' She didn't notice Wendy's dismay as she spoke.

'But it's up to Roy. I don't want to make him do anything he doesn't want.'

Roy said with the relief of reaching a decision, 'I think, all things considered, it's the right thing to do. I'm not going to pretend I'd have thought of it, left to myself, but then I suppose,' he grinned awkwardly, 'there's more for me in England than there is for Margaret. But I don't doubt we'll be very happy in Australia and, as a matter of fact, I've got a good pal in Sydney, a chap I used to know in Cairo. So it's not quite like it would be going among strangers.'

'After all,' Gerald put in, trying to make the whole thing seem a normal ordinary decision, 'any number of people are going out there now every week. They say that Old England's finished, and I'm not so sure they're far wrong.'

They weren't wrong as far as the Major's sort went, thought Roy: it was *him* and *his* sort England belonged to now. But he'd said he'd go and he'd stick to it, and maybe it wouldn't be so bad. Anyway, he'd have Margaret, which was what he wanted most, and he'd just have to make up a good reason for his parents, because it wouldn't be fair to tell them the truth, wouldn't be fair to the Major and Mrs Trevor, whom for the first time he regarded with understanding pity.

'I'll go to Australia House as soon as ever I can and find out about it,' he said, 'and I'm sure you'll understand that we'll want to get married now as soon as we get things fixed.'

'Of course,' said Wendy, and the bargain was struck.

'What about a glass of beer?' asked Gerald, trying to pitch the right note, but Roy said, 'I don't think we will just now, if you'll excuse us. I'd like to take Margaret out and talk things over a bit.'

Outside the house, walking down the hill, he said to Margaret, 'Now there's one thing we've got to get straight, once and for all. We've agreed we'll go to Australia and we know why we're going and it's not very nice. Well, we've got to forget about that part of it. If we're going to be happy, we've got to make it so's we're going because we want to, and I don't know but that if we look at it that way, it mightn't give us a fairer chance than we'd get here. Agreed?'

'Oh yes,' said Margaret fervently and then she nervously added, 'Roy, there's just one thing I'd like to ask you, if you won't be offended. Did you ever think of marrying Alice Evans?'

Roy was silent for an almost unnoticeable moment. Should he tell Margaret that that time he first went to the pictures with her, it was Alice Evans who'd failed to turn up, the first time he'd asked Alice out since he was demobbed? Should he tell her that, only this afternoon, fed up with the delay and the insults, he'd been in two minds whether or not to give in, to succumb to Alice's cheery vulgarity, make do with an easy second-best and call the other thing off? He didn't want to deceive Margaret, to bear the burden of keeping things from her, but he discovered he wanted to be kind to her more than he wanted to confess. He put his arm round her and said, 'I wouldn't marry Alice if she was the last girl on earth.' But Margaret had noticed the pause, and now she had a secret too, the knowledge that courage to act had come to her in the very nick of time. Roy pulled her closer, as though to diminish the gulf of their separate thoughts. 'You're the only girl in the world for me,' he said, 'and d'you know what I'm going to do now? I'm going to take you to the Month-Of-May and show everybody once and for all, that you *are* my girl and no nonsense about it.'

So Roy took Margaret to the Month-Of-May. They walked arm in arm up to the bar in the middle of a sudden silence, a silence that fell on Jim and Edie and Reg Summers and Alice Evans and Ted Pickering who'd left his pregnant Rosemary at home with her mother otherwise he'd be at the Master-At-Arms, which was where the gentry went and the tradespeople when their wives were with them. 'What'll you have, Margaret?' said Roy, loudly, and then everyone knew for sure it was true when Roy Wilson could address Miss Margaret like that in a public bar. The engagement had been officially announced.

CHAPTER NINETEEN

For the rest of that autumn Margaret's engagement and Miss Evadne's death overwhelmed all other topics of public interest.

Miss Evadne had had yet another of her heart attacks only a week after Margaret had been to see her, and this time she had died of it before the village had even wakened up to the fact that she was seriously ill. The uneasy distress that everyone felt when they heard was more than personal sorrow for the loss of her awkward kindly personality. 'It won't seem the same without Miss Evadne,' people said, half realising, now she was gone, that the presence of Squire Graham's daughter at the Hall had pointed the pyramidical social structure of the village, and that without its apex this pyramid must shift, change its shape, perhaps even collapse to a uniform level. 'There's Green Lawns,' people would say doubtfully, not even sure why they were saying it, and someone else would answer, 'Well, it's not quite the same thing, is it?' and then everyone would agree in speculating about whom they'd get at the Hall.

It was quickly known, in the way these things do get known, that all Miss Evadne's property passed to a nephew in

Kenya and that he had written to old Mr Stalybridge, George Bruce's senior partner, to sell the house and the furniture since he was settled out there and not likely ever to come back. And Mr Stalybridge had placed the sale in the hands of a big London firm, which was galling since quite a few people in Priory Dean had some kind of a contact with the Walbridge estate agents, but now there was nothing on which to base speculations or check the rumours that soon were flying around. Someone had heard that some woman was after it for one of those advanced schools where the children did just as they pleased; it was said that the Council were considering it, though no one quite knew what for, and other people talked about a stockbroker from London. Most conversations in the village that autumn sooner or later turned on the possible fate of the Hall, and when the topic had been exhausted, the next, which was felt in some unexplained way to be linked with it, was what the Trevors would do about the wedding.

On this latter subject there were more facts to play with. It was known that the Trevors had formally agreed to the marriage and that Miss Sheila was playing up and walking around with a face like a thunder-cloud. It was known that Mrs Trevor had gone down to see Edith Wilson and though no one could ever find out just what they had talked about, it was agreed that when Mrs Trevor came back up Station Road again, she looked, so people said, as if she'd been eating something that didn't agree with her. It was soon known that young Roy had got a passage to Australia for the week before Christmas, and that the marriage was to take place the day they sailed so that they could have the journey as a kind of honeymoon. But what, people endlessly speculated, was Mrs Trevor going to do about the wedding?

It was a problem that nagged at Wendy all the time. She and Gerald had decreed, with guilty generosity, that the money from the sale of the field should be spent on a trousseau for Margaret, and there was something practical she started on right away, taking Margaret, who had given up her job, not to Walbridge but to Harrods, where Wendy had always shopped as a girl, buying her sheets and bath-towels and tablecloths, buying her, for the first time since Margaret could remember, outfits of clothes that were new from head to foot. And there wasn't any difficulty about the coupons, for though those Margaret got from the Board of Trade as an engaged girl didn't really go anywhere, Maureen had quite spontaneously done a whip-round among her friends and produced more than Wendy knew what to do with. But despite Wendy's occasional light comments that it was amusing how these people always seemed to have coupons to spare, both she and Margaret enjoyed and were drawn together over the shopping until one day when Wendy in the Household Linens said with a sigh of relief, 'Well, I really think that's everything now,' Margaret shyly asked, 'Mummy, when are we going to see about my wedding-dress?'

At first Wendy really didn't see the problem. The child's so muddled she doesn't know whether she's on her head or her heels, she said to herself and she reminded Margaret, 'Don't you remember when we chose that blue two-piece, we agreed it would do for the wedding-day?'

'But I thought you meant for going away in,' protested Margaret. 'I'm going to be married in white, aren't I?'

It was then that Wendy began to perceive all the new difficulties that lay in her path. It was funny for church-going people like her and Gerald, but they'd somehow taken it for granted that Roy and Margaret would be discreetly married in the registry office in Walbridge and then, perhaps, a quiet lunch at Fuller's and off to the ship. 'You weren't thinking of getting married in Priory Dean, were you?' she asked and Margaret, her eyes wide open in surprise, answered 'Yes, of course we were. We talk about it all the time. And Maureen wants to be a bridesmaid and I was hoping –' Margaret's voice faltered a little, 'that perhaps Sheila would come round and be a bridesmaid too.'

'Well, we can't very well discuss it here,' said Wendy hurriedly. 'Let's get home and think it over quietly.'

'You won't leave it too late about the wedding-dress?' begged Margaret, following Wendy into the lift, and Wendy said quickly that there was plenty of time, a good six weeks to go and after all Margaret was lucky, she was stock-size, not like Wendy herself who had always had to have everything made for her.

That evening Wendy and Gerald talked it over – or rather, without going into any of the reasons that led them to this decision, decided definitely that the registry office was the only sensible idea and that somehow or other Margaret had got to be talked out of this nonsense. 'I think the best thing,' said Wendy at last, 'is for me to go and see Edith again. I can't say I look forward to it, but I've no doubt she'll feel as we do, that the less fuss made about it the better.'

'What did she say when you went before?' Gerald asked at last. When Wendy had come back from her first visit to Edith, saying only 'Well, that's done,' and quickly going on to talk about the WI Christmas Fair, Gerald had been only too glad to evade a subject redolent of distaste. Now Wendy wrinkled up her nose and said, 'It was all very stiff and formal and proper. Edith had her sister-in-law, Mrs Taylor, to support her and it took place in the parlour, but really, we all felt so very uncomfortable I only stayed ten minutes and left it at that. I mean, I'd done the proper thing and it was all they could ask of me.' Neither she nor Edith had been able to recognise anything each had known in the other during this stiff painful call.

But the question of the wedding was obviously an important issue that had got to be settled once and for all, and so unwillingly Wendy made herself go down the hill to Station Road again. 'I thought we'd better have a talk together about the wedding,' she said to Edith at the door, and Edith, looking a bit more like her old self, said, 'Well, I was only saying yesterday we'd have to be getting a move on soon if everything's to be ready in time,' and again she led Wendy into the dark overcrowded parlour.

Wendy sat down on the hard stiff sofa of the three-piece suite which had to be pushed right up against the piano if there was to be room for everything, and Edith sat by her on the edge of one of the matching armchairs. Wendy began lightly, 'I find our young people have got a lot of fancy ideas in their heads, Edith, so I thought it was about time we got together over it and made them see that they'll have to come down to earth. I'm sure you'll agree that under the circumstances the best thing will be the registry office in Walbridge and a nice quiet lunch for just the two families afterwards.' She was annoyed that Maureen came in while she was finishing her sentence and went and sat on the arm of her mother's chair. She took it for granted that Edith would send her away but she didn't, didn't even check Maureen when she said insolently, 'Under what circumstances?'

Wendy said as coldly as she could, 'If you don't mind my saying so, Maureen, it's your mother I'm discussing this business with, not you; and your mother knows sufficiently well what I'm referring to for me not to need to explain myself any further.' She looked at Edith for approving acquiescence, but Edith didn't meet her glance. Instead she patted Maureen's hand and said, 'Well no, Mrs Trevor, now you come to mention it, I'm not at all sure as how I do understand what you're driving at.'

Wendy changed her tactics. She leant forward and said confidentially, 'Edith, I know we're both agreed that we want to give Roy and Margaret the very best start we can. But I don't feel we'd be doing the right thing by them if we let them set themselves up as a show for all the village to gossip and tittle-tattle about. We can have a nice quiet dignified wedding in Walbridge without it being anyone's business but those of the people concerned.' Maureen looked at her with scorn and Wendy, trying to avoid her gaze, said earnestly to Edith, 'You do agree with me, don't you?'

Edith looked up and met Wendy's eyes. 'No,' she said, 'I don't agree with you and I'm not going to pretend I do. There's been a lot of things I haven't agreed with over this business and I've kept my mouth shut so's not to cause trouble, but there are some things that have got to be said. I don't agree with them going to Australia, and no one can tell me they'd have thought of it of their own accords if somebody – I'm naming no names – hadn't put it up to them. It's not very nice to feel your only son's going all that way away when there's no good reason for it.'

'He'll be better off there, Mum, all things considered,' urged Maureen, surprising Wendy, who never thought of Maureen as a girl who'd bother to comfort anyone, and it fitted better with her estimate of her character when Maureen added with a sharp laugh, 'There'll be no one to know he's no better than dirt when he gets to Australia.'

At last Edith said, though with tenderness not admonition, 'Be quiet now, and let me talk to Mrs Trevor. Me and Dad have stood for a lot of things without opening our mouths,' she said to Wendy, 'but there's one thing we won't stand for and that's any hole-and-corner business about the wedding. I don't want anybody to be able to say afterwards that there was any funny business about it and that it wasn't all open and above-board.'

There was no doubt but that she was adamant. With a little laugh that desperately tried to minimise the tension, Wendy quickly said, 'Well, if you feel like that about it, Edith, there's nothing more to be said. As I told you, I came here to discuss the matter, not to present you with a cut-and-dried decision.

We'll marry them in the church here then, shall we, a quiet little wedding, and afterwards perhaps you'd let me give a quick lunch, just for our two families, so that they can go straight off on to the boat.'

'I'd have pulled it off,' Wendy said angrily to Gerald afterwards, 'if it hadn't been for that girl.' She knew when Edith opened her mouth she was going to agree, but before she could speak Maureen heaved a heavy theatrical sigh and said in the mock-refined voice that had infuriated Sheila, 'Ah well, I suppose all our plans must go by the board, now that we've been issued with our orders by our social superiors.'

Edith shut her mouth and started again. She said firmly, 'I'm afraid that's not quite what we had in mind, Mrs Trevor. We've just given our Edie a real good send-off, and we don't want it said that less was done for our Roy. And I know that Margaret's set her heart on a proper wedding in white and I don't see why she should be done out of it. You needn't worry about us presuming, Mrs Trevor, once it's over and they've gone off, you and the Major needn't have no more to do with us than you have in the past. But what we want to see is a real proper wedding with all their friends around them afterwards as is right and proper, and if you don't fancy doing it at your house, Mrs Trevor, I'm sure I'll be only too glad to give the reception myself.'

There was nothing Wendy could possibly do. If the Wilsons' friends were coming, then the Trevors' friends must come. It was unthinkable that the Wilsons should give the reception, that, if reception there must be, it should be given by anyone but the parents of the bride. With the help of her insolent daughter, Mrs Wilson had manoeuvred Wendy into a position that had only one way out.

She rose and said with as much dignity as she could muster, 'Well, I'm delighted we've been able to reach agreement. I take it that Roy will go and see the Rector about the service. And of course the Major and I will deal with the reception. I'll order some invitation-cards and perhaps you will let me know whom you'd like me to ask.' There was some satisfaction in drawing the social reins into her own hands again, but Edith quickly diminished it by saying, 'You don't want to go to any trouble and expense about the invitation-cards, Mrs Trevor. You let Roy know just what you want, and he'll run them off for you in no time. Then we can send ours out ourselves and save you the trouble.'

It didn't seem worth embarking on the argument that must ensue if she told Edith that wedding-invitations should be not printed but engraved. 'And there's one more thing, Mrs Trevor,' said Edith at the door. 'We'd like to see a notice in the papers, as is usual. Will you see to it or shall we?'

'I'll see to it right away,' said Wendy hurriedly. 'The *Walbridge Gazette*, I suppose?' and secretly thanked providence that Edith agreed and didn't think of insisting it was put in the *Telegraph* as well.

She got out of the Wilson house with a modicum of dignity, but once home she let herself go. 'I can't face it,' she said to Gerald, 'I just can't face it. Just think what it'll be like having all those people in our house, treating us as equals. I mean, if there's going to be a reception at all, we'll have to ask everyone. We can't just have the Wilsons' friends and leave our own out. Well, can you just imagine what it'll be like with Trixie Beltram, say, and Mrs Paynter-Smith rubbing shoulders with people like that awful vulgar Ted Pickering and Mrs Wilkins? That brings it home to you, doesn't it, having to entertain my char as an equal in my own house.'

If Margaret had been there, she could have explained to Wendy that there wouldn't be any question of entertaining Ted Pickering or Mrs Wilkins, that the tradespeople were as much above the Wilsons as labourers were below them; but Gerald, like Wendy, could not perceive that as subtle social nuances existed outside their own social circle as within it, and the only comfort he could offer was, 'At least you won't have to cope with Trixie. I'm told she's had a row with Miss Porteous and has gone off to stay indefinitely with some cousins in Torquay.'

'I wonder what about?' said Wendy, but she wasn't really interested. Her thoughts were tied up in her own troubles and she said, 'What we really want is someone else who'd give the reception, someone quite outside. You'd think the Wetheralls might have offered, since they always pretended to be so fond of Margaret,' but there was no question of the Wetheralls offering. Martha had been deeply affronted by Roy's refusal to mount on the ladder of success, and the silver cigarette-box from Asprey's that had arrived a couple of days before marked the extreme limit of her interest in the Trevor-Wilson wedding.

'If only Miss Evadne were still alive,' Wendy sighed. 'I'm sure she'd have seen how it was and helped us out.' Like the rest of the village Wendy had already accepted Miss Evadne as the legendary symbol of times past and would concur in saying, as long as she lived in Priory Dean, 'Of course it was very different when Miss Evadne was alive.' But Miss Evadne was dead, and try as they would, they couldn't think of anyone who would help them out of their agonising social dilemma.

'Roy was wondering if you were ready to tell him what you wanted on the invitation-cards,' Margaret said now and again, obviously, Wendy thought, prompted from elsewhere, and irritably she would answer, 'Don't nag me – there's plenty of time yet.' And on each occasion she would read in Margaret's face that she was longing to ask when, oh when, could they see about the white wedding-dress, but still she put it off and prevaricated, hoping for some miraculous solution, though what she could not imagine, to the appalling problem of entertaining such infinitely varied people under her own roof without implying an equal acceptance of them all.

She had still not yet brought herself to tell Roy about the cards when, in the middle of November, the village heard that the Hall had been privately sold and that an auction sale of the contents would take place the next week. The most diligent inquiry failed to discover who the new occupant could be; but in the interest of being able to go all over the Hall when the goods were open for inspection on the Saturday before the sale, everyone felt that this other focus of curiosity could well be postponed until the present excitement was over.

Practically everyone in the village that day went over the Hall from attics to cellar. 'It's really rather distressing to see them all flocking in like this,' said Miss Porteous to Mrs Paynter-Smith, diligently turning over piles of curtains in the hopes of finding something that would do for the dining-room. 'It's just vulgar curiosity that's brought them, and one hates to think how Miss Evadne would have loathed to see all this rag-tag-and-bobtail fingering her most dearly-cherished possessions. Now, would this do?' she muttered, holding up a curtain. 'I'm afraid it's badly worn in the middle,' pointed out Mrs Paynter-Smith, wondering whether it wouldn't, all the same, cut up for the little window on her own top landing, and Miss Porteous put it back regretfully and commented, 'One would hardly have expected Miss Evadne to buy such poor-quality stuff. Surprising, isn't it?'

Martha, who had gone with encouraging memories of people who picked up Duncan Phyfe chairs in dilapidated Massachusetts farmhouses, was not disappointed. 'Look,' she said proudly to Mrs Green, who happened to be in the kitchen at the same time that she was, 'a wheelback rocking-chair!' and Mrs Green smiled at it tolerantly and said, 'a quaint old thing, isn't it?' 'Have you come across anything you fancy?' asked Martha, remembering a little tardily that it was improvident to draw attention to what one hoped to buy, but Mrs Green shook her head and said, 'I'm afraid it's all a bit too out-of-date and shabby for my liking.'

Edna Pickering was upstairs with her husband marvelling at the bathroom with its old deal-encased iron bath and the purple flower-sprays decorating the round washbasin. 'It's really not much better than a slum for all it's the Hall,' she said. 'You'd think the old lady would have done herself a bit better than that,' but Mr Pickering, who knew good stuff when he came across it, said, 'You just look at those floorboards now – a good foot wide if they're an inch and all solid wood.'

'Those are elm, those are,' said old Birch, who, wandering dolefully around like a lost ghost, still liked to deal out dollops of proprietary information wherever he got the chance. 'Every day of her life Miss Talbot was down on her hands and knees polishing those boards to keep them as Miss Evadne liked them. Been there a good three hundred years, they have, those boards, but I wouldn't fancy them myself.'

'Why ever not?' asked Mrs Pickering, and Birch shook his head and said, 'Coffin wood, that's what they are. Elm boards are unlucky as I was always saying to Miss Evadne, and so it's proved.'

In the best bedroom next door, Ted Pickering was saying to Rosemary, 'I've heard there's going to be some of those London dealers at the sale, though what they can see in this old junk beats me. I wouldn't be surprised,' he added confidentially, 'if whoever bought the house wasn't going to pull it down and put up a cinema as soon as ever the building restrictions are lifted.'

'But there's hardly enough people here to keep a cinema going,' Rosemary objected, but Ted said, 'Bloke with an eye to the future, see. That's what I'd do myself if I'd got the money,' and if he hadn't remembered her condition he'd have given her a nudge in the ribs.

'Mind you, it's silly for us to buy things when we can get them out there,' Roy said to Margaret, wandering hand in hand through the attics, 'but if there's any small object you take a fancy to, as a memento, like, I don't see why we shouldn't go after it.'

'No, I'd sooner just have the locket she gave me,' said Margaret; she knew that she wanted the new life to be wholly new, not laden with souvenirs from the old. 'Look,' she said at the little round attic-window, 'you get a marvellous view from here,' and Roy came and stood beside her, his arm round her waist, looking out.

'You can see right down the hill to Walbridge,' he said, and they looked at the bright red roofs shining four miles away in the valley, at the ribbon of road meandering up the hill from Walbridge to Priory Dean. 'I hadn't realised there was so much new building going on on our side of the town,' said Margaret, looking at the raw patches that had until very recently been copses each side of the climbing ribbon, looking at the scaffolding and the corrugated roofs of the builders' huts. 'There won't be any real country between here and Walbridge much longer,' said Roy, and then they looked closer on to the village green with the old houses on its north side, the new shops on the south, and the stagnant duckpond in the middle. They looked right down, down to the front garden of the Hall under their feet and Margaret said, 'Funny, there's Mummy talking to the Rector. I wonder what it's about.'

'Perhaps it's about the wedding,' said Roy. He looked round quickly. There was no one else in the attics, and he caught hold of Margaret and kissed her with a passion born of an uncomprehended regret as he looked at the village still isolated and intact, and the new raw roofs climbing up the hill to engulf it.

The Rector said with his usual awkwardness, 'I wonder if you could just spare me a few minutes, Mrs Trevor. I had it in mind to come and see you this evening, but now I've caught you, so to speak, perhaps we could take a turn in the garden if you won't find it too chilly.'

'Not at all,' Wendy said unwillingly but politely, and they walked round to the back of the house and paced the worn mossy lawn under the old cedars.

The Rector cleared his throat and said, 'My wife and I were thinking, Mrs Trevor, if it so happened you hadn't made your final arrangements yet, that it might be a help to you to hold the wedding-reception at the Rectory.' He looked at the ground, and stammered excuses. 'We've got the room, you see. It wouldn't be any trouble. I know your house can't hold a lot of people.'

But Wendy's gratitude was so deep that it lifted her beyond pretence. For the first time since Mr Robinson had come to the village, she spoke to him with complete sincerity. 'You've saved my life,' she said, 'at least, you've saved me from the most utter social embarrassment and I'm afraid that at the moment that seems more important. Yours is the one house in the village where we can all come and mix without any awkwardness.' She put her hand on his sleeve and said earnestly, 'Believe me, I don't know how to thank you. I never thought – I never imagined –'

The Rector met her eyes. He said, 'I'm grateful you'll let me do it. I owed it, you see,' but Wendy didn't hear his last sentence, she was beckoning to Roy and Margaret who had just come round the corner of the house.

'Roy,' she called, 'Roy, Mr Robinson's going to lend us the Rectory for the reception, and if you'll come back home now, I'll give you the wording for the cards. And, Margaret, we'll go on Monday and choose the wedding-dress.'

CHAPTER TWENTY

'Just a small friendly gathering to keep you from brooding after the bird has flown,' said Miss Porteous graciously, inviting Wendy and Gerald to the party she had planned for the evening of the wedding-day, when the reception would be over and the Trevors back from the farewell trip to Tilbury with the Wilsons in Porter's taxi to see the young couple right on to the ship. 'They'll be glad to be back among their own,' she said to Miss Moodie who, in view of Trixie's continued dudgeon at Torquay, was helping with the preliminary arrangements, and certainly it was with undisguised relief that Wendy sank onto the Morris chintz and found herself once more surrounded by her friends, her old friends, her own friends, the rift closed and the Priory Hill circle, though modified, intact and welcoming.

'Well, it's nice to be all together again,' said Dr Gregory, voicing the general feeling, and Miss Moodie looked at her hands and smiled in prim satisfaction.

'I hesitated whether or not to ask the Wetheralls,' said Miss Porteous, 'but somehow one feels they've never quite fitted in.'

'They think a bit too much of themselves for my liking,'

said Mrs Paynter-Smith, who occasionally prided herself on speaking her mind, and Daisy put in, 'Well, from all I hear they'll have even less time than ever for us poor folk now they'll have their own friends on their doorstep.'

'Why, what do you mean?' everyone asked, leaning forward eagerly, and Daisy said, 'Well, I've heard – and I didn't hear it from George but from Mrs Green –' she put in with such discretion as befitted a solicitor's wife, 'that the people who've bought the Hall are those friends of theirs who used to be after Broomfields. Mrs Green says she understands he's the managing director of a big engineering firm.'

'It will be a sad comedown after Miss Evadne,' sighed Miss Porteous, and Dr Gregory snorted, 'Those business people are the only ones who've got the money these days.'

'By the way,' said Gerald uneasily, 'did anyone else see those men with rods this morning?'

'Men with rods?' repeated the Doctor. 'What men with rods? I didn't see any men with rods.'

'They were in that field I sold,' said Gerald, 'walking about with rods and tape-measures. I saw them from the bathroom window when I was dressing and I meant to go and ask them what they were doing, but then the car came and I hadn't got time. I wondered whether perhaps Rowe was going to put up a cow-shed or something?' He looked round the room interrogatively.

'It wouldn't be Rowe,' said the Doctor. 'Rowe's sold those fields. Didn't you know?'

Gerald asked, 'Who did he sell them to?'

'He didn't know who it was,' said the Doctor. 'He just got

the offer through some agent or another, and he told me it was too good to refuse.'

'You don't think –?' began Wendy slowly, and there was no need to finish the sentence, for it was quite clear that reluctantly, apprehensively – no, with doomed certainty, everyone thought exactly the same thing.

AFTERWORD

VE Day, victory in Europe, 8th May 1945. Bunting hung between buildings, Union Jacks were run up flag poles and tied onto garden gates, crowds poured through the streets, arms linked, children had the day off school and scoffed cakes and jellies at hastily arranged street parties. The King and Queen appeared on the balcony of Buckingham Palace with Winston Churchill to acknowledge the cheers of the hundreds and thousands of people who had surged along Piccadilly and the Mall. That evening bonfires were lit on hills, in parks and on village greens and people forgot the exhaustion of six long years, and danced and sang. The war was over!

Priory Dean, the imaginary village of Marghanita Laski's novel, was no exception. 'Since the King had spoken on the nine o'clock [as everyone called the main BBC news bulletin of the day] . . . the village had poured spontaneously into the streets to celebrate' and 'Mr Jenkins, the schoolmaster, had touched off the bonfire that the children had been amassing all day on the messy bit by the pond.' A loud-speaker 'blared out dance music, and suddenly people were dancing on the cobbles in the forecourt, dancing right out in the village street.'

By eleven thirty that night the bonfire had died down, and most of the villagers had drifted home to bed, all save a few of what later would come to be called 'teenagers,' but were still then called 'village boys and girls', who continued to dance to the music of a wind-up gramophone in the pub forecourt.

But long before that, Mrs Trevor and Mrs Wilson had left the celebrations to go home and change 'into their thick navy serge trousers and tunics' ready for duty at the Red Cross Post as usual. The war was not over of course. Hostilities continued in the Far East until the surrender of Japan on 15th August 1945. In fact Marghanita Laski does not actually specify that the novel's opening scene takes place on 8th May 1945, but the details all point to that day. As far as most Britons were concerned – though not, of course, those who had men still fighting in the war against Japan, or in POW camps in south-east Asia – Germany's surrender meant the coming of peace. There was, as the two village women themselves recognised, 'no need in the world' for them to take up their vigilant wartime responsibilities that night. There were certainly not going to be any air raid casualties who might require the services of two middle-aged housewives trained in First Aid.

The women's reluctance to let their wartime world go is central to the theme of *The Village*, which tells the story of an English village that is losing its bearings. Wendy Trevor is typical of thousands of middle-class women who had not worked outside the home since they had married but who, when war came, had responded to appeals for help since, in such uncertain times, one felt rather better with a definite task to perform and, preferably, a uniform to wear. Women flocked in their thousands to join the WVS, the Red Cross, or other voluntary organisations such as the Women's Institute, or the Townswomen's Guild, all of which were involved in the war effort, and found usefulness and comradeship in so doing. First compelled by patriotism, and then from 1941 by conscription and compulsory direction, well-brought up young women, who might never have thought of doing so in peacetime, worked long hours in munitions factories, or hospitals, or drove ambulances or went into the auxiliary forces, and thus came into contact with all sorts of people they might never have met otherwise. And often if they were young so-called 'mobile women' without family responsibilities, they could be sent to live away from home in hostels in remote areas of the country where many war production factories were sited, well away from family surveillance and influence.

It became a commonplace during – and after – the war to suggest that class differences had been suspended for the duration: that there was unity in struggle. It had, after all, been named as 'the people's war' in which civilians from all walks of life were commended for standing shoulder to shoulder on the front line. But with the coming of peace, would the old conventions, the traditional hierarchies, the pre-war social niceties resurface? And what would be their currency in the post-war world? Would the much-vaunted 'equality of sacrifice' survive in peacetime? How would the building of a 'new Jerusalem' challenge those Britons who had believed that they were fighting to keep the country as it had always been?

In the election held in the months between victory in Europe and the end of the war with Japan, the Conservatives, who had pleaded to be allowed to 'finish the job', were swept from power in a landslide Labour victory. Attlee's government promised a fairer future for all, greater state involvement in society and no going back to the inequalities and inequities of the pre-war world. How would it be in Priory Dean, where 'the Labour Party woman got a deal too many votes' for some people's liking, and with 'every jumped-up Jack thinking he's as good as his master,' in the words of the village doctor?

Huddling round the gas-ring in Priory Dean village hall, making a 'nice cup of tea' on the night of VE Day, as they had done so many times during the war, Wendy Trevor and Edith Wilson epitomise class differences. Wendy, the wife of an ex-Army Major, back from the colonies, and now struggling to make ends meet as a chicken farmer, her headscarf knotted under her chin, makes her way down the hill from Wood View, Priory Hill 'where the gentry live', while Edith, her headscarf tied in a turban, trudges up the hill from her rented house, 15 Station Road, where she lives 'among the working-classes' with her van driver husband. On that last night of the war, they meet in the middle, in the porch of the village hall. They will never meet on an equal footing again. From henceforth Mrs Wilson will cease to be Mrs Trevor's co-worker in the war effort, and Wendy Trevor will recall the days before the war when Edith Wilson 'did' for her every morning, and came back in the evening to serve at table if the Trevors had a dinner-party, a life style that they can no longer possibly afford.

Four of Marghanita Laski's other novels apart from *The Village* are concerned with wartime themes and these, like all her novels and much of her journalism, are shot through with barbs at the English class system. *Love on the Supertax* (1944), her first book, is an elegant, extended joke about the world turned upside down in wartime with an aristocracy who had lost everything – money, prestige, influence – and a working-class that will inherit a state-dominated future. *To Bed with Grand Music* (1946), written under the pseudonym Sarah Russell, is the story of a young wife and mother who finds that the war offers her undreamed-of social, sexual and financial advancement, and that behaviour that is distinctly *déclassé* in peacetime, is what a girl does to get on during the war. *Tory Heaven* (1948) is a satirical look at a post-1945 Britain with the Tories having won the general election. *Little Boy Lost* (1949), also published by Persephone Books, begins with a satirical portrait of the hero's family in England but then becomes a moving description of his visit to post-war France as he searches for the son who had disappeared after the German occupation of Paris.

The Village was published in 1952, a year after the fall of the post-war Labour government and the return of the now not-far-off-eighty year-old Churchill as Prime Minister. The years of post-war austerity were almost over, although rationing continued until 1954, fourteen years after its introduction; by 1948 rations were lower than they had been during the war, with bread rationed for the first time. 'Don't you know there's a peace on?' was the bitter post-war parodic response to continuing rationing and shortages. There were many issues that the war had thrown up that had been left unresolved. Some of these – Britain's role in the post-war world with its increasingly restless Empire, and its uneasy relations with the new super powers, Russia and America; questions about how children should be educated; the extent of state intervention in people's lives; the need for a new entrepreneurial class to revive Britain's fortunes; women's uncertain role in the home and in the workplace; the acute shortage of affordable housing – find a place in *The Village*, some overtly, others more obliquely addressed.

Marghanita Laski came from an intellectual aristocracy whose political sympathies were firmly with the reformist left – and although her portrayal of the working-classes can seem snobbish and patronising to us today, it is the middle-class pretensions and philistinism, those 'clinging to the wreckage' of a lost and unlamented past, that are her real target. She lived for most of her married life on the edge of Hampstead Heath but spent much of the war in Abbots Langley in Hertfordshire, a village whose experience of the war must have been very similar to that of Priory Dean, and which had been losing its rural character since the 1920s too, as the voracious sprawl of the metropolis crept ever nearer. In 1945 Marghanita Laski's village could no longer pride itself on 'not just being a London dormitory' with the threat of a new housing estate and a 'whole lot of those pre-fabs [pre-fabricated houses, supposedly temporary, often used to house those who had been bombed out] in the field beyond the churchyard.'

Like so many rural communities Priory Dean had been

host to children from London during the war. A dispropor-
tionate number of evacuees came from the most impoverished
areas of Britain's urban conurbations, and brought eye-
opening revelations about the conditions of inner city life
to the country. Although reports of verminous, bed-wetting
slum urchins were grossly exaggerated, evacuation tended
to reinforce the divide between town and country, and
strengthen social bonds in the countryside. Smug contrasts
were drawn between the thrifty rural poor who had taken
these school children – or a mother and her brood of under-
fives – into their homes for scant reward, and their feckless
urban counterparts. Now the evacuees – 'more like hooligans
than children' according to the village policeman – had gone
back home to London, and the social cement that had bound
the village community together in adversity had one more
reason to dissolve.

During the war not having much money did not matter
very much – or at least it did not show very much. Rationing,
which was introduced in January 1940, had been generally
welcomed since it meant fair shares for all, as did the points
system by which a housewife at least retained *some* choice
about what she could buy to feed her family. And though
queuing for anything up to two hours for a precious piece of
fish, or fruit, with no guarantee that when you got to the head
of the queue there would be any left, was onerous, there could
be something companionable about it. Standing there in all
weathers, with a basket and a piece of old newspaper to wrap
your purchases in, since shop keepers were not permitted
to supply that any more, broke down barriers and was an

opportunity to complain and to compare notes about the war and its hardships. Of course there was always a flourishing black market, things kept 'under the counter' for favoured customers, coupon scams and paying over the odds. Those in the country were thought to fare better anyway with more space to dig for victory and keep chickens and pigs – and not always declare how many – and get fresh milk direct from the farms; not that there were many farms any more around Priory Dean, most had been split up into small-holdings. Clothes rationing meant that everyone had the same number of coupons for clothes – unless they did heavy manual work in which case they got more. So that should have been a great leveller too. Except that if you could afford to buy good quality clothes, they would last longer than cheaper ones, and they both took the same number of coupons. But it was patriotic to look shabby, and lots of things could not be had for love, nor money, nor coupons any more. There was so little to spend money on towards the end of the war with most of the factories turned over to wartime production rather than making consumer items. But now the war was over, money will start to talk again, and Wendy Trevor is one of those who won't be able to join in the conversation.

Counterpoised to the Trevors are some newcomers to the village, the Wetheralls, who had come to Priory Dean by 'pure chance' to live in a newly-built house with every modern convenience. Martha is an American married to an Englishman, and in the novel the couple represent modernity. Britain could not have won the war without American help, as the presence of over a million and a half GIs stationed in

Britain prior to D-Day in June 1944 demonstrated, and post-war Britain continued to be in hock to America financially and permeated by US culture – films, music, dance crazes, consumer choice, even the economically-empowered teenager – or 'bobby soxer' as the imported phrase had it.

The story of the romance between Wendy Trevor's daughter Margaret and Roy, the printer son of Edith Wilson, forms the central narrative of the novel, and the attitude of the other villagers when the news gets out, illuminates their understanding – or rejection – of the village's elaborately calibrated social stratification. It is left to Miss Evadne, the last remnant of the 'real gentry' in the village, to give Margaret the courage to confront her parents. '"Class" said Margaret with a new contempt. "What's class? What's class ever done for you or me or any of us? Roy and I are people . . . and a thing called class isn't going to stand between us."'

When *The Village* was published the anonymous reviewer in the *Times Literary Supplement* complained that 'love between persons of different social classes is an age-old literary subject...though here approached by Miss Marghanita Laski as if no one had ever gibbed at the class barrier before 1945.' But with her prodigious and catholic reading and formidable erudition, and her reverence for the novels of Jane Austen, Miss Laski was without doubt well aware of 'age-old literary subjects': however her preoccupation is a historically-specific one.

The Village is a finely observed novel about the losses and gains of the Second World War, how hopeless and how isolating it would be to hold onto the past, how illusory was the notion that the war had broken down class barriers, or had managed to save 'deep England' from the future and how peace, too, would produce its own list of casualties.

Juliet Gardiner,
London, 2004